STITCHED UP

MICHAEL CLOWER

$\mathcal{C}_F$

Published for Michael Clower in 2023, by Christel Foord, Self-Publishing. (cfoord@yebo.co.za)

Cover design and layout by Jakobie de Wet (jakdesignco@gmail.com)
Cover photo: www.shutterstock.com

ISBN: 9798851620379
Available as an eBook and paperback on Amazon.com

More titles by Michael Clower
MICK KINANE – BIG RACE KING
CHAMPION CHARLIE
THE LEGEND OF ISTABRAQ
KINGS OF THE TURF
RIDING FOR A FALL

WITH SPECIAL THANKS TO

Nick Craven of Weatherbys
Nick Godfrey, editor of Thoroughbred Racing Commentary
James Burn of the Racing Post
Mark Scully of the British Horseracing Authority

1

'Hi Rod.' The man stopped me in my tracks as I made my way from the Newbury winner's enclosure to the press room.

He held out his hand for me to shake. 'John Roberts,' he announced as I silently cursed. I'd been deep in thought, mentally writing my report and working out how the trainer's explanation for the improved form of his 20–1 big race winner should be fitted into the story. An interruption I didn't need.

But you can't ignore the public. I smiled as I shook hands with a man I took to be in his fifties. About medium height and build, wearing a mac, flat cap and a grey scarf he was barely distinguishable from an army of others at any end-November racemeeting. I was pretty sure I had never seen him before.

'Rod, I want to congratulate you on your tips. You've won me a fortune.' Obviously he had me mixed up with Gerry Robson, my colleague on *sports-all.com*. He did the tipping. My brief was news and reports.

I was about to explain to John Roberts that he had the wrong man when he pulled a bulky brown envelope out of his mac pocket and began extracting a wad of what looked like fivers. 'I want to give you a present.'

He thrust the money towards my right hand and, as I grabbed it to stop it falling, I smiled again and said: 'No John. I can't accept that.'

He took the money back, looking a little disheartened. 'John,' I began, anxious that he should not take offence at my refusal to accept his generous gesture. 'I'm delighted to meet you – and equally delighted that things are going so well for you. But I'm only doing what the website pays me for.'

He still looked disappointed. I reached forward to pat him on the shoulder. 'See you again, John. Let's talk then,' I said cheerfully. 'I'd better get on with my report or I'll be in trouble.'

I resumed my path towards the press room and mentally returned to the preparation of my story. I didn't give John Roberts another thought.

It was the biggest mistake I ever made.

'You're 6–4 on. The horse's form makes him a stand-out. The question is are you fit enough?' Tom Cameron, sitting in his usual place, laptop open in front of him, was clearly working on his preview of the next day's card, a much more glamorous affair than the relatively routine Friday fixture.

'Should be,' I said, hoping that the *Racing Post's* on-course reporter was not able to sense that I was being economical with the truth. I hadn't ridden in a race for the best part of a year and I hadn't done as much preparation on the gallops as I should have – but I couldn't wait to get back. And back into the winner's enclosure.

'I've been running four or five miles a day for the last eight weeks. I've been riding exercise every day for the last month – as soon as the doctors gave me the all-clear – and I resumed riding work a fortnight ago. I'll be fine.'

The red-haired Cameron made notes on his pad as I spoke. 'That's great. I reckon Brave Soldier is a good thing,' he grinned as he flipped over the pages. 'You deserve to come back with a winner after all you've been through.'

I was so confident that I hardly needed his positive assessment. But the hard-working Cameron – he was invariably the first of the press to arrive and always the last to leave – was recognised as a shrewd judge of form, and I felt a warm glow running through me.

I was only too aware that I wasn't anywhere near as fit as I would normally be but Brave Soldier was a good jumper and an easy ride. He didn't pull hard and he invariably gave his best without too much effort from the man on top. Also his last run, when third on his return at Sandown, suggested he would be spot-on for the next day's opener.

The other two scribes in the press room, who had been listening carefully to Cameron's questions and my answers, echoed his sentiments and wished me luck. I said nothing about the extra incentive the horse's owner had promised me but my excitement was soaring.

I had feared I wouldn't sleep a wink but the small brandy the evening before must have done the trick because I went out like a light, and I didn't wake until the alarm went off at 7.00am. By half past I was in the village newsagents collecting my pile of papers. 'Morning Mr Hutchinson,' said the turbanned Joshi Shah. 'Big day today.' He flipped open the *Racing Post* to an inside page and pointed to an article headed: 'Cheltenham bomb victim aiming to be back with a bang.'

The jangle as the door opened heralded the arrival of other customers. I hastily gathered up my papers and hurried out. I didn't want to be drawn into a general discussion on my prospects. Mr Shah, a keen racing enthusiast, liked nothing more than chatting about what was going to win.

Over a good breakfast – I wasn't planning on eating lunch – I studied the papers, or rather their racing pages. I was disappointed not to find any mention of myself or my race anywhere except in the *Post*. The others concentrated on the day's big race, the sponsored handicap chase – the feature of Newbury's 2025 two-day November jumps meeting, and seemingly didn't consider the Berkshire Amateur Riders Steeplechase worth any space at all. But Cameron had done me proud, recalling my Exeter win in the colours that were to be carried by Brave Soldier and my lengthy fightback from the injuries I suffered in the bomb explosion that had made headlines round the world.

He was already ensconced in his customary seat, laptop open, when I arrived at the racecourse almost two hours before the first. 'Going to walk the course?' he asked. I shook my head, explaining that I had done that a fortnight ago and again yesterday. In fact, I hadn't needed to. I'd ridden at the Berkshire course a few times before although I had never ridden a winner here.

In truth I'd only ridden four winners altogether, excluding my ten point-to-point victories, and my lack of success on the racecourse proper meant that I claimed a 7lb allowance – a factor that only added to my conviction that my mount was a good thing.

Brave Soldier had only 10st 9lb under the conditions of the race whereas he would have been allotted 10lb more had the race been a handicap. Over three miles that meant he should win by the best part of 15 lengths. Little wonder that he was odds-on!

I was one of the first into the jockeys' room and my valet, ex-jockey Jim Simons, directed me to a hook on the wall at the far end, handing me the red and white squared jersey of Christopher Mayhew.

My opponents began to filter in and occupy the spaces on either side of me. Some I knew well, others I'd hardly heard of. I tensed as I saw Ben Walters approaching. Champion amateur for each of the last three season and 16 winners clear already this campaign, he disliked me intensely – and the feeling was mutual.

Much to my surprise he broke into a smile as he neared me, hand outstretched in greeting. 'Good to see you back, Rod,' he said as I tentatively gripped his and shook it. 'You should win this.'

I just nodded. You often read in books of people saying 'words failed me' but that was exactly how I felt. In my mind Walters was a sworn enemy, an opponent who grimly gave no quarter and – so far as I was concerned – received none either.

I silently finished dressing and, finding I had a good half hour to kill, put my overcoat on over my colours and wandered outside to savour the atmosphere. The crowds were beginning to pour through the turnstiles and, as I walked down the row of bookmakers, several of them called out my name and shouted greetings. They clearly fancied my chances. Brave Soldier was odds-on with every one of them, and as short as 1–2 with some of those at the far end.

I started to feel nervous. Supposing I didn't win? Supposing the horse made a mistake and I fell off? I would look stupid or, even worse, incompetent. I decided to retreat to the press room.

That proved no better. The place was filling up fast and many saw my arrival as an opportunity for leg-pulling, plus jokes at my expense. 'Cor, it's Tony McCoy re-incarnated' and 'Walters must be shivering in his boots' were two of the more printable, the speakers and their audience roaring with laughter.

I went back to the jockeys room, got my saddle ready, stood on the trial scales and called for Jim Simons to help. The bald, aproned figure fussed around me like the proverbial mother hen, tut-tutted at my efforts to make the weight up to the required 10st 2lb, slotted a few bits of lead neatly into the compartments of the weight cloth, reached for the number cloth on the table behind him, checked the reading on the scales one final time and pronounced me ready.

From there I went to the official scales, stepped on them and, glancing at the needle, informed the tweed-suited Clerk of the Scales: 'Brave Soldier 10st 9lb, number five sir. Rodney Hutchinson, claiming seven.'

The slightly overweight, bespectacled figure peered at the scales, looked at the printed list in front of him and put a tick by the horse's name. 'Welcome back,' he said smilingly.

Charles Charterman was already waiting to collect my saddle. Tall, cheerful and charming, Charlie was trainer Paddy O'Reilly's assistant. In his early twenties, he had already had increasingly important jobs with two of the top jumping trainers in the country. He was also the nephew of Christopher Mayhew, owner of not just Brave Soldier but of the yard where the horse was trained and of the majority of the stable's other thirty-plus inmates.

'Hi Charlie.' I handed him the saddle. 'What news of Paddy?'

'Not so hot.' Charlie's grim-set expression answered the question. 'They've moved him to the Rutherford in Reading for some special treatment. But,' he shook his head. 'It doesn't look good.'

'Bloody hell. I hope he makes it. He's too good a man to go.'

Charlie nodded in agreement, turned on his heels and headed off, presumably to the saddling boxes.

Less than ten minutes later, a shout of 'jockeys out' saw me and the nine other amateurs making for the door as eagerly as lemmings on the move, and heading towards the parade ring. The horses were already there, circling quietly and being eyed by punters all around the outside while the trainers chatted to their owners. Christopher Mayhew and Majorie were, as always, smartly dressed: he in a camel hair overcoat and his wife in a warm-looking well-cut dark red coat.

After the usual pleasantries, Christopher said: 'Rod, I need you to know that I went to see Paddy yesterday, and he agreed with me that it's not doing him any good worrying about the stable when he is fighting the cancer, and so Charlie will take over the licence some time next week. I've told Charlie about our own arrangement and he's fully in agreement.'

'That's right,' Charlie added. 'We've got a stable of good horses and we're going to get plenty of winners.'

Further conversation was interrupted by the bell. Charlie and I headed for the horse, now tossing his head up and down in a clear signal that he wanted to get on with things. Charlie legged me into the saddle, saying: 'The trip's no problem, Rod. But it's a long way home here. Don't go too soon.'

I slipped my feet into the irons and began knotting my reins as the horses were led round the ring. 'He's in great shape,' said the horse's lad, looking back at me. 'You should win ten lengths.'

'We still odds-on, Jerry?' I inquired.

'Unfortunately. I was going to put fifty on, but not at 4–6 in a steeplechase. Not,' he added pointedly, 'with amateurs riding.'

The horses were led out onto the tarmac walkway, which gave way to woodchips before we reached the actual racecourse. 'Good luck,' said Jerry, unclipping the lead rein, and Brave Soldier broke into a canter as he followed the horse in front along the narrow strip on the outside of the course.

The horse's pounding hooves and powerful action, coupled with the air rushing past my face, sent a surge of excitement through me and my mind went back over what Christopher had said – not just now in the parade ring but on a visit to the yard one Sunday some weeks ago – when he was there with a small group of friends who part-owned some of the horses.

'One of my ambitions for this season is to make Rod champion amateur,' he informed them. 'He is one of the most talented I've seen for years but he's had a truly annus horribilis.' I noticed some of his audience nodding in agreement. 'I've told Paddy that I want him to ride most of the horses whenever he thinks they are in with a decent chance.'

'Whoa now lad. Steady.' Brave Soldier, turning into the back straight, tried to quicken. I had to pull him back quite sharply to stop him taking off. Being run away with going down to the start was an ignominy I was determined not to suffer.

Fortunately he got the message, and he switched off completely once we neared those already circling at the start. Leaning forward and reaching down, I managed to squeeze two fingers between the horse's stomach and the girths. Not tight enough. I pulled Brave Soldier out of the circle and made for the starter's assistant. Not needing to be asked, he took hold of the girth strap and pulled it up two notches. 'You'll be fine now,' he said as he turned away to attend to another horse needing the same treatment.

I saw the starter looking at his watch and then heading for the rostrum on the other side of the rails. He ducked under them and called out 'Jockeys' as he went up the steps. We all moved forward into a very rough sort of line, with some riders deliberately hanging back. 'Come on,' he shouted as he sharply lowered his flag.

Brave Soldier had pricked his ears at the first shout and at the second he broke straight into a gallop. I hastily eased him back behind a couple of other equally impatient rivals as we thundered towards the first fence. He quickened again as he neared it, soared over the fence with a foot to spare and landed running.

Again I eased him back, more determinedly this time, and steered him nearer the inside rail. As the second fence loomed up I steadied him slightly, and this time he jumped it much more economically.

'Good lad,' I said to him as he settled in fourth. We began to turn out of the back straight and towards the cross fence. I knew this one could be tricky but Brave Soldier made light work of it, so much so that I was able to glance back and see where the others were. Ben Walters was immediately behind me. I was convinced he was my one real danger – and obviously he felt the same about me.

Heading into the straight for the first time, I could sense that the pace was sensible – but strong enough to separate the talent of the likes of Brave Soldier from those of lesser ability when the tap was turned on in a circuit's time. He took the open ditch cleanly and, as we neared the stands, I briefly heard a few shouts of encouragement from the punters. But soon the only sounds were the pounding of the horses' hooves, the crash as the horses brushed through the tops of the fences and the shouts of their riders, cursing or encouraging – depending on how well, or otherwise, they were travelling. I glanced back again as we passed our starting point. All ten horses were still standing but the field was strung out, and some were many lengths adrift.

Heading towards the cross fence, we were still fourth but travelling easily. I glanced back. Walters was directly behind but a bit further away and beginning to niggle. Seconds later the picture changed dramatically.

The leader met the fence all wrong, and put out a leg on the landing side to save himself. But it crumpled under the horse's half-ton weight and he fell sideways, bringing down the second horse. I just had time to steer Brave Soldier towards the outside of the fence. He soared over it and swept past the fallers. Looking back, I saw Walters' mount having to switch to avoid the fallen horses and losing several lengths in the process.

Turning into the straight for the second and final time, I had only one horse in front of me and he was starting to come under pressure. I must have been ten lengths clear of Walters, with the rest of those still standing strung out with the washing. I knew I had it in the bag.

I decided to wait until after jumping the open ditch before going past the leader and heading for home. Brave Soldier, still travelling well within himself, jumped it cleanly. I shortened the reins and went to give him a kick to give him the message to quicken. But, frighteningly, my legs wouldn't move. They were like jelly. I just couldn't get them to respond.

Brave Soldier faltered for a stride or two before galloping on at the same pace. I glanced back. Walters and another rider were together, some eight lengths behind but beginning to close. Again I shortened the reins and tried to kick.

My hands were as weak as my legs. I picked up my whip – and promptly dropped it. As we came to the second last, I could hear the two pursuers quite clearly. I didn't dare look back but my advantage couldn't have been more than three lengths. And it was narrowing by the second.

My strength was completely gone. It was all I could do to stop myself falling off. I sat still as Walters, and then his rival, swept past and headed towards the final fence, passing the end of the false rail. There was now a space on the inner big enough to drive the proverbial bus through. I was vaguely aware, and slightly puzzled, when I saw them veering off a straight line and heading towards the inside corner of the fence. Walters was almost a length up on his opponent who was trying to get through the dangerously narrowing gap. Suddenly the white plastic running rail spectacularly exploded into several pieces as the horse hit it and ran past the inside of the fence while Walters' mount jumped it cleanly.

I followed suit, some ten lengths behind, but I was just a passenger, unable to do anything more than sit motionless as I concentrated on not falling off. As I passed the post I hadn't even the strength to lift my head to see how far I had been beaten.

Brave Soldier knew the race was over and pulled himself up without any assistance from me. As I turned him to head for the unsaddling area, I saw the jockey of the horse who had smashed the rail ride up alongside Walters and forcefully crack him across the back with his whip.

A few of the crowd began shouting as I rode in. 'You useless fucker. Pity you didn't stay away a bit longer,' yelled a bald man, waving a rolled-up racecard in his right hand. I tried to shut out most of the other abuse. But I was clearly the subject of considerable hatred.

'I'm so sorry,' I said as Charlie took hold of the reins and gave the horse a pat. Christopher joined him, looking at me inquiringly. 'I thought I was fit enough but my muscles went to jelly in the last half mile. I've let you down badly.'

I slipped off the horse and made a feeble effort at unbuckling the girth. Charlie had to do it for me. 'Maybe we were all expecting too much,' said Christopher. 'Better luck next time.'

At least he was talking of a next time. 'Partly my fault,' added Charlie. 'I should have insisted that you were fully fit before returning.' He glanced uneasily at the angry punters now beginning to crowd round.

'Rod. I think you'd better go and weigh in,' Christopher added, the concern in his voice echoing that of Charlie as the angry punters closed in, their abuse intensifying.

I pushed my way through, close to the man with the rolled-up racecard who thumped me on the arm with it, and headed determinedly for the weighing room. My mind was so preoccupied with my own personal disaster that I ignored the scales. Failing to weigh in is a criminal offence in racing, and punished more severely than a shoplifter. Fortunately my path was blocked by a white-coated official.

I silently told myself to get a grip, and concentrate on what I should be doing, as I stood on the scales while the bespectacled Clerk ticked the sheet of paper in front of him. 'Hard luck,' he smiled. At least somebody wasn't after my blood.

As I entered the jockeys room I saw a group of riders around Ben Walters, naked from the waist up, displaying a nasty-looking red weal on his back. The modern so-called horse-friendly whips weren't meant to hurt but this one had certainly left its mark.

'You could have killed me, forcing me into the rails like that,' said a rider I now recognised as Bob Farthing. He did most of his racing in point-to-points and was seldom seen on the racecourse proper.

Walters advanced on him menacingly only to be restrained by two of the senior professionals and a call from the doorway. 'Mr Walters, Mr Farthing. Stewards room. Now.'

The despair hit me as I slumped down on the bench beneath my peg. I was physically exhausted, mentally drained and in the depths of depression. I'd waited over eleven months to return to what I liked doing best of all, been offered the chance of achieving my ambitions and blown the lot – all because I'd been in such a hurry. I knew Christopher: he might have been putting a brave face on it out there, and been careful not to pull the rug from under my boots, but he dearly wanted racecourse success – and you don't get that using unfit amateurs. Charlie would remind him too – his own success in his new role as trainer would depend on using the best jockeys available. The last thing he wanted was an unfit amateur who had only ridden four winners. My career was as good as over.

'Cheer up. There's always another day.' Robbie Bolton, the current champion jockey, sat down on the bench beside me. 'I've had worse days. Most of us have.'

I was surprised he had taken the trouble to commiserate, particularly with someone whose race-riding ability was as nothing compared with his own.

'Sometimes you think it's the end of the world,' he continued, in the same understanding tone of voice. 'And we've all come back too soon after injury. We have to, otherwise somebody else takes the rides – and you don't get them back.'

'But....'

I didn't get a chance to explain. Bolton stood up and, patting me on the shoulder, said: 'Give it another two or three weeks, ride as much work as you can, and you'll soon be on a winner.'

I watched his retreating back, already feeling a new man. And, by the time Jim Simons came up and told me that I was wanted in the stewards room, I felt I could face anything.

There were three of them. All professionals. I would rather have had the amateurs. At one time most of the stewards were unpaid, gentlemen who did it out of a sense of duty and because they loved racing. Many of them had ridden in races in their youth, as amateurs like me. They would have been more likely to sympathise than the present trio for whom the rule book was God.

I knew all three by their first names. I would often ask them to explain how they arrived at their decisions and, where necessary, to show me the replays of controversial incidents.

'Rod,' began the grey-haired James Robinson. At least we were playing on Christian-name terms … no Mr Hutchinson. 'We would like you to have a look at the film. Take a seat,' he pointed to a nearby chair.

The huge TV screen lit up and the film started with me approaching the open ditch, three from home, and travelling strongly. At least my mount was. I was sitting motionless and looking like a complete novice. Not once did I push the horse with my hands or my legs. Even the time I picked up my whip, it was a half-hearted effort. The film froze as the whip flew out of my hand.

'What happened there, Mr Hutchinson?' Mister now. Things were getting serious. I could see a suspension coming.

'Look, James.' I turned to the other two and looked them each straight in the eye. 'Richard.... John.... I have to put my hand up. I thought I was fit enough but, as you know, there is no substitute for race-riding and by that stage in the race I was as weak as a kitten. I've let a lot of people down – Mr Mayhew, Paddy O'Reilly, all those who backed the horse, and yourselves. I can only apologise.' My voice was, embarrassingly, beginning to croak – and I felt close to tears.

'OK,' said James Robinson slowly. 'We are giving you a caution to make sure that you are properly fit before you ride again – and we will require the trainer you are riding for to provide us with a written assurance that he, or she, believes you are fit enough to do the horse justice.'

No suspension, then. Thank God for that. I breathed a mental sigh of relief.

Robinson's tone softened as he broke into a smile. 'It's good to see you back, Rod. You've had a rough time.'

'Thank you,' I stood up. 'By the way, what happened between Ben Walters and Bob Farthing?'

'We'll show you,' he nodded in the direction of the steward who was operating the replays at the far end of the long table. This time the huge screen began with the two leaders approaching the final fence. Walters could be seen quite blatantly steering left to narrow the gap between the challenger and the rails. The way the rails were sent flying in all directions was even more spectacular on the big screen than it had been from my vantage point several lengths behind.

James Robinson smiled. 'You've seen nothing yet,' he chuckled. The picture was fast-forwarded until it showed an angry-looking Bob Farthing shouting something as he rode his horse alongside Jenkins' mount, raise his whip and crack it down across his rival's back.

Robinson turned back towards me, the smile gone. 'We gave Walters six weeks for dangerous riding and Farthing three months for striking another rider.'

Six weeks. I wouldn't ride 16 – now 17 – winners in three months even in my dreams but, if I could get properly fit inside three weeks, I could make serious inroads into Jenkins' lead by the time he resumed. I re-entered the jockeys' room – where most had gone out for the next race – feeling on top of the world.

Jenkins and Farthing were still changing. Taking out my notebook, I tackled Walters first. 'Were you expecting to be hit with the whip, Ben?' I asked as I sat down beside his peg.

'Of course not.' His fury was still there and, I felt, in danger of being transferred to me. I softened my approach. I needed to get a lot more out of him yet.

'No, sure,' I agreed. 'It looked terrible on the film. But the stewards said Farthing felt you had closed him up and that that had a lot to do with forcing him off the course.' A slight embroidering of the truth but diplomacy was needed to keep him talking. It worked.

'Listen Rod.' His voice was quiet. He didn't want Farthing to hear. 'You know as well as I do the unwritten rule is that you don't try and come up someone's inside. And, if you do, you deserve all you get. I was in front and I was clear. I simply made it difficult for him – as I was entitled to.'

I wasn't at all sure that he was right. Things had changed in recent years following a court case when a Flat race jockey was left paralysed after trying to come through a narrow gap on the inner. He won substantial damages.

I returned to my own peg and wrote down all Walters had said before going to Bob Farthing to get the other man's viewpoint.

Farthing was putting on his shoes and socks. 'Bob,' I began purposely. 'The stewards showed me the films of what happened from the second last fence to the line, and of the whip incident after you both pulled up. I take it you felt very hard done by. Was that why you hit Ben Walters?'

He sat down beside me. 'I presume you are writing about this?' He didn't wait for my answer. 'Well, let me tell you something. I've been race-riding for five years and never before have I seen such a blatant piece of dangerous riding. He deliberately ran me out of room and through the rails. If they had been the old wooden ones I could have broken my leg, or worse. And my horse would have been injured.

'Ok, I lost my rag,' he continued. 'I shouldn't have hit him – but I'm not sorry I did. He deserved it. He deserved to be strung up, certainly to have his licence taken away. All he got was six weeks, and I got more than twice that. It's enough to make you sick.'

'Will you appeal?'

'Nah. There's no point. They would take the same view at the

BHA, I'm sure they would. Anyway I won't miss all that much of the point-to-point season.'

I stood up. 'OK, Bob. Nice to have met you anyway. Maybe we'll both have better luck next time.' He didn't answer but turned away to resume putting on his shoes.

At least I had a story. Most of the press room had gone out to watch the main race, only the few who preferred the TV version remained. They scarcely noticed me as I sat down to make sure I could read my scribbled notes.

Reporting the race was the prerogative of Gerry Robson. My brief was a report on my race and any news I could pick up. I briefly noted down the main points of my story, and the order I was going to put them in, as those watching the race began to get excited. I interrupted my thoughts to look at the drama unfolding on the large screen on the wall.

The hot favourite – and, judging by the noise, the one most of the journalists had their money on – was four lengths clear approaching the final fence. But he was getting tired. He tried to put in a short one to get his stride right, but he couldn't get high enough. He hit the top of the fence and, to the collective groan of the press room audience, came down too steep, crumpled on landing and ejected his pilot. His nearest pursuer made the most of his change of fortune, jumped it cleanly and strode up the run-in to win comfortably.

Looking at my racecard I saw that the rider was none other than Robbie Bolton. As he waved his whip in triumph I felt that I was somehow sharing in his delight.

Now in a considerably cheered frame of mind, I began my story with the sensational end to the amateur chase. I painted what I hoped was a vivid picture of Ben Walters riding his rival off the course, Bob Farthing taking the law into his own hands and administering a particularly painful form of justice, and the stewards showing neither of them any mercy. I quoted the stewards as well as both riders.

I then turned to my own part, explaining what had happened and why, and added that I was barely able to lift my head as I exhaustedly neared the line. 'If it looked as if I was hanging my head in shame that was certainly how I felt. I promptly expressed my apologies to owner Christopher Mayhew and to Charlie Charterman who will be taking over the licence next week so that Paddy O'Reilly can concentrate on fighting the biggest battle of his life.

'Some of the crowd forcefully, angrily and quite correctly, expressed the view that I was the cause of them losing their money. I owe them a considerable debt and, while it may not be much consolation, I can assure them that they will not see me in action again until I am fit enough to do them justice.'

After reading it through, I filed it with the suggested caption: WHIPS FLY IN DANGEROUS RIDING – AND OUR MAN TAKES THE BLAME.

2

My appearance in the yard first thing on Monday morning was akin to that of a comedian's straight man. I seemed to be the butt of all the jokes, and even on the gallops it didn't let up. One of the lads pulled up his mount at the end of a canter and promptly called out to the rest of the string: 'Did you see me riding a finish Rod Hutchinson-style? I didn't move a muscle.'

But there was almost nothing malicious. It might have been a different story if Brave Soldier hadn't been too short to be a betting proposition. Only the head lad was unpleasant. 'You mucked out yet, Rodney?' he greeted me unsmilingly as I walked in ten minutes before we were due to pull out. It was by no means the first time he had said this, even though he must have known that mucking out the stables was no part of my arrangement with Paddy O'Reilly who had always treated me like one of the owners.

In fact I did own two of the horses and, so far as I was aware, I paid the same training fees as any of the other owners. But I was pretty sure I knew why the head lad had such an obvious chip on his shoulder.

He said exactly the same thing on Tuesday morning when I again rode out first lot, and had a quick breakfast with Charlie Charterman before heading back home to start the day job. I was in front of my laptop, and going through my emails, shortly after ten when I saw the letter from the British Horseracing Authority. It was dated today and read:

Dear Mr Hutchinson,

Berkshire Amateur Riders' Steeplechase, Newbury

The Disciplinary Panel of the British Horseracing Authority has decided to reopen the inquiry into the above race following receipt of new evidence.

You are requested to attend the reopened inquiry at Holborn Gate on Wednesday next (December 3) at 9.00am. Please confirm that you will be present and whether you intend being legally represented. The BHA will not be legally represented but there will be an independent legal assessor present to assist any party if so required.

Yours sincerely,

The signature was indecipherable but he, or she, was secretary to the Disciplinary Panel. I cursed. I had better things to do than spend an hour driving into the middle of London, searching for somewhere to park, listen to either Ben Walters or Bob Farthing explaining some complicated reason why they were unfairly treated, and should have their sentence shortened or dropped altogether. I could see it taking up the whole morning.

Anyway what could I contribute? I saw almost nothing of the offences they committed other than on the film.

I reached for my phone, dialled the number on the letterhead and asked for the secretary of the Disciplinary Panel. The illegible secretary proved to be a man.

'Listen, I've got this thing from you just now,' I began, the irritation in my voice obvious to myself let alone the official at the other end of the line. 'Do you really need me at this thing tomorrow. I am due at Paddy O'Reilly's at 8.00am and then I've got a full day's work in front of me.......'

The secretary tried to interrupt, but I had more to get off my chest. 'I saw almost nothing of the incident beyond what little I told the stewards at Newbury. In fact it was them who explained the incident to me when they showed me the film. And they only did that because I asked them what had happened.'

I paused, and the secretary took advantage of the brief let-up to get across what he wanted to say. 'I'm sorry Mr Hutchinson. I know you have a full day's work ahead of you, and I understand and appreciate that. But it is essential that you attend.'

I could see I wasn't going to get my way with this and, as I struggled to come up with another excuse, the secretary continued: 'I just need to know if you intend to be legally represented.'

The exasperated explosion that I let fly must have almost taken his ear off, or at the very least forced him to hold the earpiece several inches further from his face. 'Listen,' I began. 'I'm a qualified solicitor. I don't need a bloody lawyer just to say I didn't see what happened.'

'Mr Hutchinson, please.' The secretary sounded hurt, as if he had taken my outburst personally. 'The legalities simply require me to point out that you have the right to be legally represented should you so wish.'

'OK.' I was mollified only slightly. My biggest annoyance was still the unnecessary waste of time. 'I'll be there at 9.00am and, if there is any need for legal representation – and I can't for the life of me think why, then I will do it myself.'

I found a multi-storey within striking distance of Holborn Gate – and winced when I saw the hourly rate – but I was at the offices of the British Horseracing Authority with fifteen minutes to spare.

'Good morning. Mr Hutchinson, I presume?' smiled the smartly-dressed, middle-aged lady behind the desk. She took me down a corridor and ushered me into what was obviously some sort of waiting room with four chairs, a table and a copy of the *Racing Post*. I was asked if I would like tea or coffee. I opted for the latter, with milk and two sugars.

No sign of either Ben Walters or Bob Farthing. Either they were cutting it fine or, more likely, they were being kept apart from the witnesses – and certainly from each other. I was just finishing my coffee and the *Racing Post* when there was a firm knock on the door as it opened and in swept a man I knew as a recent addition to the list of professional stewards. He was a small, busy-looking man in his early forties, almost bald and unusually fast-talking. I seemed to remember that his name was Gavin Chesterfield. According to those journalists who prided themselves on knowing everything about everyone, he was an ex-solicitor.

He certainly wasted no time on pleasantries. 'Come this way', he commanded as I stood up to follow him through, presumably, to where the inquiry was taking place. He said nothing more, not even when we entered a large room with three men seated on the far side of a long table.

I glanced round. There was a large screen taking up half of the wall opposite the three men, and a much younger man – who I presumed to be a technician – was fussing over a table of electrical equipment. I assumed this included some sort of recording device and projector or video player.

At a small table nearer the door was a grey-suited middle-aged man in glasses beside a woman of about thirty who looked as if she might be his secretary.

'Good morning Mr Hutchinson. Thank you for coming and for getting here on time – no mean achievement in the London traffic.' Lord Greenstone was the centre figure of the three at the long table, a tall, slim grey-haired individual with a prominent roman nose. I was on nodding terms with him on the racecourse. I knew he had been recently appointed as chairman of the BHA's new disciplinary panel and that he was a man held in the highest regard by racing's officialdom. The two men either side of him I didn't know.

Gavin Chesterfield unsmilingly pushed a chair in my direction. 'Sit,' he said as if he was talking to his dog. I sat. I wondered where Walters and Farthing were. Then it occurred to me that they probably wanted to hear my evidence first so that I could be free to go as soon as I had given it. My spirits rose.

'Now Mr Hutchinson,' Lord Greenstone began. 'I don't know whether you are aware of this but we are making a little bit of history today.'

I wasn't. Nor did I want to. All I was concerned about was getting out of the place as soon as possible.

'This is the first case under the new procedures recommended by the British Horseracing Authority's Justice Committee, and indeed it is the first one that I have the honour of presiding over,' Lord Greenstone continued in his self-important monotone. 'The Justice Committee was established to provide additional fairness for those accused of serious misdemeanours.'

I couldn't see what this had to do with me and I pointedly glanced at my watch as if to give his lordship a hurry-up signal.

'The British Horseracing Authority has decided against being legally represented in this inquiry,' Greenstone continued pompously. 'We don't feel that it is necessary, and I understand that you have also decided not to be legally represented. Is that correct?'

'Yes... er sir.' I wasn't sure how to address him. I'd thought of 'My Lord' but that made me sound like his butler asking him what he wanted for the next course. It all seemed very formal, but I supposed he felt he had to observe every possible legal requirement.

'Nonetheless Mr Hutchinson, we have engaged a legal assessor who you are free to consult at any stage – as are we. Mr Gordon Watson.' The grey-suited man raised his right hand, momentarily breaking into a smile. 'And his colleague, Mrs Sue Tomlinson.' She cheerfully gave me a brief wave. I thought she looked rather nice.

I forced myself to concentrate as Lord Greenstone continued: 'We want to you to have a look at the film of last Saturday's race and afterwards give us your observations on it.'

The huge screen came to life as the ten runners approached the cross fence for the second time, me going easily in fourth place. Not a word was spoken when the two in front fell, and nor when I was passed between the last two fences. Only when I was halfway up the run-in did the technician operating the film freeze the picture.

'Now Mr Hutchinson,' Gavin Chesterfield's tone was unmistakeably antagonistic. It was as if he was accusing me of something. I deliberated whether I should remind him that Walters and Farthing were the wrongdoers, not me.

'Were you aware that your horse was odds-on?'

'Yes, I knew that but...'

Chesterfield hadn't finished. 'Were you also aware that many of the large crowd had backed your mount? And indeed thousands more in betting shops all over the country?'

'Of course. But, as I explained to the stewards....' Chesterfield raised his hand as if to say stop. 'Then Mr Hutchinson, why did you not at least try to encourage your horse?'

'If you would only let me finish, Mr Chesterfield.' I knew my voice was betraying my irritation. I didn't care. 'I hadn't ridden in a race for almost a year, I wasn't as fit as I should have been and nowhere near as fit as I thought I was. My muscles were like jelly by that stage in the race, and I could hardly move. As I was trying to tell you, I explained all that to the stewards on Saturday. They accepted my explanation and gave me a caution to be properly fit before I rode in a race again – and that is what I am going to do.'

Chesterfield glanced questioningly at Lord Greenstone. 'I think we should move on to the next film,' said the chairman, nodding in the direction of the technician. At last we seemed to be getting to the point of all this. But where were they, the two accused? And why hadn't they been called in?

The screen came to life again, this time starting with a shot of the Newbury grandstand and following up with crowd scenes. The picture closed in on me walking past people and then being stopped by a man in a mac, wearing a cap and a scarf. As he pulled out the sheaf of fivers, realisation dawned. Or, to be more exact, it hit me like a ton of bricks.

My first reaction was that Chesterfield was deliberately trying to frame me. The second was that he was going to look a fool, and possibly lose his job, when Lord Greenstone and his two co-judges realised that this supposed transaction took place not after the race on the Saturday, but the previous day.

Now I knew why there was no sign of Jenkins and Farthing.

'How much did he pay you, Mr Hutchinson?' Chesterfield's tone was more unpleasant than ever.

I turned to face what I now realised were the three judges, the men I had to convince. 'Sirs, if you let the film continue you will see that I refused the money and that this happened on the Friday, not on the day of the race. Please look at the date superimposed on the film.'

The technician closed in on the date in the bottom righthand corner of the screen. To my horror, I saw that the date was the 29th. Saturday.

'Well, whoever came up with this film must have altered the date.' I was only too well aware that I sounded as if I was clutching at straws. 'Anyway, it doesn't really matter. The fact is that I refused to accept the money. The film should show that.'

'Harry, play it again but in slow motion,' Chesterfield commanded, his tone of voice sounding, to me at least, unnervingly confident.

Harry did as instructed and this time the film showed only too clearly how I grabbed the money. But what the film failed to show was me handing it back to John Roberts – or whatever his real name was. It suddenly, and belatedly, dawned on me that I had been set up.

'Mr Hutchinson,' said Lord Greenstone, sounding ominously to me as if he thought he was addressing one of the accused at the Nuremberg War Trials. 'Have you anything to say in mitigation before we pass sentence?'

'Yes, my lord.' I was clearly a good deal lower down the social scale than the butler by this stage. 'I did not take a bribe – whatever that film might suggest, and the only reason I lost the race was because I was so unfit. Somebody,' and I looked hard at Gavin Chesterfield, 'has for some reason got it in for me and has set me up.

'I was not prepared for any of this when I came here today and I now need to take legal advice. You said that I was free to consult the legal assessor at any stage and I would like to do so now. Please.'

I looked at Gordon Watson who returned my gaze, and nodded.

'Very well, we will all take a break,' said Lord Greenstone, beginning to gather the bits of paper in front of him. 'Thirty minutes, Mr Watson?'

Watson nodded a second time. I felt I needed days rather than minutes. I couldn't afford for my fate to be decided on the evidence submitted so far.

We went into the small room where I had sat while I was waiting to be called into the hearing. Gordon Watson gestured me to the chair furthest from the door. He took the one on my left and Sue Tomlinson the one on the other side of me.

'Look,' I began, the irritation in my voice clear even to myself. 'Somebody is trying to stitch me up. It looks to me like that shit Chesterfield although I've no idea why – apart from the fact that he seems to dislike me intensely. God only knows why he should. I'd never even spoken to the man before this morning. But what the hell am I going to do? I can't just stand there and let his lordship warn me off.'

Gordon Watson, glancing briefly at his colleague, said: 'Mr Hutchinson, I appreciate your predicament but you must first appreciate our position. Our firm often acts as legal assessors in these BHA inquiries and our job is to provide guidance on the law – which in effect means guidance on the Rules of Racing – to all the parties involved, if and when we are asked to do so.

'But, and this is highly relevant here, we are not allowed to provide legal advice. I understand from what you told Lord Greenstone that you were offered the opportunity to be legally represented but that you chose not?'

'Yes, but I thought I was being summoned to appear as a witness to the Ben Walters – Bob Farthing whip incident. Nobody said anything about me being accused of anything.'

An idea suddenly hit me, and I immediately perked up. 'Can I get this thing adjourned? It's a horrific accusation. I'm entitled to be given notice, and prepare my defence, surely?'

Gordon Watson looked inquiringly at his colleague. 'Rod has a point,' she said. I was encouraged that she was using my first name instead of the Mr Hutchinson of the star chamber across the corridor.

'Yes,' Watson seemed to agree but there was an ominous element of uncertainty in the way he said it. 'Looking at it from the point of view of the BHA, though, they will probably take the view that they issued a warning in writing about the fresh evidence and offered you the opportunity to bring a lawyer to represent you.

'We will speak to Lord Greenstone and see if he will agree to a postponement. But,' and his tone suggested, ominously, that my suddenly cheerful expression might be misplaced, 'he may not agree. In my experience he likes to get on with things. He did once tell me that he was against anything that could delay the administration of justice. And those were his exact words.'

'What are the odds?'

'I beg your pardon?'

Sue smiled. 'I think what Rod means is what are the chances of Lord Greenstone agreeing to a postponement. Is it odds-on or odds against?'

Gordon Watson, clearly not a racing man, hesitated before answering; 'I would say that it is more unlikely than likely. But, if you agree Rod, we will give it a go.'

He stood up, Sue did the same, smiling at me and showing what looked a shapely pair of legs beneath her dark green skirt.

'I think you and Sue should stay here while I go and make a case to his lordship.' Sue sat down again as Watson shut the door behind him.

'Have you been to one of these before?' she asked, presumably to make conversation.

I shook my head, deep in thought. I was worried. The implications, if the inquiry went ahead, were frightening.

'Gordon will do his best. He's very professional.' She was clearly intent on getting me back in a positive frame of mind. I didn't answer.

'I believe you used to be a solicitor. What made you give it up?'

I looked at her. She smiled, and I was entranced. 'Well, the male members of my family had been solicitors for generations and I was six months away from sitting my finals when my parents died of Covid.'

'Oh, how awful,' she interrupted. 'I am sorry.'

'It made me think again. I realised that the law wasn't what I wanted from life. I was already hooked on racing, riding in point-to-points and writing race reports. I decided that, once I qualified, I would concentrate on racing journalism and race-riding.'

'How interesting.' She really did sound as if she meant it.

'How about you? What got you doing what you do?'

Before she could answer, the door opened and Gordon's serious expression told its own story.

'I have made representations but Lord Greenstone is adamant that the inquiry should continue and finish this morning. We are to go back in now.'

I stood up. So did Sue. When we got back into the star chamber the three judges were already seated at the long table and Gavin Chesterfield had resumed his position by the big screen.

Lord Greenstone coughed, looked at the two men on each side of him and then directly at me. 'Mr Hutchinson,' he began, his tone of voice as serious as if he was about to don the infamous black cap worn by the judges of yesteryear when sentencing a man to hang. 'We have heard, and seen, some very clear evidence of you accepting a bribe, and of making no effort to win on a red hot favourite.

'You have very clearly, and very deliberately, broken one of the most important rules in the Rule Book,' he held up the small volume in his right hand, 'Namely that every horse must be run on its merits. You have defrauded the betting public and given racing a bad name. We have to take strong action to deter others from similar wrongdoings....'

'My Lord,' Gordon Watson was on his feet. 'If I might I have a quick word before...' His voice petered out as Lord Greenstone raised a finger to beckon him.

Watson hurried over to the main table and began whispering as the men on either side of Greenstone closed up to hear what he was saying. I couldn't make out much although I did hear 'racing journalist' and something about earning a living.

'Very well,' Lord Greenstone resumed as the whispered conference broke up, the two men on either side of him returning to their places and Watson to his seat.

'Mr Hutchinson,' continued the chairman. 'As I was saying, you have clearly broken one of the basic tenets of racing, and taken money for doing so. For that, we are withdrawing your amateur licence for five years. Only after that time will the British Horseracing Authority consider an application for its renewal, and then it will need clear evidence of unblemished behaviour.'

Five years! I would be nearly thirty-three by then, almost too old to try again. All my dreams of Cheltenham and the Grand National destroyed by a chance encounter with an unknown member of the public waving money at me. Money which I wouldn't even have dreamed of accepting. 'Sir,' I began, trying to attract Lord Greenstone's attention.

But he was already standing, gathering up the papers in front of him. He gave no sign of having heard and swept out of the room, closely followed by his two co-judges who had still not uttered a word. Gavin Chesterfield was also gone.

Only the technicians were left, and they were packing up their equipment. Gordon Watson and Sue were still seated. I made my dazed way over to them, as stunned as if I'd been hit over the head with a mallet.

'Rodney,' Watson began as he got to his feet. 'I did make the point to Lord Greenstone that you earn your living from writing about racing. He wanted to declare you a disqualified person for the five years, and that would have meant you not being allowed to set foot on a racecourse. But I told Lord Greenstone that this might open the way for a legal challenge to his ruling because the BHA does not licence journalists. It might also make other members of the racing press critical of the judgement.'

I was far from sure that he was right about the last point. In my experience there was no solidarity in the press room. It was more a case of dog eat dog, with each one trying to scoop the others – and I had no real friends amongst the scribes. Tom Cameron was the one I knew best but even he would have no hesitation about hanging me out to dry, particularly if it made a good story.

I said nothing. Sue stood up and shook my hand. 'Rodney,' she said. 'I'm sorry that things didn't work out for you today. Perhaps we will meet again in happier circumstances.' She smiled. I was still struck dumb.

Watson also shook my hand. 'Don't forget,' he said. 'If you do find new evidence - maybe about that man who tried to give you the money, or that someone confirms your story about you refusing to accept it, get in touch.'

He fished a card out of his breast pocket and handed it to me. I still said nothing, and I was still wondering what had hit me. Maybe it was all a dream. Or rather a nightmare. I deliberately bit my lip. And the grimness of the reality struck me all over again.

I made my way slowly to the front entrance – this time there was nobody on the desk – and onto the street. There were people everywhere. Several times I was jostled as I unseeingly bumped into morning shoppers. Somehow I reached the car park, parted with a small fortune at the pay office and began the drive home, forcing myself to concentrate on the road.

3

The phone started ringing just after I came off the M4. The Press Association's main racing man wanted to know if the bribery offence was true and whether I was going to appeal.

I didn't mince words. I told him in no uncertain terms that I'd been set up and that I was going to leave no stone unturned until I could prove it.

'I guess you made a few enemies in the lead up to the Cheltenham bomb,' he said, his tone sympathetic. But I wasn't sure how genuine the sympathy really was. I'd been on the other end of this sort of phone call for some years now – and getting the person to talk was the main secret to obtaining a few decent quotes. 'Could it have been one of them?' he continued.

'I dunno. Possibly.'

'So will you appeal?'

'You bet I will. But first I've got work to do finding out who set me up. One thing I can tell you, though: I am totally innocent of what they accused me this morning, and I won't rest until I've proved it – and until I've made the BHA wipe out their charges. I might have ridden a bad race, and made a bad decision to ride when I wasn't fit enough, but I would never dream of taking a bribe. As I'm sure you know, Chris.'

The PA man made a few conciliatory noises before hanging up. Two other pressmen had rung by the time I reached home and two more did so while I was sitting in front of my computer working out what I was going to say in my own article for *sports-all.com*.

I needed to concentrate. But I couldn't afford to switch the phone off. Journalists unable to reach people like me in such circumstances assume the phone has been turned off so that the subject can't be quoted. And they invariably go on the attack.

I switched on my computer and read the emailed press release:

The stewards inquiry into the Berkshire Amateur Riders Steeplechase at Newbury last Saturday was reopened by the Disciplinary Panel of the British Horseracing Authority this morning following the receipt of new evidence.

The Panel, under the chairmanship of Lord Greenstone, found that Brave Soldier had not been allowed to run on its merits and that rider Rodney Hutchinson had committed a breach of Rule 37.1 (a jockey must, and must be seen to, ask their horse for timely, real and substantial efforts to achieve the best possible position).

The Panel also found that rider Rodney Hutchinson had committed a breach of Integrity Rule 4 (A person must not accept, or agree, or offer to accept a bribe).

The Panel withdrew Mr Hutchinson's Amateur Jockey Licence with immediate effect and ordered that he may not apply for any BHA Licence before five years from today.

Three more journalists rang while I was writing my piece but my mind was so full of injustice, and what I needed to say, that the calls barely interrupted my mental flow.

I went into some detail about the so-called John Roberts, the unexplained source of the film, and how it conveniently stopped before I'd handed back the money. I decided against mentioning Gavin Chesterfield and his accusatory tone – prejudice against the officials might not put me in a good light – but I finished by declaring that 'I will prove my innocence even if it's the last thing I ever do.'

I read it through again. A cracking piece, or so I thought. All sorts of material that none of the other journalists could know about. A real inside story – the sort of thing that would, in the ordinary course of events, be labelled an exclusive. And, most important of all, it would clearly demonstrate that I was the innocent party, deliberately set up for reasons so far unexplained.

An hour and a half later, though, there was still no sign of it on the *sports-all.com* website, just the BHA's press release – with no accompanying comment or explanation.

I picked up my phone and dialled Brett Marsh, my boss at *sports-all.com*. 'Yes Rod. I was about to call you.' His tone was uncharacteristically unfriendly. 'We need to talk. Can you be at my office at ten tomorrow?'

'OK. But what about my story? There is nothing on the website yet.'

'That's what we need to talk about. See you at ten tomorrow.'

'But......'

I realised I was talking to myself. He had switched off.

'Morning Mr Hutchinson.' Joshi Shah had my papers ready in a pile, the *Racing Post* on top. I winced as I saw the headline: *Journalist – amateur rider banned for five years for taking bribe to lose.*

'Is it true?' The turbanned proprietor's tone seemed to say 'surely not.' He shook his head, his expression grave, his tone sad.

'No, it most certainly isn't, Joshi – and in the next few weeks I am going to prove I was set up.'

'Good man. That's the spirit.' The choice of phrase sounded odd in his Indian-accented English. I almost expected him to add: 'Jolly good show, chaps.'

'Must go – but thanks Joshi. Appreciate that.' I picked up the bundle and hurried out to the car. I'd almost reached the M4 when I could stand the suspense no longer. I pulled in to the side of the road and went through Tom Cameron's piece.

I breathed a sigh of relief when I saw that he had quoted me at length – and with tape-recorder accuracy – on having been set up, my complete innocence of the charges and my utter determination to prove it.

A quick skim through the racing pages of the other papers revealed rather less of my side of the story – in many of them nothing at all – and a concentration on jockeys deliberately riding to lose.

I glanced at the dashboard clock. I didn't want to risk compounding my offences in Brett's eyes by turning up late. A more detailed study of the papers, and the implications of their comments in the minds of their readers, would have to wait.

I had only visited the boss once before, when I had been appointed one of the website's two racing correspondents. But I remembered the way to the semi-detached in North Finchley which had been his home for most of his 35 years on the newspaper sports desks, the only noticeable difference being that he now owned the left-hand half of the property as well as the right.

sports-all.com had taken off so rapidly that he had been able to accumulate capital at a rate that not even a working lifetime of inflation had matched, and the new purchase was used for offices for himself and his three editorial staff. The advertising, and its mushrooming revenue, was all done through an agency with Brett repeatedly supplying them with evidence of the ever-growing readership.

'He's upstairs waiting for you,' informed Michelle, the longest-serving editorial assistant.   'And the good news is that he is in a good mood!'

I grinned. I knew that this wasn't always the case by any means. As my confidence returned, I took the stairs two at a time, knocked on the door facing me and went straight in.

'Ah, Rod.' The rather overweight, almost bald man reminded me of the pictures of the Cistercian monks, a wafer-thin tonsure of grey hair going two-thirds of the way round his otherwise shiny bare skull.

He sat down on his office chair and bid me to take the one on my side of the large desk, covered in newspapers. Most of them, I noticed uneasily, were open at the reports of my sentence. Headlines like Journalist Banned, Jockey Banned and even an innacurate Bribes Jockey Warned Off sent shivers down my spine. Judging by his expression, they horrified Brett too.

'I believe you,' he said slowly, as if picking his words with deliberate care. 'Indeed I've never had any reason to suspect your integrity and, despite all this,' he pushed some of the newspapers across the desk in my direction, 'I still haven't.'

I breathed a mental sigh of relief. Clearly Brett was on my side …… and it looked as if things were going to be OK after all. Touch wood. My right hand involuntarily grasped the edge of the desk and squeezed it.

'However,' I could feel my breath giving a sharp intake - the way

Brett said 'however' sounded horribly ominous. 'It's not me, and what I believe or don't believe, that is the issue here. What is are the views of the public in general, and of our readers in particular. And also those of our advertisers. You know, as well as I do, that our racing coverage attracts more advertising than any other sport. That's why we have two full time racing correspondents and other sports have only one.

'Integrity, and an integrity that is wholly above even a trace of suspicion, is essential for any journalist - let alone one whose speciality is horseracing, an activity that has suspicion, intrigue and the possibility of corruption bursting from every pore.'

I thought he was considerably over-egging the pudding. But this was not the moment to say so, or even to interrupt the flow.

'For these reasons it is essential that there should not be even a hint of doubt about our racing journalists. However the British Horseracing Authority has blackened your name to such an extent that it cannot be mentioned without calling to mind the offences of which you have been convicted. Accepting bribes, stopping hot favourites and lying in the racing courts. It could hardly have been worse had you been sentenced for murder.'

'But Brett, for God's sake.' I couldn't let all this go unchallenged. He seemed to believe that every word of the BHA press release was gospel. 'I explained in my report exactly what happened, me being set up to make it look like a bribe when I'd simply handed the money back, and how I lost the race because of a lack of fitness. That was my only crime, if that is what you want to call it. As regards any other misdoing, I am as innocent as the driven snow.'

Brett held up his right hand towards me, palm upwards as if to stop me saying any more. 'Rod,' he began. 'As I said at the beginning, I believe you. But the public perception does not – and what our public believes is what counts. Without the public's trust in us, we are finished. It's the same with the papers. We might be a more modern form of newspaper but, believe me, the same rules apply.'

'Have we published my story?' I was becoming more and more uptight. I could feel the tension in my chest. I could also feel my face going red, not with embarrassment but with fury.

'No Rod, we have not – and nor can we do so.' I could see that he too was struggling to keep his composure. The way his fists were clenched was ominous - for me.

'We cannot allow you to fight your battles through the columns of *sports-all.com*. That would be akin to us supporting your cause – and, as I have been trying to explain, it would be totally wrong to do that. No newspaper worth the name would do so, and we are no different.'

'So what happens now?' Maybe I should have kept quiet and heard him out. But I was damned if I was going to have my life unprotestingly squeezed out of existence like the pips from a lemon.

'What happens now,' answered Brett, getting to his feet and noisily pushing his chair back, 'is that you are suspended on full pay for the next three months. If, during that time, you provide the BHA with sufficient evidence for them to publicly cancel your ban, we can discuss the possibility of *sports-all.com* re-employing you. Otherwise your employment with us will be terminated.'

I stayed seated, too shocked to move. My job, my career and my income eliminated at a stroke. Devastated hardly summed up the mental destruction.

'Now Rod, you've got a job to do. Perhaps the most important job you will ever have. As I said, I believe you. I also believe that somebody has it in for you and that this is the result. It's easy to make enemies as a journalist. Indeed sometimes you have no choice. Remember the old adage: if you never upset anyone, your stuff's not worth reading.

'Your copy is always worth reading, and sometimes you come up with explosive stuff. Literally so, on occasion.' He smiled at his own joke. 'We want more of the same. And we want you back. But I can only give you three months. Don't waste them. Find the bastard who did this to you.'

He reached forward, shook my hand and then came round the desk to open the door for me. 'Remember one thing, though.' Clearly he hadn't finished. 'People who think they have been maligned in print never forget it. Many of them bear a grudge against the journalist concerned for the rest of their lives. What I am trying to say is that this business at the BHA could well trace to something that has no connection with the Cheltenham bomb. Don't make the mistake of focussing on that to the exclusion of all else.'

I took the stairs a good deal slower than I had come up them. Deep in thought, I nodded at Michelle – ignoring her questioning expression – and walked slowly to my car.

Brett's words worried me and encouraged me at the same time. I thought through our somewhat one-sided conversation as I negotiated what seemed like a never-ending succession of traffic lights on my way back to the M4.

Three months was not long but surely it was long enough. There weren't that many people who could have been responsible. I already had strong leads, having investigated the stories before writing them, and I could surely explore them sufficiently to find the culprit.

But I would have to get on with it, not waste a day or an opportunity. I must also bear in mind that the BHA might take some convincing to publicly admit that their people had got it so wrong. That might take longer than three months – but no matter. If I couldn't get Brett to publish details of the villains and how they had set me up, I could surely find a newspaper that would. It was the sort of story that editors dream about.

And, if all else failed, I would write a book about it. Indeed I might well do that anyway. It would make for blistering reading and would surely see me back as a racing journalist, possibly with one of the broadsheets.

By the time I reached my rented cottage just beyond the end of the village, the edge of the Downs stretching out in front of me, I was in my best frame of mind for days. A cup of coffee had me at the computer, compiling a list of possible suspects and preparing an action list.

I remembered the card Gordon Watson had given me. It was still in my suit pocket and I rang the number. 'I'm sorry, he's in court today,' said the girl on the switch. 'Can anyone else help you?'

'Yes. Is Sue Tomlinson in?'

'Hold on, Mr Hutchinson. I will see if she is available...........
Putting you through.'

'Hello Rodney. How's things going?' The friendly voice conjured an instant picture of the attractive brunette with the lovely legs.

We exchanged pleasantries – extremely pleasant in my mind – before I decided I had better get to the point of the call. 'Sue, you know that film that appeared to show the man in the mac handing me money. Would it be possible to get a copy of it from the BHA?'

'I don't see why not. It's material evidence so I don't think they could reasonably refuse. Do you want me to speak to them?

'Yes please, Sue. They might not give it to me, if I asked.'

'OK. What's your number? I'll ring you back.'

She did so less than ten minutes later. 'They are going to have a copy made this afternoon and will courier it over first thing in the morning. Do you want me to courier it on to you?

'No. I'll come and fetch it. If I'm there around eleven?'

'That should be OK but I'll ring you when it arrives just in case it's late. And, if you haven't heard from me by ten, ring me. I wouldn't want you battling with all the Friday morning traffic only to find there's been a hitch.'

Next on the list was Charlie. I'd called off riding out this morning as soon as I received the summons from Brett but I was due to resume tomorrow.

'Charlie,' I began. 'I'm changing plans for the next few weeks. I'm not going to ride exercise at all because I want to devote every minute of every day to finding out who set me up and to clearing my name. Only then can I concentrate on race-riding.'

There was a few seconds' silence from the other end, presumably while Charlie worked out the implications from his point of view. 'OK Rod. I fully understand. Pity about the riding, though. We value your input. But look, why don't you call round? Might help to run through things with somebody else. Also, Rod, we've got plans for your two horses to work out. Why don't you come round after stables this evening? Say around six? And have a drink.'

We agreed on 6.00pm the following evening. By that time I should have a copy of the film, and would feel that I had made some progress – enough to warrant taking an evening off.

Over the next few hours I made a list of possible suspects, their reasons for holding a grudge against me and how I might contact them in a manner that would encourage them to talk. But I was surprised how many there were.

By this stage I was mentally exhausted. I went out for a walk to clear my head, and I'd reached the edge of the Downs when an idea occurred to me. When I got back I googled 'Susan Tomlinson, London solicitor.'

There was a lot about her, including pictures of her wedding five years earlier to a fellow solicitor who worked in the same firm. What I found even more interesting was a newspaper report of her divorce three months ago.

My imagination of what the romantic future might hold was wiped out by the gathering cloud over my finances. And it was a dark cloud. The prospect of no income after the next three months was frightening. True, I had a bit of capital to fall back on but drastic savings were going to have to be made. My two racehorses were costing me something like £140 a day.

I'd bought them out of the money left to me when my parents died in the first few months of Covid, and I had put a chunk of the inheritance aside to pay for their training costs for three years. By which time I'd hoped to have become a reasonably successful amateur rider, good enough to get decent outside rides. Nine months out of action had knocked that ambition for six – and now I was sidelined for a further five years.

Even if I succeeded in persuading the BHA that they had got it all wrong, it was going to take time for them to cancel the ban. They wouldn't exactly be rushing to do so because any climbdown or retraction would be seen as a loss of face on their part. It would also expose them to criticism in the press.

No, the horses would have to go – and at a decent price. That meant running them to sell rather than to win. Racecourse success would, of course, be a good shop window but the shrewder owners would prefer to buy a horse who looked as if he was ready to win – rather than one who had just won, and whose consequent handicap rise might make it difficult for him to do so again for quite some time. In other words they needed to be not trying too hard but running on in eye-catching fashion when the race was as good as over. Just what eagle-eyed officials like Gavin Chesterfield were trying to stamp down on.

I could end up in even more trouble!

I was on the Chiswick flyover when the phone rang. Sue had received the copy of the film and she would be in her office all morning.

I found Johnson, Kerson and Lawson just off Chancery Lane, the firm's heavy black door at the top of three stone steps. It swung slowly open as I neared it. 'Good morning, how may I help?' politely inquired the grey-haired lady behind the front desk.

'I've come to see Sue Tomlinson. She's expecting me. Rodney Hutchinson.'

The receptionist picked up her phone and I heard her say my name. She directed me to the three armchairs a few feet from her desk, saying 'Mrs Tomlinson says she won't be a minute.'

It was nearer three when the smart grey-suited figure in high heels came clicking across the parquet flooring, a padded envelope in her right hand. 'Morning Rod. How's things?'

I could have said, and perhaps should have: 'All the better for seeing you.' But I was mesmerised, and embarrassingly tongue-tied, by her dazzling smile – and even more by those legs. All I managed was a feeble 'Hello Sue.'

'I've had a look at it,' she said as she handed over the envelope. 'It looks the same as the one they showed at the BHA. But I think you were hoping for a bit more, weren't you?'

My response was inaudible, even to my ears. I glanced at her left hand to make sure I wasn't going to make a complete fool of myself: no ring. I steered her a few yards further from the ears of the receptionist. 'Sue.' This was the bit I had rehearsed on the drive up. 'Will you come out for a meal with me one evening?'

She didn't hesitate, but her expression had my hopes dashed even before she spoke. 'Rod, I'm sorry but I can't. It would be totally against professional ethics to discuss a client's business – in this case the BHA's business – with anyone outside the office. And particularly with someone who has been the subject of a hearing.'

I felt my ears and cheeks going red. I tried to force myself to relax as I glanced at the receptionist who was clearly attempting to listen to every word.

'Sue,' I said as quietly as I could without risking her being unable to hear properly. 'You misunderstand me. My fault, I'm sure. But I like you. I find you extremely attractive, and I would like to get to know you. I won't be saying a word about the BHA or anything to do with the hearing. I promise you.'

I felt I'd made a complete hash of it. I should have sent her a letter instead of trying to talk to her at the office, particularly with other people around.

She looked at me inquiringly for a few seconds then, to my surprise, broke into a smile. 'In that case,' she said. 'I would be delighted. When are you thinking of?'

'What about Sunday evening?'

'Perfect. Will you pick me up? And what time?

'Seven o'clock if that is OK with you. Where do I find you?'

She glanced at the receptionist before saying quietly: 'I'll text you. OK?'

She smiled again before turning on her high heels, and going back the way she had come. I watched the retreating shapely rear view, totally entranced. I was still smiling as I bid the receptionist a cheery farewell and headed back to the car.

4

Brown River noisily munched the large carrot I'd given him and pointedly ignored both my pats on his neck and the sweet nothings I was murmuring into his ears. I knew then I wasn't going to sell him, not unless I was economically forced to. And even then he, and Ezekiel in the next box, would be the last luxuries to go. Both horses had loyally given their all for me, both had carried me to victory, and both had done their bit for my finances by winning during my many months out of action.

My earlier vow to put them on the market had gone by the board as soon as I walked into the yard and seen them inquisitively sticking their heads out of their boxes. Brown River had even given me a whinny of recognition.

'Charlie, just keep them going the way you and Paddy have been doing. And if you can win with them, so much the better. It 'll help towards paying their keep.'

'Sure.' Charlie came alongside me and rubbed Brown River's nose. 'They're no stars but they've both still got potential.'

He turned towards me and, in a slightly more serious tone, said: 'Are you sure you don't want to come and ride work? You are allowed to, you know. I rang the BHA just to make sure.'

I shook my head. 'Not yet Charlie. When I look like getting things wrapped up, I'll be here like a shot and badgering you for rides.

But for now, no. The all-consuming priority is to find out who set me up and prove it to the satisfaction of the BHA.'

We moved off on a path that was new to me, out of the right-hand side of the yard towards a house I hadn't noticed before. Charlie led the way, through an unlocked side door and flicked a switch that seemed to light up just about every room on the ground floor.

'Impressive, eh?' Charlie grinned as he slipped off his Puffa and hung it on a nearby row of hooks. 'Uncle had it built during the year. Said he and Marjorie were going to use it at weekends, but when I came he told me to move in. The old trainer's house, where Paddy O'Reilly lived, has become the head lad's house – and it's great to have Barry on the premises. He's close enough to the yard to hear anything if a horse hurts himself during the night.

'Come through.' He led the way along the passage and into a medium-sized sitting room, the three-piece suite tastefully upholstered in Dralon, and asked me that I would like to drink.

'Just a beer please, Charlie.'

'Fine, I'll have the same.' He went to what was clearly a well-stocked drinks cupboard, extracted two bottles and, handing me one together with a glass, said: 'I'm at Fontwell tomorrow. Bigasbrass goes in the three-mile hurdle – and he's in with a good chance. I suppose you'll be at Cheltenham for The Major's race?'

I nodded. 'It would be wrong not to go, despite all that's happened this week.' The race Charlie was referring to was the first running of the Charles Alvernon Memorial Handicap Chase, run in honour of the man who was killed by the bomb that was intended for me.

A highly successful amateur jockey in his younger days, Charles became even more famous as a tipster under the pseudonym of The Major and won the naps award four times in his last five seasons. He was something of a legend, particularly with the punters. He had also been my colleague on *sports-all.com*. But he had made the mistake, quite literally fatal, of assuming that two tours of Northern Ireland at the height of The Troubles, decades earlier, qualified him to tell what was – and what was not – a modern-day car bomb.

'So, who's at the top of the suspect list? Jimmy Brownson?' Charlie's long, slim frame sank back into the armchair as he took a drink of his beer and smiled. His cheerful outlook was infectious.

'Hardly,' I smiled back as I began to relax. 'The judge put him away for life, with a 15-year minimum.'

'Yes, but look where he is – and the company he's keeping,' Charlie's expression was now serious. 'In Belmarsh, or wherever they put him, he'll be mixing with some of the most accomplished, and most ruthless, criminals in the business. If he can pay for it – and he's surely still got plenty of money – he will be able to get anything done. The fact that he's inside will be only a minor inconvenience.'

Hmm. I hadn't looked at it that way. Obviously I should have done. Charlie had me worried.

Jimmy Brownson, convicted of the murder of Charles Alvernon and the attempted murder of myself, was a highly successful businessman who had built up a large shareholding in the bookmaking firm Hedgers under false names. Somebody in the firm (the trial did not reveal who) had blackmailed Charles into revealing his daily tips before they appeared on the *sports-all. com* website. As the tips had a big following, the information was hugely valuable, and it enabled Hedgers to steal a march on its rivals on a daily basis.

'And what about Trevor?' Charlie had obviously been giving my plight some serious thought. 'He's taken a massive knock in all this. I gather his numbers are down from over eighty to no more than twenty.'

'Yes,' I said thoughtfully, more to myself than to Charlie. 'He would have good reason, alright. You know I took Brown River and Ezekiel away from him? Brown River he stopped at Bangor-on-Dee. Took the horse's water away two days beforehand and gave him nothing more until shortly before the race when of course he drank bucketfuls. Was tailed off by halfway and I had to pull him up.'

'Bloody hell.' Charlie was shocked, as well he might be. It was a horrific thing to do. I had been convinced the horse was doped until a disgruntled stable lad told me what had happened. 'And Ezekiel?'

'He was going for a pipe-opener at Ludlow to get him right for when I returned after breaking a bone in my arm. He told me the horse wasn't off and I said as much in my column. Bugger me, if he wasn't backed off the boards. Billy Black had the ride and of course he won. Made me look a complete crook.'

Those last few words made me think. The running of Brave Soldier at Newbury, and the film given to the BHA, had had the same intention behind it – and the same effect. Even more so. Maybe it was the same person who was responsible. Trevor again? I said as much to Charlie.

'Yea,' he said thoughtfully, rubbing his chin. 'I certainly wouldn't put it past him. But I thought he was cutting back on his jumpers anyway, to make room for all the expensive Flat horses that Jimmy was buying.'

'So did I. He never quibbled when I told him that I was taking my two elsewhere. Didn't even ask why.'

Charlie said nothing, just sat there deep in thought. I looked round the room and, as I did so, I realised what was strange about it. The furniture and carpets were of a high standard but the walls were completely bare. Not a photograph or a painting to be seen.

Most racing people's houses were full of them. I mentioned this to Charlie.

He looked round as if noticing it for the first time. 'I guess Marjorie hadn't got that far with the furnishings by the time Paddy O'Reilly got taken ill and I was brought in.

'Barry was let go, you know. Trevor told him the day after Jimmy was convicted. The stable suddenly had no horses, no more than twenty or so anyway. Only a handful of the staff were kept on.

'The stable here was growing rapidly, Paddy took on half a dozen lads including Barry. He still bears a grudge and he seemed to blame you for a while. It all came out when I ticked him off for being offhand with you one day.'

I must have looked surprised because Charlie continued: 'Maybe you didn't notice but I did. I told him that I expected all the staff to treat the owners with respect; it's the owners who are paying their wages. Less owners: less staff, less wages. And less wage increases.

'Sorry,' he got to his feet. 'I was so engrossed I didn't realise your glass was empty. Have another.'

'No, Charlie one is enough. I've got to drive.' I stood up. 'But thank you for all your help with my problems. You've certainly given me plenty to think about. And plenty to work on. When its just me saddled with it all, I tend to get a bit overwhelmed and I don't seem able to separate the wood from the trees – if that's the right expression.'

'Sometimes you need to be able to talk things through,' said Charlie, looking straight at me. 'It helps to bounce ideas off other people and get their opinion. I've found that myself when I have problems.'

He went with me, torch in hand as he led the way to my car. 'Come round anytime. I will be most interested to hear how you are getting on. And if I can help in anyway I will.' He shook my hand and, as I got in behind the wheel, he boosted my spirits by adding: 'We want you back riding out and riding in races. That 7lb allowance will be like gold dust.'

I walked slowly to the brick wall on the racecourse side of the press car park. I don't know what I was expecting but I felt a slight disappointment that, so far as I could see, there wasn't even a mark on it. I'd been thrown against it so hard by the force of the explosion that it had broken my ankle in two places, and broken my elbow so badly that I had been unable to ride a racehorse for nine months.

I retraced my steps back to the car, and from there to the end of this particular section of the car park. I knew the bomb, and its sheets of flame, had left a large black patch – the grass had been burned away completely– but now there wasn't even a suggestion of fire. I felt as if I had been somehow deprived of what I had a right to expect. All that was left was the nightmare in my mind: the scream as the human ball of flame sailed through the air, and the deafeningly loud explosion so powerful that it lifted me off my feet and crashed me against the brick wall with the force of a piledriver.

I made myself get a grip. I was the lucky one. It was Charles who had lost his life, and his wheelchair-dependent daughter who had lost her father, to a horrible burning death. This day was for him, not for the person his bravery had saved.

I looked out onto the racecourse, green almost as far as the eye could see, and thought of the great moments he had enjoyed there as an amateur jockey in a riding career that had hit the heights. Try as I might, I could not help but compare it with my own which had barely got off the ground – and was now snuffed out in disgrace.

I didn't want to look back but I felt I owed it to Charles to do so. That fateful evening he had insisted I moved further and further away as he used the remote to open the car door, and condemn himself to a dreadful and unbelievably painful death. He had demons of his own to contend with – and I still had a sneaking suspicion that what proved to be a suicidal act of bravery was, to some extent at least, occasioned by a belief that his reputation was about to be blown apart in the same way as his body.

The ace tipster had been told a year or more before that, if he did not give his daily selections to someone in Hedgers before they appeared on the *sports-all.com* website, his daughter's face would be disfigured with a knife. He felt he had no choice but to co-operate. However what he had done – a betrayal of thousands of loyal followers as well as of his employer – was in danger of becoming public knowledge at the time he stepped in to save my life. He knew he could never have borne the shame had he survived. I said a silent prayer as I gazed out over the racecourse, seeing nothing but his screaming body in a sheet of flame.

This was my first visit to Cheltenham since that fateful November day and I had been nervous about coming. Not because of what happened but because of the reaction I feared I would face after the BHA press release and all the adverse newspaper comment, in some cases blatantly antagonistic and condemnatory. My fears were made worse by not having any journalistic duties to take my mind off them although, not wanting to look like the proverbial spare prick at a wedding, I had brought my laptop with me.

No-one seemed to show the slightest sign of recognition as I produced my pass at the entrance, but I was sure it was going to be a different story when I went into the press room. However nobody seemed fussed and, even when I took off my coat and draped it over my usual seat at the same table as Tom Cameron, the *Racing Post* man only stopped typing long enough to say: 'Hi Rod. Am I glad to see you?'

I looked questioningly at him.

'Mike Johnson of the *Mirror* was offering 2–1 that you wouldn't show, and I put a score on,' added Cameron in smiling explanation. 'I knew you'd come as it's The Major's day, and you wouldn't miss that – no matter what trouble you might be in.'

As he said this, he pointed in the direction of a table at the far end of the big room where a group of journalists seemed to be in animated conversation. The *Sunday Mirror* reporter looked my way and threw up his hands in mock horror. Then, grinning broadly, he raised a thumb in my direction. Clearly not all the press corps was anti my presence. I began to feel a little better.

But I had work to do, and it wasn't in the press room. I got up, went out into the general racecourse area and headed for the weighing room. I passed a few trainers who nodded in my direction. Only two deliberately ignored my polite hellos, both turning the other way. I spotted the man I was looking for just as he was breaking away from what was clearly a friendly conversation with one of the top trainers.

Arthur Jackson, the public face of Hedgers Bookmakers, was one of racing's diplomats. Always cheerful, always helpful, he was there to convey a favourable image of his company – and, although other bookmaking firms had people in similar ambassadorial roles, few were as well liked as the tall figure with the fashionable but uncomfortable-looking four-day growth.

'Hi Rod,' he said, extending his right hand and grasping mine in a firm grip. 'Good to see you. How's things?'

'Arthur, I need to talk to you. Privately.' I steered him away from the gathering number of listeners, and towards the racecourse. 'Arthur,' I began. 'I was set up at that hearing on Wednesday.'

He listened carefully and, I thought sympathetically, as I told him about John Roberts, the film showing him trying to give me money and ending before it got to me handing it back. 'I need to find out who was responsible for doing this – and the trials of both Jimmy Brownson and Tommy Thompson (the man who planted the bomb) strongly suggested a link with somebody in Hedgers.'

Arthur gripped my right arm as he looked behind him. 'Rod. Let's keep walking. Those two trials, and all that was said at them, nearly destroyed Hedgers. Several people lost their jobs and, however unfair this might seem, many of those that did hold you responsible. So did some of the shareholders who saw their investments all but wiped out, with the share price tumbling from over £10 to little more than ten pence at one stage.

'Rod, what I am trying to say is that the people who bear a grudge against you are legion. So far as they are concerned, you are public enemy number one. I know that sounds tough but,' he gripped my arm a second time, only on this occasion far more firmly, 'that is the fact of the matter.

'Rod, take the advice of someone who has seen it all before. The racecourse is a burial ground for reputation. Once you get a bad one, it never leaves you. I know you believe you don't deserve yours but, no matter how hard you try, in most people's minds you will always be the racing journalist who took bribes. Even if you prove your innocence, human nature being what it is, your name will be tarnished for ever more.'

'But Arthur…. that's balls.'

'Rod.' My arm was gripped again. 'Let me finish. You are one of the few lucky ones. You have another career already waiting to welcome you back. A career where the racecourse, and all its rumours, doesn't exist. Go back to the law, Rod. Forget about racing. Unless you do, racing won't forget about you.'

With that, he turned on his heel and headed back in the direction of the weighing room.

I stood where I was, as rooted to ground as a turnip in a winter field. And as stunned as if I'd been struck on the head with a cricket bat.

Only a public address announcement about a jockey change in the first race brought me back to reality. I headed slowly to the weighing room and from there to the press room. I was passing the former when I saw Gavin Chesterfield coming towards me. As he glanced at me his lips turned down. It was his only sign of acknowledgement, and it pierced my already-depressed state of mind like a poisoned arrow.

I sank into my seat, opened the laptop and stared at the blank screen. I was just glad that Tom Cameron was out of the room, presumably hunting for news. I didn't think I would have been able to keep a lid on my feelings had he started his questions.

'Rod.' I looked up and into the friendly face of Graham Gordon of *The Sunday Times* and the current chairman of the Racing Writers' Association. 'Just to let you know: we're going to have a group photo of the presentation immediately after The Major's race, and then we've been invited to the directors' box for a drink. OK?'

'Sure Graham,' I acknowledged. 'And Graham – thanks.'

At least I was still part of the RWA. Not a total outcast – despite what I was supposed to have done. Even so the first race passed me by, on the various TV screens, without me seeing any of it.

I had one more person to see and, after Arthur Jackson, I was hardly looking forward to it. Indeed dreading was the operative word.

I found Christopher Mayhew, camel hair overcoat on and coming out of the directors' dining room. For once Marjorie wasn't with him. I was still trying to work out whether that was a good sign or not, when he spotted me and raised a finger as if to say 'I want a word.'

'Rod. Just the man I'm looking for. I've been talking to Michael Greenstone – I sat next to him at the lunch – and I was pressing him about the evidence presented at your hearing on Wednesday. He told me the whole thing, or what I presume was the whole thing.' He paused, eyebrows raised as if waiting for a response from me.

'Did he say where the film came from? And why it was stopped before the end instead of showing me handing back the money?'

'No, he didn't.' Christopher's response was slow, as if he was casting his mind back to what he had been told. 'But he did say that there was no doubt about the evidence. 'Totally conclusive,' were the words he used. But apparently not?'

'Not at all. Christopher,' I was speaking from the heart, with total sincerity as if my life depended on it. My future certainly did. I told him about the letter summoning me to the hearing, and about me wrongly assuming that it was the Walters-Farthing incident that was being looked at.

'I'm disappointed you didn't see fit to tell me this before.' 'His deep-set frown somehow seemed to emphasise the words. 'Apart from anything else, I could have made these points to Greenstone instead of listening to him telling me about bribes and corruption in my racing colours.'

What he said made all-too-obvious sense, and made it clear that I should have kept him informed from the very start. I said as much, and apologised again.

'It's a bit late for that now.' His tone suggested he wasn't mollified one iota. 'You are going to have to get yourself out of this mess – and clear my name too. It was my horse that you were convicted of stopping. The next thing is that I will be up before the beaks too, accused of benefiting from your criminal activities.'

His face was reddening as he said that last bit, his blood pressure clearly rising.

'Christopher.....' He waved me and my protests aside, clearly intent on not listening to anything more.

I watched him go, annoyance evident in every step. I cursed myself. I had deliberately waited until I had a chance to speak to him face to face before explaining what had gone on. How many more mistakes was I going to make before I completely ruined my future? Or was that now gone beyond recall?

Back in the press room, I opened my laptop and stared at the screen deep in troubled thought.

'Any luck?' inquired Tom Cameron, typing away as busily as ever.

'Hmm. What do you make of Gavin Chesterfield?' It was nothing more than a train of thought on my part. I wasn't expecting much of an answer. 'Is he above board, do you think?'

'He's a shit of the first order. A horrible piece of work.' The words were spoken with a venom totally out of character for the normally mild-mannered Cameron. 'Was he involved last Wednesday?'

'Involved? He was the chief prosecutor and the hangman rolled into one.'

'Tell me,' said Cameron quietly, pushing his laptop to one side. 'What were you actually accused of at that hearing? What did they say in the letter summoning you to the BHA? I presume they sent you a letter?'

'It was an email. It just said that they were reopening their inquiry into the Newbury race and I was required to attend. Like a bloody fool, I assumed that they were referring to Bob Farthing hitting

Ben Walters with his whip. I only realised that I was the accused when they showed the film.'

'The film of the race?'

I knew I was on dangerous ground talking to someone who would, in all probability, blaze his version across a newspaper. But it could be a gamble worth taking. True, I had plenty to lose, particularly if I was misrepresented or misquoted. But, as Arthur Jackson had so cruelly pointed out, my reputation was already shattered almost beyond redemption.

I looked round to make sure no-one else was in earshot and quietly told Tom about the approach from John Roberts the day before the race, how I had refused to accept the money, how – unknown to me – this had all been filmed, and how a doctored version had been shown by Chesterfield at the inquiry.

'And that was the first you knew that you were accused of anything?' Cameron's tone was full of disbelief, not of what I was saying but that such a thing could have happened at the BHA. 'Nothing at all in that email?'

'Not a word. Look, I've got the letter here. What's your email? I'll send it to you.'

'OK. tomcameron@racingpost.uk.'

I promptly forwarded the letter.

'Got it.' I waited while he read it through. 'That all there was? No wonder you went in unprepared. I would have done the same.'

'Course you would. Anybody would – particularly if they weren't guilty of any offence in the first place. And, when I realised what was going on, I asked for the inquiry to be deferred so I could prepare my case and get a lawyer to properly defend me. They refused point blank.'

'That's terrible.' I could see Cameron was genuinely appalled. 'I know the BHA can be dictatorial. They probably have to be in a business like racing. But they also have to abide by proper legal principles – and behave fairly. You think Chesterfield was responsible?'

'I don't know, Tom. But on Wednesday he treated me like something the cat brought in.'

'Little bastard. It couldn't have been just him though. He wouldn't go to all that trouble on his own. Somebody must have supplied him with the film. Any idea who could have been behind it?'

'I've been thinking of little else since Wednesday. I think it must have been somebody in Hedgers, or somebody who used to be in Hedgers. Several people lost their jobs, and more of them after everything came out in the open at the trial – as Arthur Jackson made a point of telling me when I quizzed him earlier this afternoon.

'Ambitious Arthur,' Cameron chuckled. 'It certainly knocked some of the varnish of the veneer.'

But his smile didn't last more than a few seconds. 'What about *sports-all*,' he asked, serious once more. 'Are you still writing for them?'

'Not for the next three months. They've given me that on full pay. But, during that time, I've got to prove to the satisfaction of the BHA that I wasn't guilty of anything – and get them to publicly admit it. Otherwise I'm out on my ear.'

'Hmm,' said Cameron thoughtfully, scratching his red hair with the blunt end of a biro. 'Getting them to admit it could be the hardest part. They don't like to be shown up. But,' his tone cheered. 'You will surely find the culprit inside three months. And, if you can do that, the newspapers will do the rest.

'Listen Rod,' he leaned towards me, his voice dropping to no more than a whisper. 'I'm going to put something about all this in the *Post*. I can't do it for tomorrow – I want to do a proper story and I'm tied up today. But I will have it in on Monday. On one condition.'

'Meaning?'

'Meaning you don't talk about it to any other journalist in the meantime.'

'That's no problem.' I grinned. 'Most of them don't want to know me at the moment.'

An hour or so later a couple of them made this blatantly clear by pointedly moving well away from me, when we all lined up for the group photo of the presentation to the winning connections after The Major's memorial race. Not wanting to risk more of the same, I gave the directors' drinks a miss, collected my laptop and went home.

5

The Rutherford proved an impressive place. I arrived shortly after 11.00am, as agreed with Paddy O'Reilly, and was shown to a seat amongst the modernistic mauve and grey armchairs, a grey sofa in similar style and a pair of unusually-shaped small tables. But what struck me most was the general air of professionalism. And everywhere was spotless, as were the nursing staff in their white clothing.

But Paddy's appearance shook me to the core. Christopher Mayhew's former trainer looked a good ten years older than the sixty-one I knew him to be, his sparse grey hair was gone altogether, and he had lost a lot of weight leaving him looking as weak as a kitten and as sickly as a man on his last legs. In dressing gown and slippers, he grinned from me to the nurse alongside him.

'Rod, great to see you,' he exclaimed, his voice little more than a whisper as I stood up to greet him. 'My amateur jockey – and a good friend,' he said enthusiastically to the nurse as she eased him into the chair facing me. The nurse, dark-haired, dark-skinned and in her thirties, smiled at me. 'Paddy's been telling me all about you.'

As she headed back to what I presumed were the wards, I asked Paddy how he was feeling. 'I've been better,' he replied with masterly understatement. 'Colon cancer, but it's the bloody chemotherapy that's killing me. I've an operation in the morning and they tell me that will help me a lot.'

'How long have you had the ….er…. cancer?' Somehow it didn't seem tactful to mention the dreaded C word.

'Ah, for sure, a few months.' He still had traces of the Tipperary accent of his youth before it was adulterated by spells in Australia, California and Yorkshire. 'When I first went to a specialist I was told my chances were 6–4. I said that was just as well because I never backed anything at odds-on.' He smiled weakly at his joke. 'Here, they won't quote a price, they just tell m e to be positive. I reckon I'm in with a chance once I can get the bloody chemo behind me. What I really need, though, is to be back training the horses. That would put me right.'

His tone was wistful, reminiscent of a man who does the football pools every week, dreaming of the big pay-out that he knows in his heart of hearts will never come.

'Anyway, what's happening with yerself? I've been reading some terrible things in the *Post*.'

I told him about John Roberts, the following day's race, the BHA inquiry and the verdict. Paddy nodded frequently but said nothing other than the occasional heartfelt 'beyjaysus,' and 'the feckers.'

'So, what are you going to do? You've got to get this put right, Rod – you can't let them get away with it. That would be like hooking a certainty race after race, and never getting to put the money down.'

I smiled at his analogy. Despite his life-threatening illness, Paddy O'Reilly was still entertaining company. I told him that I was trying to find out who was behind it. I told him of my suspicions that it was probably someone formerly connected with Hedgers, and now either sacked or in prison.

'Nah,' Paddy shook his sickly-looking bald head. I looked at him questioningly. 'My money's on the jigger twins. I'd make them odds-on.'

That made me think, and curse myself for my stupidity. The jigger twins were trainers Tom Swarter and Bob Arrows. They both used the same gallops and the same horrifically cruel methods. One morning I'd watched from a nearby hill as they brought out electric whips for their work riders to use, giving the horses a loud shout before they applied the electric shock. The horses soon associated the shout with the shock, and all the jockey in the race had to do was give the same shout at the moment when he required the horse to quicken. The effect on the horses was frightening. They would return from winning their races with the sweat pouring off them, and dancing around on their toes, as the mental impact of the electric shock dominated their thoughts.

An electric whip was known in Australian racing as a jigger and was banned the world over. Both Swarter and Arrows trained for the same man, George Rickards, who I had never met but I was convinced was in on the terrible practice. According to Paddy, the trio had an arrangement with a bookmaker that they were given a good price – much better than they would have got otherwise – up to a certain amount in return for the information that the horses couldn't lose, and the bookmaker concerned was rumoured to be Hedgers.

Swarter and Arrows had left me in no doubt about their ruthlessness. One morning, after I had been watching them from the hill unobserved – or so I thought – I returned to my car to find a knife had been taken to my tyres and a note on the windscreen saying 'Next time it won't be just your tyres that get slashed.'

'Think about it, Rod,' urged Paddy quietly. 'Everybody connected with the bomb is either in prison or fully exposed. Whatever you write can't make it any worse for them but the jigger twins are fully aware that you know what they have been doing – and that you can expose them for what they are. They would get warned off, even put in jail. That's a real motive for discrediting you and, better still from their point of view, ending your career as a journalist.'

Such a long speech was almost too much for Paddy. His face was red and he was struggling to get the words out before the end. I reached forward and put my right hand over his. 'Steady Paddy,' I urged. 'I can see you are right. I was blind not to see it before. I will concentrate my efforts in their direction from now on.'

'But be careful Rod. Those men are ruthless. They wouldn't hesitate to kill you.' Paddy had his voice back, or at least most of it. He gave a cough and drops of spittle ran down his chin.

'Paddy, I've tired you enough. It's time I left you in peace.' I made a move to stand up, pushing back my chair.

'Wait Rod.' Paddy's words stressed urgency. I sat down again. 'Have you explained everything to Christopher Mayhew?'

I said how I had tried to at Cheltenham the previous day, and how he had expressed annoyance at not being kept fully informed.

'You must go and see him, tomorrow if not today. Tell him everything. Hide nothing. His support will be vital. Don't forget, he's been on the board of the BHA and, if anybody can make them see your side of things, bejaysus it's Christopher.'

I assured Paddy that I would, getting to my feet as I saw his nurse coming towards us, a look of concern on her face.

'Time for your pills, Mr O'Reilly,' she said, helping him out of the chair.

'Wait, Rebecca,' he commanded and, turning to me, he continued: 'Christopher Mayhew is one of the best men I've ever come across. He is paying for all this' – Paddy waved an unsteady hand around the whole area – 'and he has told Mary that he will give us the choice of a flat in Reading or a house he will build for us near the stables. Tell him everything, Rod, and he will help you with everything.'

Nurse Rebecca took him by the arm and led him unsteadily away. I sat down again, thinking about the jigger twins. As Paddy had pointed out, they had motive far more pressing than any of those already convicted or sacked. I thought of the knifed tyres and the note. And I shuddered.

As I made my way towards the exit, nurse Rebecca came up to me smiling broadly. 'Mr Rod' she began. 'Please come again, and soon. Your visit has done wonders for Paddy. I know he is tired but you have given him a new lease of life. If, between us, we can keep him like that he will sail through tomorrow's operation and make a good recovery.'

I told her I would ring tomorrow evening to see how the operation had gone and find out when I could visit again. I smiled at her. 'He's done wonders for me too, you know.'

Sue had her coat on, ready to go, when I picked her up from her first floor flat on the outskirts of Twickenham almost on the dot of seven. The coat was smart – fawn with just two large buttons on the front – and open to reveal a white ruffle blouse above a bright red skirt and dark brown stockings. She looked sensational, and I said so.

'Glad you approve,' she said, smiling as she shut the flat door behind us.

'Where are we going?' she asked when I switched on the ignition and eased into a road almost empty of traffic.

'Richmond, The White Swan. Do you know it?'

'No, but I'm looking forward to it,' and, after a pause, as she looked my way: 'How have you been since I last saw you?' The companionable small talk continued for the next few miles while I relied on my GPS to guide me through streets that were completely new to me, and made even more strange by the darkness.

The white-painted pub was well lit up and, as luck would have it, there was a parking space right outside. We went to the upstairs bar where I told an approaching waitress that I had a table booked for 7.30pm. There were several tables in this area and we were shown to one overlooked by a wall of pictures. The waitress pulled out a chair for Sue who declined the offer to have her coat hung up for her. 'Thanks, but I feel the cold.'

The waitress took our drinks orders and two minutes later was back with my beer and Sue's gin and tonic plus the menu, saying she would return once we had had a chance to decide.

The place was busy and quite noisy. I could see only one vacant table and it had a reserved notice on it. 'Seems nice,' said Sue, looking round her. I noticed at least two men at nearby tables glancing in her direction with evident interest. If she saw them, she took no notice.

'So,' she said smiling. 'Have you made any progress on finding out who set you up?'

I didn't answer. I was amazed that she should ask about this. 'I thought the subject was out of bounds for this evening,' I said diffidently, not wanting to risk annoying her. Maybe this was a test to see if I was going to keep my promise.

'Look Rod,' she leaned forward, as if she didn't want anyone at the nearby tables to hear what she was saying. 'I only said that because I thought you were after some free legal advice. When you said what you did say….well, I was embarrassed. I realised I'd completely misjudged you. Insulted you in fact. And, well, I have to admit, I saw you in a new light – a light I liked. Very much so.'

I reached forward to squeeze the hand she had around the stem of her glass. She put the glass down and returned the squeeze. 'Rod,' she smiled. 'You haven't answered my question.'

The arrival of the shrimp cocktail starters delayed my reply. 'I've got several suspects, and the number one are two trainers known as the jigger twins.' I told her about the electric whips they used when training their horses and how the jockey's shouts in a race galvanised the animals into producing more than the form book suggested they could.

She was horrified. 'But that's animal cruelty, surely. What about the RSPCA? Do they not get involved? And the BHA – isn't there a rule against that sort of thing?'

I explained that the trainers concerned would probably get warned off if they were caught, and quite likely face a prison sentence. I also told her about my slashed tyres, and the windscreen note.

'Good God, Rod. You were taking an awful risk. They might easily have killed you.' She was silent for a few seconds, seemingly digesting what she had just said. 'No wonder you think they might have arranged that film and given it to the BHA. They certainly have a pretty powerful motive for wanting you out of the way.'

'They have got that alright.' I told her about being unable to continue with my job at *sports-all.com*.

That shocked her even more. 'So what are we doing here?' She looked round the now packed dining room. 'We should be at the fish and chip shop down the road.'

My explanation of the three months' grace coincided with the arrival of the main course: dover sole for Sue and fillet steak for me. I waited until the waitress had finished serving before explaining about the three months I had to find the culprits and satisfy the BHA.

'That's cutting it tight,' she said. 'What about the thugs who planted the bomb?'

I was surprised how much she knew about my history, and said so. She smiled. 'I looked you up on Google. A woman needs to know about a man when he asks her out.'

It was my turn to smile. 'I looked you up too. Very interesting but a bit traumatic.'

'A bit?' Her voice raised, she continued: 'It was a living nightmare, and it went on for ever. Rod, whatever you do, don't ever get divorced. Better still, don't get married in the first place.'

'How come you didn't take your own advice?' I chuckled at the leg pull.

Sue was not amused. 'I should have known better,' she said with feeling, 'and I certainly won't let it happen again. I thought I was in love' she added, her tone now almost wistful. 'Correction, I was in love. But we had too much in common. We both studied law at the same university, we were articled at the same firm and we both stayed on there after qualifying. We had the same interests and the same views – we could have been twins. It was a terrible mistake.

'Eventually we got on each other's nerves, and soon we were avoiding each other. Not just in the office but at home too. One day Richard said he had met somebody else and he wanted a divorce. I cried for days.'

I made sympathetic noises. She was close to tears. Fishing a tissue out of her handbag, she blew her nose. 'Sorry, I'm making a fool of myself.'

I reached for her hand and squeezed it. 'Don't say any more for the moment, if it's going to upset you.'

'No,' she withdrew her hand. 'You must know,' she added, blinking back the tears and trying to smile. 'Then, if you know what I went through, you won't make the same mistakes.

'The lawyers made it even worse. They turned it into a modern-day version of slaves fighting each other in pre-Roman times. And their bills! They were out of this world. They took all our money, both of us. We had a nice house in Surbiton – a huge mortgage, but it was ours. But then it had to be sold, and now we both live in rented flats.'

'Could you not have done the legalities yourselves?'

She shook her head. 'We weren't on speaking terms – and we hated the sight of each other. No way could we have sat down together to agree anything. It would have been World War Three.'

The waitress came up to take our plates as the tears flowed. 'Are you alright, madam,' she inquired, glaring at me.

'Sorry, yes, fine,' she blew her nose again. 'Thanks to Rodney here. He's such a gentleman – and so understanding.' She reached for my hand and gripped it tightly.

The waitress, suitably mollified, asked what we would like for dessert. 'Nothing for me, just coffee,' said Sue, now smiling almost happily and still holding on to my hand. I said I would have the same.

'Would you like to have it in the lounge?' The waitress, seemingly no longer regarding me as a bullying ogre, was clearly trying to be kind to both of us. 'We've only just done it up – and it's lovely. Come. I will show you.'

She led the way to a room with two armchairs and three small sofas, empty apart from a couple in their forties sitting on the furthest of the three. We took the one nearest the door, Sue removed her coat and hung it over the top of the sofa. I looked at the blouse and, from there, to the red skirt and those fabulous legs. As she sat down I wondered about my chances of getting her to move a good bit closer.

'Anyway I think I've said enough about my life and love gone wrong.' Sue didn't take the hint when I patted my hand on the cushion beside me but she was still smiling. Indeed I detected a mischievous grin. 'How about you? Have you ever been married? Or come close to it?'

'No…. I didn't make it.' It was my turn to fight back the tears. Sue, presumably sensing my change of mood, stopped smiling. 'I was engaged and we were to be married in June – June 29 actually – but almost three weeks before that, the night of June 8, Emma died.'

'Oh Rod, I'm so sorry.' My right hand was gripped again, and squeezed. By this stage I was losing the battle with my emotions and I could sense the tears running down my cheeks. Sue was also in tears, and the couple on the far sofa had their eyes glued on us as they strained to hear what was going on.

'I should never have asked,' said Sue as she took a tissue out of her handbag and began dabbing at her cheeks. 'I had no idea – there was nothing in Google about that. What did she die of?'

'She caught Covid and it affected her so badly that she had to be rushed to hospital and put on oxygen. It seemed to be working, although not well enough for me to be allowed to see her, and at around 3.00am the following day she died.'

'Oh Rod,' Sue repeated, but louder this time, and the hand squeeze was much tighter – so much tighter that it hurt. I winced and glanced across at the two onlookers who seemed totally fascinated by the drama being played out in front of them.

'She'd had the vaccine and three boosters by that stage. But she didn't have any more after we got engaged last December. She was worried that they might affect the baby if she became pregnant. But she didn't say anything to me about this, and the first I knew of it was when I was driving her to the hospital.'

'My God, poor you.' She now had both hands around my right one. 'Is that correct? I mean, about the vaccine affecting babies in the womb?'

'Not according to the doctors. I spoke to several of them. One said it was an old wives' tale. But apparently many women firmly believe in it, and stop having the vaccine.'

'Covid was a terrible thing.' This was said with feeling and louder. She glanced at the couple on the far sofa, as if for the first time. 'And didn't you say your parents both died of it too?

'Yes, very early on when there were no vaccines.'

We sat in silence hand-in-hand for several minutes before Sue looked at her watch.' Rod,' she murmured. 'It's time we went. I've got an early start in the morning. I need to be in the office by eight to do some preparation before my first appointment an hour later.'

I picked up her coat, held it for her while she put her arms into the sleeves, called out 'good night' to the still-watching couple and three minutes later we were en route to Twickenham. Most of the journey was spent in silence but, as we turned into the road where she lived, her hand grasped mine on the steering wheel. 'Rod,' she began. 'It's been a fascinating evening – and most enjoyable, despite me becoming so emotional. But I really am sorry about Emma. You are too nice to have had to suffer like that. My heart goes out to you.'

When I drew up outside the flat and switched off the ignition, I leaned across to kiss her goodnight. She responded with a passion that almost had me suggesting I go up to the flat with her. Almost – but not quite. One thing I'd learned from previous romantic assignations was not to rush things on first dates, not if I wanted more – and, despite still being in love with Emma, I was beginning to find this girl unbelievably attractive.

I'd been at my computer for the best part of two hours, reworking my original list of suspects and detailing their possible motives, when my phone pipped just after 9.00am. I glanced at the most recent message and smiled as I read it:

Ten minute coffee break. Rod, thanks for a lovely evening. Haven't enjoyed myself so much in years. Hope you enjoyed it too. Love, Sue xxx.

Things were definitely looking up. I texted back: 'Glad you enjoyed it. I love your company. Will ring you this evening' and returned the love and kisses.

I glanced at the cover of the *Racing Post* and, for the third time that morning, turned to the article on page five. It carried a head-and-shoulders shot of me in my racing colours and was headed 'Justice – or Injustice. You Decide.'

Tom Cameron had begun with the five-year race-riding ban handed out to me last Wednesday and continued:

Deliberately losing a race is one of the worst crimes in racing and accepting money to do so makes the 'offence' ten times worse. But this writer, for one, firmly believes that Rodney Hutchinson is not guilty and is appalled at certain aspects of the British Horseracing Authority hearing.

This article, I should point out, is not a balanced view in the true journalistic sense but is written by a press room colleague who has sat next to the sports-all.com racing correspondent at racecourses all over the country for the best part of two years and, I would venture to add, knows him better than any other member of the racing press.

Hutchinson has no need of bribes. He is a wealthy man by

comparison with the rest of us as he inherited a sizeable amount of money when his parents tragically died of Covid-19 in the first few weeks of the pandemic. It was enough for him to buy two racehorses – Ezekiel and Brown River – so that he could ride them himself, and enough to pay their considerable training costs (around £70 a day each!).

He gave up a lucrative career in the family legal business, despite qualifying as a solicitor, to pursue his first love – racing. And that is also why he became a racing journalist. In other words he does it because this is the life he wants to lead. Money is not his motive and, unlike most people, it doesn't have to be. A man less susceptible to bribes would be hard to imagine.

But what I find appalling is that he was given no prior notice that he was going to be accused of anything when he received an email summons to the BHA last week. And, just as bad, he claims that he was refused time to prepare a proper legal defence when he was informed at the hearing of the crime he was alleged to have committed.

Interestingly, the evidence of the bribe consisted of a film delivered by persons unknown (at least unknown to Hutchinson) to the BHA. According to Hutchinson a man who said his name was John Roberts came up to him after the second last race on the Friday of the two-day Newbury meeting, congratulated him on his tipping, said he wanted to give him a present and extracted a wad of notes from a brown envelope and thrust them into his hand. Hutchinson says that he only took hold of the notes to stop them falling to the ground. He then handed them back saying he could not accept them. The film showed all this but ended before the notes were handed back.

Nobody at the BHA – and I have mobile numbers for several of the senior staff – was prepared to comment yesterday. sports-all.com has given Hutchinson three months to convince the BHA of his innocence and get the race-riding ban cancelled.

As a journalist Hutchinson is afraid of nobody and his bold approach has made him a few enemies. In addition to the Cheltenham bomb, he was beaten up in the Ludlow car park last year – I found him lying on the ground, semi-conscious and in agony.

But, if he is a crook, I'm a Dutchman. I would be astonished if he committed any crime other than grossly over-estimating his fitness after not having ridden in a race for eleven months.

I emailed a short note of thanks to Cameron who promptly replied: 'Just glad to be able to help put the record straight. Please keep me updated – if poss before you tell anybody else!'

I then cut out the whole page, scanned it and emailed it to Brett and then to Gordon Watson. I studied the email address on Gordon's card and used the same formula (first name, surname@ JohnsonKersonLawson.co.uk) to send it to Sue. Somehow I felt it important that she should read it, and I waited an anxious ten minutes before I could be sure that it was not going to be returned undeliverable.

I debated whether to send it to Christopher Mayhew as well but finally decided against it. I knew he took the *Racing Post* and he might think I was trying to force his hand. But I decided to wait a further hour before ringing him, just in case he had had more pressing things to do on a Monday morning than read newspapers.

It was as well I did because the first thing he said was 'Just been looking at your article in the *Post* – goes a long way towards clearing both of us.'

'Yes, although I have got a lot of work to do to convince the BHA,' I said before he had a chance to say anything else. 'And Christopher, I want to apologise for not coming to see you straightaway. I wanted to get things sorted, or at least get started on that, so as not to waste your time. But I realised, when we spoke at Cheltenham on Saturday, that I was wrong not to have done so.'

'Yes, you were. It was pretty embarrassing being lectured by Greenstone, pompous ass that he is. Seemed to be trying to imply that I was somehow involved in stopping the horse.'

'Sorry, Christopher. But could you spare me a few minutes if I called to you sometime tomorrow that suits you?'

'Certainly. I'll be at the yard at nine to go through various things with Charlie. Could take an hour or so. Come at 10.30 and we can talk then.'

I returned to the list of possible suspects a relieved man. At least we were still on speaking terms. And I was going to need his help.

6

By 4.00pm I had the list as complete as I was going to get it, for the time being anyway. I printed it off and read through it as I sipped what I regarded as a well-earned cup of tea.

1. Tom Swarter and Bob Arrows (the jigger twins) use the same gallops at the foot of Green Hill, seemingly employing the same highly illegal methods and would be warned off – probably for life – if the BHA discovered what they were doing. Both know that I knew, and had shown that they were capable of threats and extreme physical violence, eg the slashing of my tyres and the windscreen note.

2. George Rickards owns several horses with each trainer including some that were the subject of electric whip gambles. Not much more known about him. Deliberately secretive?

3. Jimmy Brownson, given 15-years minimum for masterminding the Cheltenham bomb. Being in prison may not stop him from trying to exact his revenge; sufficient opportunity for contact with murderers etc to arrange something and has the money to pay for it.

4. Man who planted the bomb. Was also given a 15-year minimum. Presumably not as well off as Jimmy but could be sufficiently motivated to want to damage me and my career.

5. Trevor Brownson. As Charlie said, has suffered a massive loss of horses as a result of his brother's actions. Had shown himself to be ruthless enough to stop Brown River and to back Ezekiel after telling me the horse was only having a run.

May well have it in for me as I took the horses away and was partly responsible for him (a) losing so many horses and (b) his huge drop in income.

6. Barry who lost his job as Trevor's head lad and has since shown considerable animosity towards me.

7. Gavin Chesterfield went all out to convict me at the hearing, refused to listen to anything I said. Trying to make a name for himself in the eyes of the BHA top brass? Or has he an alternative agenda? If so, why?

8. Hedgers' staff who lost their jobs or were demoted. Could be any one of several. Given Arthur Jackson's uncooperative manner it might not be easy to find out who they all are.

9. Ben Walters. Uncharacteristically pleasant at Newbury but has shown in the past that he hates me.

10. John Roberts. Obviously paid by somebody but who? Contacting him could be difficult but he could well hold the key.

11. A journalist who dislikes me and wants me out of the way.

12. Somebody who I have criticised in an article and whose resentment has been festering ever since. The fact that nobody comes to mind needs to be ignored. People can take offence at a seemingly innocuous comment and some never forget it.

I looked at my watch. I rang the Rutherford and asked to be put through to the ward that Paddy O'Reilly was in.

'Hello, how can I help?' answered a female voice that I thought I recognised.

'Is that Rebecca?'

'Yes, who's speaking?'

'Rodney Hutchinson. I met you when I came to see Paddy O'Reilly yesterday.'

'Ah, Mr Hutchinson. How are you?' I could picture the dark skin and the so-natural smile. 'Paddy had his operation this morning. He has come through it well and the doctors are pleased with him. He's still a bit sleepy though and I wouldn't want to disturb him. Have you got his mobile? You could maybe try ringing him a bit later.'

I said that I was planning to visit him around this time tomorrow. 'Would that be alright?'

'That would be perfect. I will tell him. Give him something to look forward to.'

I waited until 7.00pm before ringing Sue. I had no idea what time she normally left the office, or indeed how long it would take her to reach Twickenham by train – and I wanted to get her at home.

'Hi Sue, how are you,' I asked when she answered and, as there was a lengthy pause, I hastily added: 'It's Rod.'

'Sorry, I've only just got in. Just moving to a chair. I'm absolutely bushed. It's been a long day, one intense meeting after another.'

'Will you have recovered by Wednesday evening, do you think? Recovered enough to come out on a date with me?'

She laughed. 'Of course, love to – but Rod, on one condition.'

'Oh, what's that?' Was there again something we were not to talk about? Or was it to the effect that I was to keep my hands to myself? I began to get worried.

'It's on me – and also that we eat at Chez Sous.'

I rather like French food – but obviously she was concerned at my prospective absence of earnings – so I happily agreed.

'Is that article in the *Racing Post* going to sway the BHA, do you think?' she asked.

We talked for several minutes about that, what I was planning to do over the next two days and how she had another busy schedule tomorrow, but was going to take it a bit easier on Wednesday and leave a little earlier. 'See you then, Rod. Good hunting in the meantime.'

I could see Charlie walking towards me from the yard while I parked at the side of the head lad's house. 'Morning Rod,' he enthused, smiling broadly as I opened the car door. 'Uncle's in the house.' He pointed to the new building set some way back from the side of the stables. 'He's expecting you.'

We walked together towards the yard before he directed me onto the concreted new pathway branching to the left, and to a small but tasteful Georgian-style two-story, clearly quite newly built. It looked very different in daylight. The front door was shut but, as I knocked and turned the handle, it opened to reveal the passageway that we had come along on the previous Friday.

The door to the sitting room was ajar. I knocked and walked in. 'Ah, good morning Rod,' said a smiling Christopher Mayhew indicating the armchair next to his own. Wearing a check shirt, club tie, sports jacket and cavalry twills he was obviously in his day-off country apparel. I still didn't know what he did for a living, let alone whatever it was that made enough money to support a racing stable. But, I told myself, I was here with a job to do and it was vital that I regained his confidence. And, if possible, secure his help.

I began by repeating my previous apology for not putting him fully in the picture immediately after the inquiry.

A raised open hand halted me in my verbal tracks. 'Don't worry about that now. The important thing is to clear your name. And clear mine at the same time. It doesn't exactly look good for a former member of the BHA board to be involved in stopping a hot favourite.'

'But Christopher, you weren't involved......' The hand was raised a second time.

'Not so far as any inquiry, no. But in the eyes, or rather minds, of the present board I detected a definite suspicion at the lunch on Saturday. After all, it was my horse.'

I could see his point. But his use of the word former had me worried. I was counting on him to find out what had led the BHA in the direction of John Roberts – or vice-versa.

'I was amazed about that bit in the *Post* saying there had been no mention of the reason for you being required to attend the inquiry. Was that true?'

I assured him it was.

'And about your being refused time to consult a lawyer in order to prepare a proper defence?'

Again I told him that it was.

Christopher shook his head before saying quietly, almost as if to himself: 'That's not like the BHA. It always prides itself on fairness, and in giving any person accused of anything full notice in advance. Also, when I was on the board, we always made a point of suggesting they be legally represented.'

I explained about how the initial letter had covered this particular point, how I had thought it unnecessary as I assumed my presence was only required as a witness to the Walters-Farthing incident.

'Hmm.' Christopher rubbed his chin, seemingly deep in thought, before saying: 'Greenstone's got a lot to answer for. Always seems to make up his mind in advance, and then can't wait to get the hearing over with.'

He looked up as he abruptly changed tack. 'What are you doing to find out who set you up?'

At least he didn't appear to be harbouring any doubts about my innocence. I told him that I was trying to dig into the possible Hedgers involvement while he listened carefully. I was just starting on the jigger twins and George Rickards when Charlie cheerfully breezed in, mug of coffee in one hand and *Racing Post* in the other.

'Sorry uncle – want coffee? Rod, how about you?'

It was just what I needed but the open hand went up again. 'No Charlie. Thanks, but I've got to move. I'm due at the dentist in Reading in just over half an hour.'

He got to his feet, turned to me once more and asked: 'Is there anything I can do? I might not have the same influence at the BHA as before but I know who to ask if I need a favour.'

'Yes, there is.' This was the moment I'd been waiting for. One of them anyway. 'I need to trace John Roberts, or rather the man who said his name was John Roberts. It presumably wasn't but he's an obvious lead to the instigator of the whole thing. I want to know who delivered the film to the BHA offices, what he or she said when they took it in, was there a covering letter and – if possible – what steps the BHA took to find out if the person was genuine.'

'Hmm.' Christopher seemed to be mentally repeating my requirements, as if to commit them to memory. 'I'll see what I can do. I'll be in touch. Probably won't be today, though. I'll try and ring them tomorrow.'

I stood up, shook his hand and thanked him. After he had gone out of the room, I turned to Charlie and said I would welcome that mug of coffee.

'Thought you could.' He grinned. 'Come on, let's go into the kitchen.'

Once there – a modern affair and rather more tidy than one might expect for a bachelor – he filled the frother, switched it on and – once it had finished – poured the contents into a mug which he put on the table in front of me. 'Help yourself to sugar.' He pushed the bowl in my direction.

'Ezekiel worked well this morning. He should be ready to run in about a fortnight. But Brown River,' Charlie shook his head. 'He was blowing a lot – he's nowhere near as fit as I'd hoped after his break. He's going to need at least another month before I can even make an entry.'

'I'll leave it all to you Charlie, – I've got other things I must concentrate on.'

'Of course. Any further word on the suspects?'

'Yea, there is actually.'

I told him about the jigger twins, what they had been doing to their horses on the gallops, their successful betting coups, the slashing of my tyres and the windscreen warning.

'By God, I didn't know about any of that.' He was horrified.

'Have you heard of a man called George Rickards?'

'No, I don't think so.' Charlie said the words slowly and thoughtfully, as if searching through his memory. 'Who's he?'

'He's the owner of several of the horses trained by Bob Arrows and Tom Swarter including, so far as I can make out, most of those that were gambled on. But I can't find out who he is, let alone where I can contact him.'

'Tried Weatherby's?'

'Yea, but they don't give out owners' addresses or telephone numbers. I even asked Swarter before he knew I suspected anything. But he wouldn't give me the man's number. Fobbed me off saying Rickards doesn't like publicity.'

Charlie chuckled. 'I'll bet he doesn't!'

Charlie then looked me straight in the face. 'But Rod,' his expression was serious and I detected an urgency in his tone. 'For God's sake go carefully. If what you say is correct – and I'm sure it is – having you unable to publish what they get upto means they can resume their electric whip activities without any fear of being exposed.'

'Obviously,' I smiled, downed the rest of my coffee and stood up. 'Time I went.'

'Rod, sit down.' Charlie's tone was, if anything, even more serious. 'Don't you realise? If they believe there is any chance of the BHA lifting your ban, they will want you out of the way permanently. They know you are almost certain to write about them.

'That means a straight choice between stopping what they are doing – including no longer making a packet out of their betting coups – and killing you.'

I pulled into the lay-by at the foot of Green Hill with no little trepidation. I intended to climb the hill to look again at the gallops where the jigger twins terrified the horses that were being laid out for a gamble. This lay-by, identified to ramblers by a footpath sign, was the only one for miles around and was where one of the two trainers had slashed my tyres last year – and left that horrific warning note.

I'd been optimistic – over-optimistic I now realised – that a different car and better camouflage would not alert them that I was back on the trail of their betting frauds and animal cruelty.

When Cheltenham's insurance company (and mine) reached agreement on how much they would pay for my burnt-out car, I swapped the highly conspicuous red BMW for a black one. But all the foliage on the lay-by's many trees had been wiped out by autumn and the approach of winter. Parking here would make the car as conspicuous as Father Christmas in the snow. Tom Swarter and Bob Arrows would immediately have my name at the very forefront of their minds – and in flashing red lights.

Previous scouting missions last year had revealed no other suitable pull-in place and so I reluctantly drove on towards the stables. Bob Arrows' converted farmhouse and yard came up first with its two rows of boxes, largely hidden from view by a thick privet hedge and a big dark brown gate. Visitors seemed to be positively discouraged, particularly with a wooden board announcing 'Green Hill Stables – Private Property.'

I drove slowly past, and I had to go a further half mile before I could find a field gateway fronted by a firm-enough patch for a car. Getting stuck, and having to call for help, would be sure to alert my presence to the stable staff, even if luck was with me and the trainer was out.

Pulling a cap down over my eyes I walked back the way I had come. I could hear, rather than see, the stable lads talking and jesting as they carried buckets of food and water to the equine inmates. The thick hedge blocked any direct view. Maybe that was the intention.

I walked on for another hundred yards or so, before making the return journey. Again I could see very little. The one saving grace was that nobody would have seen me.

Tom Swarter's Hillside Racing Stables was based a few miles further round the foot of Green Hill and was quite different. It was purpose built with two lines of boxes – each with stables back and front – and the trainer's modern bungalow at the back. The whole place looked smart with white post-and-rail fencing all round and an electric-powered sliding gate at the front, plus a large notice announcing 'Hillside Racing Stables. Proprietor Tom Swarter. Visitors by Appointment.' It even gave his telephone numbers, both landline and mobile.

This time I could see as well as hear the stable staff. And they could see me. Several looked curiously in my direction. I doubted if they had many passers-by. I hurried past and on the return journey, five minutes later, I kept my head down to make sure there was no eye contact. I was only too well aware that I was still news in the racing world and all of them would have seen my picture in the *Racing Post*.

Driving slowly back past that fateful lay-by I couldn't help but shiver – and my thoughts of how to tackle the jigger twins were swamped by Charlie's warning.

It was beginning to get dark when I walked into the Rutherford, and I was still on edge. But this time it was Paddy O'Reilly's health, not my nerves, that was the reason. When I had rung him on his mobile the previous evening he had hardly been able to speak and, going into what was clearly a private room, I was prepared for the worst.

Paddy was sitting up with a wad of pillows behind him. 'Ah Rod. Jaysus it's good to see you.' He was grinning like the proverbial Cheshire cat and looking as happy as if he had just won a race at Cheltenham.

Seemingly with good reason: 'I'm going to be fine,' he declared buoyantly. 'They've cut out all the bad stuff and they tell me I'll be allowed home in a week or so.'

'Paddy, that's great news.' I smilingly took the chair beside the bed, pulled it a couple of feet away and sat down.

He was at death's door two days ago and, if the doctors had fed him with optimism, I certainly wasn't going to disillusion him. Maybe that was one of the secrets of the Rutherford's renowned success rate. But I'd read up about colon cancer in the meantime and Paddy's age meant his chances were slim.

'I've gone from 10–1 against to odds-on,' he said, as if reading my mind and smiling happily. I looked more closely. Always a bit on the thin side, he had lost a lot of weight, his face was white and drawn, and parts of the skin on his neck were loose. Recovery looked a long way off.

'Charlie is keeping the horses on the go for you,' I remarked, as something to say more than anything else. I found I couldn't, in all honesty, continue with the pretence of recovery.

'Huh. He's a bar trainer,' Paddy shook his head, or rather tried to. I could see even that was taxing him physically.

Further conversation was halted by the arrival of a nurse. Not Rebecca, but an older woman with grey hair. 'Now Mr O'Reilly, time for your tablets.' She held what looked like three largish capsules in one hand and a glass of water in the other.

'Sure. I'd rather have a Guinness but I guess this is better for me.' He managed a wink in my direction as he downed both the tablets and the water.

'That's lovely, Mr O'Reilly,' said the nurse. 'Your supper will be in half an hour.'

'That Charlie, he's a useless bugger.' This was said with some force, the subject seeming to give Paddy strength. 'Good at chatting up the owners but that's bugger all he is good at.'

'He should know a fair bit after spending time with those two top trainers, shouldn't he?' I didn't want to put too much of a strain on Paddy by disagreeing with him. But I felt I couldn't have Charlie's undoubted ability run down. And the last thing I wanted was Charlie going to see him and hear Paddy say words to the effect that I'd told him he (Charlie)was useless.

'He couldn't train ivy up a wall,' Paddy continued to vent his feelings with a passion that belied his poor health. 'He's had it too easy in life. That bloody Eton and then his uncle's influence. And now he's got my job. Took me a lifetime in the school of hard knocks to get that.'

Paddy's fists were clenched and his face had gone from white to puce. I wondered if I should call the nurse.

'He won't last. And you couldn't trust him further than you could throw him,' Paddy continued in the same emphatic tone. 'Certainly further than I could throw him.' He grinned at his own joke. 'I'll be back training soon – now that I'm putting the cancer behind me.'

I was astonished, not at the words or the venom with which they were spoken, but at the way his outburst had affected him. Far from nearing collapse with the effort, he seemed to have gained strength from it. He pushed himself up against the pillows and grinned broadly.

Conversation switched to the jigger twins and more particularly George Rickards. 'He's the man with the money, financing those two dirty bastards. Pin him up against a wall and knock the shit out of him until he talks. Record what he says, take it to the BHA, and you'll be back in no time.'

This was said with the same force but this time it did seem to drain him. He sank back against the pillows, although he still managed a happy grin.

I assured him that I would do as he said and, standing up, said how delighted I was that he was recovering so well. And now I could see that perhaps it could be true.

But, getting into the car, I wondered about the reason for the anti-Charlie sentiments. Seemingly, in Paddy's mind anyway, Charlie had taken away Paddy's position training good horses without the financial struggle that he had faced for so much of his working life. Therefore Charlie had to be shown up as no good – both as regards ability and character – so that he, Paddy, could be reinstated.

I was just coming off the M25, and little more than ten miles from Lingfield, when my phone rang. As soon as I realised it was Christopher Mayhew I reached forward and pressed *9 to record what he said. With a bit of luck it was going to be important.

'I've called in a few favours and got some of the information you are looking for,' he began as I headed down the A22, slowing down my speed as much as I dared given the traffic behind.

'The film was delivered by Paddington Couriers at 9.32am on the Monday after the race and the package was addressed to Gavin Chesterfield, British Horseracing Authority, Holborn Gate.

'Chesterfield studied the film, rang Lord Greenstone as he is chairman of the Disciplinary Panel and recommended reopening the inquiry. Greenstone told him to set things up. So far as I can ascertain, no attempt was made by Chesterfield or anyone else to establish the validity of the film or to trace the sender. When someone did query whether it was genuine, Chesterfield said he had suspected your integrity – apparently those were the words he used – and said he was pressing ahead.'

There was a loud hoot behind as I spotted the Lingfield turn-off at the last moment and immediately swung hard left without indicating.

'Certain senior staff – I'm not sure which ones,' Christopher continued, 'expressed reservations about taking things further without confirmatory back-up and without first questioning you. As I told you before, the BHA prides itself on fairness in general and, in particular, going into things in considerable detail before instituting proceedings. But Chesterfield again contacted Greenstone and he said go ahead straightaway. Hence that email to you.'

There was a lengthy pause. Flustered by the traffic closing up behind as I slowed still further, absorbing the implications of what Christopher was telling me, I took time to realise he was waiting for a comment from me.

'Christopher, that's marvellous – and a great help. It explains a lot. Thank you very much.'

'Not at all. My reputation is also on the line over this, don't forget. Keep me informed of progress.'

He rang off as I turned into the racecourse car park and headed for the Press & Officials reserved area.

There was no shortage of room. Quite the opposite. Even ten minutes before the first race the car parks had more empty spaces than a church on a weekday. Hopefully the day's other two meetings – jumps races at Hexham and Exeter – were making more appeal. But I'd been delighted when I rang Chris Thomas earlier and he told me that he would be at the all-weather Flat race meeting at Lingfield. Apart from anything else, I would never have got back from even the nearest of the other two in time for my date with Sue.

I found the PR for Betwins in the betting ring watching which horses were being backed.

'Hi Rod, what's on your mind?' said the small man – he couldn't have been more than 5' 3" – as he cheerfully shook hands. On the phone I had only told him that I wanted to pick his brains.

'This time last year Bob Arrows and Tom Swarter were bringing off a number of heavily-backed gambles with horses that were in a highly nervous state by the time they were led into the winner's enclosure.'

'You're telling me,' Thomas interrupted feelingly. 'Took us to the cleaners on several occasions. Fortunately they've been quiet for some time.'

'That was my next question. Or at least are they still at it?'

'Nah. The general belief in the ring is that they've been scared off. The world and his wife seemed to know how they were doing it. Those electric whips on the gallops and all that. The BHA seemed blind to what was going on but rumour had it that they were about to be exposed by a journalist.' Thomas broke into a broad grin. 'Namely you.'

'What about George Rickards? So far as I could make out, he owned most of the horses that were backed.'

'You think he exists?' Thomas's tone suggested considerable doubt. 'We did a lot of investigating. So did the other layers who were hit. As you can imagine, bookmakers don't like losing and when somebody is winning big bets we like to know all about him. We could find no trace of Rickards.'

'But he must exist, even if it's a fictitious name. Surely the BHA would require some sort of references before registering him as an owner?'

'You'd think so.' Thomas continued to sound dubious. 'All I can tell you is that we could find no trace of him, and nor could any of our competition. You going to do an expose somewhere?'

I shook my head. 'No. I'm simply trying to find who set me up?'

'Somebody did – I read that story in the *Post*. And you reckon it was this bloke Rickards?'

'I don't know,' I said slowly, deep in thought. 'Somebody did – and, if racecourse rumour had it that I was about to write an article concerning him, Arrows and Swarter they have the motive.'

'In a way you've been lucky, I guess.' Thomas said quietly, almost as if to himself.

'What do you mean?' I couldn't see how he could possibly think that. No job. Reputation gone. Both possibly for good.

'Well. They obviously decided to go the BHA route. The alternative would have been to silence you permanently.'

Why did so many people seem to think I could – or even should – have been bumped off? I decided it was time to move on from this conversation.

'Thanks Chris. Listen, if you hear anything more will you give me a ring? You have my number.'

The small man – rumour had it that he had tried to become a jockey in his youth and turned to bookmaking when he found that he couldn't handle horses – nodded cheerfully before heading towards the weighing room area and the press room.

I went in the opposite direction, not to avoid any further contact with him, but to think through what he had told me. The fact that the jigger twins appeared to have gone legit suggested – despite what Thomas thought – that I might no longer be a target and they might not be suspects after all.

My musing was brought to a close by one of the top trainers clapping me on the back and breaking into conversation.

'That was a cracking good piece in the *Post*,' declared Bobby Johnson, his battered trilby at a wind-endangered angle. 'Have you found out who set you up?' he inquired before asking if I had considered any of the other journalists.

He then went into a long, rather complicated account of how a rival trainer had set out to cause trouble for him with the BHA, after an owner had taken his ten horses away and sent them to Johnson.

'The BHA inspectors were told in an anonymous letter that I was using lasix on my horses to make them pee and so reduce their body weight, and that I was using a masking agent to disguise this.

'Bugger me if a team of vets didn't arrive before dawn one morning, and then kept the horses in their boxes until the vets had taken blood and urine samples. Not content with that, every horse I ran for weeks was tested at the racecourse. I knew who it was, of course. But when I tackled him about it, he sent me a solicitor's letter threatening to sue me for slander.'

Johnson's story certainly made me think and, almost subconsciously, I found myself heading towards the press room. It was practically empty. Tom Cameron had gone to Exeter, leaving just two elderly reporters who I knew only by sight.

They both recognised me and gave me a cheery 'Hello Rod.' The taller of the pair said that he covered every Lingfield meeting for whichever paper wanted him while the second said he had come after receiving a call from Brett. 'Glad of an excuse to get out of the house, really. Me and the missus are not getting on too well now that I'm retired and we spend so much time together.'

I couldn't see either as a threat, never mind being capable of setting up the John Roberts sting.

But, as I continued to walk around from the parade ring to

the winner's enclosure to the betting ring, I was struck by how many of the racing professionals now took the *Post's* view of my situation rather than that suggested by the BHA's damning verdict. Two further trainers sympathised, wishing me a speedy return to reporting action, as did a couple of the jockeys. Even two of the BHA-appointed officials nodded a cheerful 'Hello Rod.'

Fortunately there was no sign of Gavin Chesterfield or even Ambitious Arthur, both seemingly taking a day off.

7

It was just after 7.00pm when I reached the Twickenham flat. We hadn't said a specific time, but I felt much earlier would have made things too much of a rush for her and any later would have the disastrous consequence of cutting the date short, particularly if she was planning to be in her office by 8.00am the following day.

But I was glad I'd stopped to buy a bunch of flowers when her eyes lit up as she opened the door. She was wearing a tight-fitting navy skirt with a lighter blue thin jersey over a blouse of the same colour. But what struck me most were the blonde highlights in her hair, itself a glowing light brown, curling as the ends touched her shoulders.

'You look lovely,' I exclaimed rather feebly as I leaned forward to give her a kiss.

'Thank you, Rod,' she said as she gave her head a twirl before kissing me lightly on the lips. 'I took an hour off at lunchtime to get it done. But they made me pay for it by keeping me late. I only got back forty minutes ago.'

'What time are we due at Chez Sous?' I asked, not wanting us to be late for our table.

Sue looked at me, briefly in silence before breaking into a wide grin. 'We are already there.' She gave a mock bow and waved her right arm in a wide sweep, like a conjurer acknowledging the cheers of the audience as he produced a rabbit out of a hat. 'Chez Sue's!'

She laughed as realisation slowly dawned on me. Embarrassed at my own stupidity, I smiled awkwardly. She was still laughing as she reached for the bottle of red wine to the right of the cooker and topped up the half full glass in front of her.

'Would you rather have a beer? Help yourself,' she said pointing to the tall white fridge.

I did while she switched the conversation to the latest developments in my bid to clear my name. 'I was thinking,' she said. 'That man who tried to pay you money. The one in the film. Have you thought any more about who he might be? Could you have seen him before somewhere, some other racecourse perhaps?'

She opened the oven door, and then shut it quickly as a burst of hot air escaped. It certainly smelled good.

'No,' I shook my head. 'I've thought long and hard about that. So much so, in fact, that by this stage I can't be certain whether I've ever seen him before or not. I'm sure I've never spoken to him, though.'

'I don't know whether you've thought of this,' she began tentatively as if she felt I might consider it nonsense. 'But when you read about that sort of thing in books, or you are watching a TV programme, it's often an out-of-work actor who has been recruited by the villain. And the hero traces him by finding his name through an acting agency. Does that make any sense?'

'Hmm. It does,' I said slowly, considering what she had just said. 'Though finding which agency is the question. I did look on the internet. There are dozens of them in London alone. But I think I do have a lead on that front.'

As she opened the oven a second time and extracted a piping hot casserole dish, I told her what Christopher Mayhew had found out from the BHA and the Paddington Couriers connection.

'That's fantastic,' she enthused. 'And so I this, I think.' She put the dish down on a mat on the kitchen table, removed the lid and smiled. 'I think you are going to like it. At least I hope you are!'

As she replaced the lid, she gave her head a sharp shake to put back a few strands of hair that had fallen forward and then pushed them firmly back into place with her left hand. Knives and forks were extracted from a drawer next to the cooker and I was told to take a seat. 'Hope you don't mind but at Chez Sue's we eat in the kitchen.'

I topped up her wine glass and then filled one for me before taking my seat and, at her invitation, began helping myself. It tasted every bit as good as it smelled, and I told her so.

'Great. I was afraid that perhaps you might be allergic to chicken or something, and the whole meal would prove to be a disaster. Sorry,' she passed me the salt. 'I get like that sometimes. Believe it or not, I'm a bit of a pessimist underneath this cheerful exterior.'

I laughed. 'I guess we're all a bit like that, deep down. But,' I smiled. 'If you are as good a cook as you are beautiful you haven't got much to worry about.'

I felt that sounded a bit corny but I was pleased to see that she had the good grace to blush. She reached out a hand and squeezed mine. 'Flatterer. Listen, getting back to John Roberts. Have you been in touch with Paddington Couriers yet? Whoever sent the film to the BHA must have given a name as the sender. At the very least the courier company would have wanted a telephone number.'

'No, not yet. I'm going to ring them in the morning.'

She shook her head. 'Don't do that. People are never as helpful over the phone. Supposing I go at lunchtime? Paddington is only about ten minutes from our office on the tube.'

'Yea,' I said slowly. 'They're more likely to give it to you, being a woman. If I went, they might suspect I was up to something.'

'Good, that's settled. Now tell me about Lingfield today. Any further developments?'

I related what Chris Thomas had had to say, his view that the jigger twins were no longer trying to bring off gambles using electric whips on the gallops, but could well be the ones who set me up at the BHA. I also mentioned what Thomas said about them going this route rather than having me killed.

'Good God Rod!' She was horrified. 'Why do you insist on leading such a dangerous life? Is it the same for other racing journalists? Surely not?'

It was a good question, one I had asked myself several times in the past 12 months, and without coming up with a wholly satisfactory answer. I tried again. 'Dunno, maybe because I don't shirk the dangerous questions.' I thought some more. 'Maybe it's that I don't give up when I find something that needs exposing.'

'You've nearly been killed once already. Please don't take any more risks.' She reached for my right hand and squeezed it a second time. 'Please.'

Trying to change the subject, I told her about Paddy O'Reilly and the improvement in his condition, how he was determined to resume training and how little he thought of Charlie. It seemed to do the trick. She certainly cheered up, told me to go into the sitting room and she would bring coffee.

I sat on the sofa and, when she appeared with two mugs on a tray, I patted the space beside me and she didn't hesitate about sitting close. We were chatting pleasantly with me determined to keep the conversation away from the dangers of the racecourse when she suddenly burst into tears. When I tried to put a comforting arm around her shoulders she pushed me away.

'I'm so sorry,' she said, convulsing in misery, her shoulders giving great heaves of distress, and tears pouring down her cheeks as she dabbed at them with tissues from the box on the same small table as the mugs.

I put my arm around her shoulders and this time she seemed to take comfort from being so close. But the tears were still flowing. This time it was me who took tissues out of the box and held them to her nose.

'Give it a good blow,' I advised. And she did.

'I'm so sorry,' she repeated. 'I can't help it.'

'Is it me?' I thought that perhaps she was crying at me repeatedly placing myself in danger. Maybe she liked me more than I thought. But I was wrong about that too.

'It's Richard,' she said through the tears which continued unabated. 'He's going to get married and have children. I only heard about it today.'

'Is it to the woman he said when he told you he had met somebody else?' I desperately tried to recall exactly what she had said in the pub on Sunday evening.

'No. It's another one and she's pregnant.' The tears turned into more body-shaking convulsions but, when I gave her what was intended as an encouraging squeeze, she silently buried her head in my chest.

'Sorry,' she said again, this time looking me straight in the eyes and then giving me a peck on the lips. She got to her feet, picked up the cups and took them back to the kitchen.

'I know it sounds ridiculous,' she said when she returned. 'I was so relieved when the divorce was finalised but hearing that he was going to be a father brought it all back to me – my dreams of being happily married with a family in a home of our own. Now he is going to do just that – and forget all about me.'

The last few words were uttered with an intensity so strong that it seemed to be bringing the tears back. Seemingly she still had some love for her ex-husband. As I also stood up and held her tighter still, I pondered over the remarkable difference between the sexes. Sue's dream was a home, a husband and children. Mine was to ride in the Grand National.

'Sue darling, I'll look after you,' I whispered, my hands moving down to her bottom.

'I know you will, Rod.' She looked up at me and smiled. 'You're such a good man, and you've been through so much.'

When I kissed her, she responded with passion. An hour or so later my arm was round her bare shoulder, her jersey, blouse and bra were at the other end of the sofa and my lips were exploring the nipple of her left breast. 'I think it would be best if I stayed here with you tonight,' I murmured.

She sat up with a start. 'Not tonight.' She smilingly, but determinedly, pulled the jersey over her head. 'I've got to get up in the morning. And so have you.'

But when we were both on our feet she held me close and squeezed me tightly. 'Rod, thank you for being so patient with me. You are so good to me.' We kissed again. 'Ring me tomorrow. Please.'

Maybe it was George Rickards and the jigger twins. But only maybe. As I sat in front of the computer, my list of suspects on the screen, I decided I must not overlook the others with powerful motives. Jimmy Brownson, for starters.

Clearly totally ruthless, and now in the company of some of

the most notorious criminals in the world, he was an obvious candidate. Probably burning for revenge. I must go and talk to him. Come nine o'clock I would start trying to find out which prison he was in and the regulations regarding visitors.

That settled, my mind wandered back to yesterday evening and to what had brought Sue to tears – and from there to my own ambitions. I had begun to realise that I was wrong to give up riding out and so sacrifice the race fitness I had struggled to achieve. Or rather failed to achieve, with such disastrous consequences. If ever there was a warning not to let it happen again, that was it. Once I succeeded in proving my innocence in the eyes of the BHA I needed to be properly race-riding fit.

I now had no doubts about achieving the former. It was just a question of whether I could make it happen within Brett's three months. Also I was missing the enjoyment of riding out and the thrill of the gallops. There was no reason, I now realised, why I should not do this as well as all the detective work. I would ring Charlie when he came back in for breakfast.

I looked at my watch. Just after 8.00am. An hour before I could reasonably get on the phone to the Prison Service. I started on Google and, while Belmarsh – to the south of the Thames and not all that far from Greenwich – looked the most likely, I found there were others where he could be. Wakefield in Yorkshire for instance.

I went to get the newspapers – I'd cut down my order to just the *Post* and the *Express* as an economy measure – and by the time I had got back and eaten a bowl of cereal, I started on the phone.

I rang the press office of HM Prison and Probation Service in Petty France, South West London, explained that I was a student at Reading University writing a thesis entitled Crime and Punishment in present-day Britain.

Once I was put through to the right person I learned a lot. Anybody wanting to visit a Category A prisoner at a high secure unit like Belmarsh had to submit a visitor application form together with two passport photographs. A security check on the would-be visitor was then carried out, and only after that was a decision taken on whether or not the visit could go ahead.

When I asked if the victims of a crime could be given clearance to visit the prisoners who committed it, the man at the other end laughed. 'Hardly,' he said, a broad smile clearly evident in his voice.

By this time I realised I was barking up the wrong tree and, after a few further questions – I didn't want to leave the official concerned with the impression he had received a call from a crime victim planning his revenge – I thanked him profusely, said he had been most useful and the information would be a big help in ensuring the accuracy of my thesis.

I switched to Plan B – Jimmy Brownson's brother Trevor. I glanced at my watch and cursed. It was 9.45am. Charlie might well be back in the yard by this stage, and be busying himself and the staff with second lot. I rang anyway. Charlie answered straightaway: 'Hi Rod. How are you this morning?'

He seemed relaxed and in good form. I went straight in: 'Charlie, the reason I'm ringing is because I've re-thought things. I'm making good progress with my investigation and I would like to come back to ride out, say one lot three days a week – to begin with anyway. Would that be alright?'

Charlie didn't hesitate. 'That's great news Rod – on both fronts. When do you want to start? Tomorrow? We could certainly do with your expertise in the saddle.'

I knew there was a bit of flattery in the last comment – most of his staff were better riders than me. But Charlie's natural charm played a major part in making him such a likeable character.

'Tomorrow would be fine. But just first lot. Then I need to don the Sherlock Holmes cap for the rest of the day.'

Charlie laughed. 'Of course,' he said. 'We pull out at 8.00am. If you could be here five minutes beforehand. Better still ten. Then we can get you organised.'

'Will do.' Something about the ten minutes struck a warning bell. 'But Charlie, I would prefer not to have to muck out.'

He laughed. 'Shit no. You're the owner. You don't pay training fees to do the work yourself. I'll speak to Barry now. Rest assured, there'll be no problems on that score.'

Picking up the *Racing Post*, I found the next day's runners and saw there were three meetings – Bangor-on-Dee, Cheltenham and Doncaster.

There was nothing trained by T.J. Brownson at the first two, but he had three runners at the day's prestige meeting. In the 12.40, the 1.50 and 2.25. He wouldn't send his assistant to the likes of Cheltenham, he would be there himself. The one doubt was whether his wife would be going with him.

Only one way to find out. I had Sarah's number in my phone. I'd never used it but it was not so long ago that I fancied her like crazy. A good fifteen years older than me, she always looked stunning with her dark brown hair invariably worn long. Indeed I could only recall her once with it up and then she had appeared every bit as desirable. What's more she seemed to fancy me too, and on one unforgettable occasion she had talked of wanting me to make love to her. But that was to be at some future unidentified date and in the meantime I'd taken my horses away from her husband. And gone a long way towards destroying his business.

I might well be about as welcome as a swarm of wasps at a picnic.

But, I mused – with a smile on my face – a faint heart never got anywhere with a fair lady, let alone a dark-haired one. I cautiously pressed my forefinger against her name, heard the ring tone and tried not to tense up.

'Rod. Is that you?' She sounded disbelieving, as if she had never expected to hear from me again. But obviously she still had my number in her phone. A hopeful sign.

'Hi Sarah. It's lovely to hear your voice after all this time.' It was. An image of her beautiful face and fanciable figure filled my mind.

We continued to exchange general pleasantries. She made no mention of all the contaminated water that had flowed under the bridge in the past fifteen months. I decided I had better get to the point before she switched the conversation to unpleasant specifics.

'Sarah,' I began cautiously. 'Could I come and see you sometime? There are some things I would like your opinion about.'

'Of course. It would be lovely to see you again. When did you have in mind?'

'What about tomorrow? Say around two?'

There was no answer for a good two seconds. It seemed like an eternity. And I feared the answer was going to be no.

'I was thinking of going to Cheltenham. We've got three runners. You won't be there, no?'

'No.' I cursed myself for not suggesting a different day. 'Maybe next week, say Monday?'

'Listen Rod, I do so want to see you. Come tomorrow. Come for lunch. I don't have to go to Cheltenham. Only the owners of The Minstrel Boy are going to be there. The owners of the other two aren't going, and Trevor can handle the Harrisons. They're very easy to deal with.'

We agreed that I should be at the Lambourn house around 12.30pm. 'We can have a drink and catch-up before lunch. I'm looking forward to it already.'

So was I but, I told myself as I disconnected, the purpose of my visit was to find out what Sarah knew about her brother-in-law's mental state and whether he was likely to have engineered the bribe attempt, and its consequences. It was most definitely not to be sidetracked by her beauty.

Also Trevor had been quite blatant about stopping Brown River at Bangor-on-Dee, and about gambling on Ezekiel at Ludlow while telling me that the horse was just having a run to get him ready for my return from injury. Sarah's husband certainly had the form to do me down and, now that his stable was reduced to little more than a quarter of its previous size, he also had the motive. What is more he would have known how the BHA works. He might also have known about Gavin Chesterfield's apparent penchant for putting the boot in.

I wasn't sure what to expect when I rang Sue at 7.00pm. Her early afternoon text had read: 'Visited Paddington Couriers. Got info about sender. Details proved fake but have suggestion. Love and xxx, Sue.'

'I got there about 1.15pm and fortunately they weren't busy,' she said after we had exchanged pleasantries. 'The Pakistani behind the counter was a bit suspicious at first so I produced my Old Bailey pass with my photo on it, and that seemed to spur him into co-operation. He looked up the details on his computer. The sender was listed as John Roberts who had only given a mobile number. Paddington Couriers don't require anything more from senders – apart from, of course, the money. For this delivery it was £17.50.

'I rang the mobile number afterwards. It proved to belong to some man in Brighton. He said I must have the wrong number and I reckon he was genuine. I chatted with him for a bit just to make sure.'

'Pity but the sender's use of the name John Roberts must be significant,' I answered. 'Somehow I've got to track him down. You said you had an idea?'

'I'm not sure I do now.' Sue spoke the last few words slowly, and I thought I detected a note of disappointment. 'My teenage brother is a computer whizz kid. Reckons he can get into anything. I was going to suggest he hacks into Paddington Couriers. But all he is going to find is John Roberts' false number.'

'Hmm.' What she said had me thinking. 'Supposing he tries to find out who John Roberts is by hacking into the various actor agencies? Even better, get him to try George Rickards.'

'Who's he?'

'George Rickards? He's the man who owns the horses that the jigger twins have been bringing off gambles with. Those two trainers with the electric whips. Some of the bookmakers seem to think that Rickards doesn't exist, that he's just an anonymous front. But he must exist. Weatherbys registered him as an owner and they wouldn't have done that without first checking him out.'

I spelt out his surname. 'But Sue, tell your genius brother not to risk anything illegal. I don't want him to get into any trouble on my account. Or cause you problems with the Law Society.'

She assured me that she would and I switched the conversation to tomorrow evening. I suggested picking her up at seven and going out for a meal.

There was a long pause. Immediately the doubts began to sweep in. Was she getting fed up with me and all my problems? Was there someone else in her life? My mind filled with all the opportunities her work gave her to meet eligible men, solicitors who had not packed it all in for a dubious career on the racecourse – and who had not made such a disastrous and dangerous mess of their lives.

'I've got a better suggestion,' she said. 'At least I think it might be.' There was a lengthy pause. 'Supposing I come to you? I could get the train to Swindon on Saturday morning and perhaps stay the night at your place. If you like.'

Would I like? Was the Pope a Catholic? 'That would be fantastic, Sue. What time does the train get to Swindon, do you know?'

She didn't. She hadn't wanted to tempt providence, she explained, by planning that far ahead in case I said I didn't want her to come.

We agreed that I would find out the train times and ring her in the morning. When I rang off five minutes later I was as excited as a kid on Christmas Eve. So much so, I realised, that I had almost forgotten about my lunch with Sarah Brownson.

Brown River was led out for me – already saddled and bridled – by Brenda, a blonde girl of no more than twenty who had played a leading part in the set-up as travelling head girl under Paddy O'Reilly. I assumed she still had the same role. She cheerfully gave me a leg-up and I steered my horse in the direction of those already circling. I slotted in behind the last one and adjusted my stirrup leathers to a length I felt comfortable with.

There were a dozen of us by the time we peeled off in single file through the open gate at the back of the yard and headed up the path to the Downs. There were grey clouds everywhere I looked. 'Not due to rain until around 10.00am,' said Charlie as he rode up alongside me on a bay horse I didn't recognise. 'We're going to canter four furlongs and come back at a nice half-speed, quickening up for the last bit.'

He gave his mount a barely perceptible nudge in the ribs and trotted up to ride alongside Brenda on the lead horse.

'Good to be back?' grinned the lad I knew to be Jake as he came upsides me on a chestnut with three white socks. His mount was playing with his bit and tossing his head around but Jake took no notice and happily chatted away about a tip he'd been given for Cheltenham that afternoon. It turned out to be one of Trevor Brownson's, and the tip had come from Barry who had pointedly ignored me when I arrived in the yard the required ten minutes before the string was to pull out.

When we reached the top of the path the horses began circling around a five-barred gate whose purpose had long puzzled me. It stood on its own. Just a wooden gate fixed to an upright by a row of hinges.

Jake, seeing me staring at it, said: 'Goilin's Gate. Been here for as long as anyone can remember.'

'Shaun Goilin jumped it before he won the Grand National in 1930,' said a lad I hadn't seen before as he joined us on a grey horse who was jigging excitedly. 'At least that's what Harry in the Hare & Hounds says. There's a picture of the horse behind the bar.'

'Huh. If you believe that you'll believe anything,' said Jake dismissively. 'Old Harry 'll say anything if it brings more customers. I looked it up. Sean Goilin was trained at Weyhill, and that's a long way from here.'

'I was told it was put up here as a memorial to a jockey who committed suicide after Shaun Goilin won,' said Charlie as he rode up alongside us. 'Thought the ride should have been his and, when the horse won the National, he came up here that same night and shot himself.'

He gave his horse a kick and trotted up to rejoin Brenda, seemingly to give her instructions. She and the second rider in the string peeled off and began the canter. In fact it was more of a steady gallop. The next two horses followed some twenty yards behind, and two more followed at roughly the same interval. Brown River and Jake were the last pair to leave Goilin's Gate.

The speed of the work-out, the pulsating muscle-power of the horse beneath my knees and the wind rushing past my face combined to send a surge of excitement through my veins. There was only one thing better, and that was doing it for real in a race. As we pulled up I knew I was grinning broadly. I felt like a drug addict who had just had his latest fix.

'That good, Rod?' inquired a smiling Charlie as I pulled up almost beside him. 'Ten minutes circling and then we'll go back but at a half-speed.'

The horses were all on their toes once more when Brenda and her gallops partner set off together. They knew that this was going to be faster and exciting. Also they were working towards home, something that invariably filled every horse with enthusiasm. Brown River took a firm hold and he was blowing hard at the end.

I reported as much to Charlie as one-by-one each rider rode up to him and told him how his or her horse had worked.

'Yea, Rod. As I told you the other day, he's still some way off a run,' Charlie replied. 'Three or four weeks, I should think.'

Ten minutes of circling later we were on our way back down the path. Charlie came upsides. 'Any progress on the sleuthing?' he inquired.

'Yes, I reckon so.' I told him what I'd found out from Chris Thomas at Lingfield and his belief that Tom Swarter and Bob Arrows had gone quiet on the gambling front, but may well have been waiting for me to be removed from the reporting scene – 'Much as you said yourself, Charlie.'

But I was careful to say nothing about my plan to find out what I could concerning Trevor Brownson, and his brother in particular, from Sarah later in the day. I didn't know to what extent Charlie could be relied upon to keep everything secret. In my experience very few people could.

'You coming again tomorrow?' he inquired as we rode into the yard.

'Monday – if that's OK with you?' I had other plans for Saturday. I wasn't going to tell him about those either.

8

I was greeted with an exclamation of delight and a kiss on the lips. When I returned the greeting with an enthusiastic hug, Sarah Brownson responded with her whole body. It pressed against mine for several pleasurable seconds. As she stepped back, with her hands on my arms, I took in the dark hair, the still-shapely figure and the facial beauty. She was about the same five foot ten inches as me and I found her incredibly attractive.

'You're in good time, Rod. Lunch won't be ready just yet. We've got time to talk,' she said happily as I followed her into the sitting room with its Dralon-covered matching chairs and sofa, deep pile carpet and walls dominated by paintings of the famous horses trained by her husband.

'What can I get you to drink, Rod?' she asked, her back to the sideboard and the drinks cabinet. I spotted her three-quarter full sherry glass and said I would like the same. I didn't normally drink sherry but seeing her again – after all the torrents of horror that had flown under the bridge in the past twelve months, driving a painful wedge between us – made me want to be in tune with her once more.

As she poured my drink, I studied the back view. I remembered the tartan skirt but the white jersey was new to me, and I hadn't seen her in black stockings before. The overall effect was like a magnet to my now over-heated imagination.

'Cheers Rod,' she smilingly lifted her glass and walked over to sit on the sofa. 'Now, I know you didn't come here just to see me – unfortunately.' The smile seemed coquettish in the extreme. I told myself to concentrate on why I was here as I sat down next to her. 'But you did say that there are things you want my opinion on. Or was I wrong?'

'No, you're not wrong. I'm trying to find out who set me up with the BHA, and why. One of those I think might be responsible is Jimmy even though he's in prison.'

'He's in Belmarsh, in London,' Sarah intervened. 'Trevor went to see him a couple of months ago. He said never again.'

'Oh.' That had me wondering. 'Why?'

'Well, as you might imagine, Jimmy came close to ruining us. We lost three-quarters of our horses, we had to let many of the staff go and it's only now that we are beginning to climb up the ladder again.' Her expression changed, her voiced raised a notch, and I could detect a harshness on her face that I hadn't seen before. 'But was there the slightest sign of remorse from Jimmy? No, not even a sorry. Trevor was upset and annoyed for days. He said he would not visit him again.'

'God. You would think he would have shown some regret by this stage. Particularly to his brother.'

'No,' Sarah shook her head. 'Not a bit of it. There is something evil about that man. It was there the first time I met him all those years ago. But I was too inexperienced in the ways of the world to detect it – and what it could mean for anyone involved with him.'

I nodded, but said nothing.

Sarah was in full flow. 'He persuaded Trevor to switch to the Flat and get rid of most of our owners – to make way for the Flat racehorses that he had this hair-brained idea would make him even richer than he already was. And then he tried to murder you and ended up killing The Major. I hope they never let him out.'

'What about the wife? Margaret was it?'

'Gone to America. She changed her name so that nobody would connect her with Jimmy. But Rod,' her tone changed as she looked me straight in the eye. 'How could he have had anything to do with that business of offering you a bribe to stop that horse? He's in a high security prison. Hardly allowed any visitors.'

I explained Charlie's theory about Jimmy having access to some of the most ruthless criminals in the country, and having the money to pay for just about anything that he wanted.

'Hmm,' she said, sipping her sherry for the first time since sitting down on the sofa. 'I see what you mean. It could be possible. And Jimmy is evil enough to do anything. In fact Trevor said he was blaming you for him being in prison. And I remember now – he told Trevor that he would kill you even if it was the last thing he ever did.'

That last comment shook me to the proverbial core. It was all I could do not to shiver.

'Sorry Rod.' Sarah's concerned expression reflected the frightened look on my face. 'I shouldn't have told you that. Anyway he can't do anything from there. Those big-time criminals have got more on their minds than to pander to the whims of a horrible nutcase like Jimmy.'

She stood up. 'Come and keep me company in the kitchen while I put the finishing touches to our lunch. And let's talk about more pleasant things than my horrible brother-in-law.'

Her still shapely figure, and her lively conversation, certainly helped to take my mind of the threat now so clearly posed by the imprisoned Jimmy. So did the food: fillet steak and vegetables followed by fruit salad and ice cream. But I still had questions to ask about Barry ... and Trevor.

'I see Barry is now working at Paddy O'Reilly's stables – or rather where Charlie Charterman now holds the licence,' I said in a tentative tone that clearly suggested a reply was expected.

'That's right. He was one of the many we had to let go. He was the deputy head lad here. We kept on George as he had been head lad for over ten years. We operated on a basis of last in, first out with many of the staff.'

'Seems a bit of a surly bugger,' I fished as I cut off a tasty piece of one of the tenderest bits of steak I had eaten in a long time. 'Never has a polite word to say to me.'

'He was always like that. Even with me. But Trevor said he was brilliant at his job. Swore by him.'

'I thought it was just me he didn't like. My accent or something.'

Sarah smilingly shook her head. 'No, you'se all fookers.' She laughed at her impersonation of Barry's accent. So did I.

Two down, one to go. Questions about her husband next. I didn't want to upset her but I had to find out.

'Trevor was hard on me, you know.' I began. 'He made me look a complete fool by winning with Ezekiel after telling me that the horse was only going for a run at Ludlow – and then stopping Brown River with buckets of water at Bangor-on-Dee.'

'I know. That was all part of the arrangement to create space for his Flat horses. He told me what he'd done when you transferred them to Paddy O'Reilly. I was furious with him, and I'm still ashamed that I didn't make more of an effort to explain things to you.'

My raised eyebrows seemed enough to persuade her to elaborate.

'I know trainers don't tell their owners everything – just what they want them to know, or think. That's where the trainer's wife has to come in sometimes, and smooth things over. But Trevor deliberately drove you away. I was furious, even hinted at divorcing him – at least I did until it dawned on me that Trevor would rather have had Jimmy's horses than his own wife!'

I found myself unable to stop smiling.

'You may well laugh, Rodney Hutchinson,' she said, still decidedly unamused. 'But it wasn't funny, and I still haven't forgiven him.'

'Do you think he bears a grudge against me? Or that he wants to get even with me for the bomb destroying the size of his stable?

'You mean did he set you up with the BHA?'

I nodded.

'No way.' She was adamant. 'Trevor's not like that.'

She glanced up at the clock on the wall. 'Almost 1.50,' she said, reaching for the TV remote. The horses were at the start at Cheltenham. 'Brigbok Boxon can win this.'

We watched in silence as the TV commentator gave his own observations on the chances of the principal contenders. As the nine runners for the three-mile chase were called into line he handed over to the racecourse commentator.

They were away at the first attempt and no-one seemed in any particular hurry as the horses swept towards the first fence. A good jump from Brigbok Boxon earned him a 'good boy' from the trainer's wife who added her own comments at most of the fences and several times in between. Her voice rose to a crescendo coming to the last where Brigbok was level with the leader and seemingly going the better. He soared over it to an appreciative shout from the sofa and was clapped all the way up the hill.

We watched companionably, but in comparative silence, as the winner was led in. Then the clothes of the owner's wife's were dissected item by item. Silence returned for the interview with the winning trainer and, as soon as that was over, the TV was switched off.

Sarah, her cheeks pink with excitement, looked again at the clock. 'We've got all the time we want,' she said as she turned to give me a kiss on the lips. My arms went round her body and we embraced with passion. When my right hand began caressing her left breast, her's responded by going round the back of my neck and pulling me closer.

After what seemed like several pleasurable minutes she whispered, 'Let's go upstairs. It'll be more comfortable there. And more private.'

She got to her feet, grasped my hand and led the way, like Eve with Adam in her thrall. Maybe I was being fanciful but that was the analogy that struck me. Once on the landing we headed off to the bedroom at the furthest end. As we turned into it I was relieved to see that it faced into open country and did not look out onto the yard.

Sarah promptly eliminated all possibility of anyone looking in by drawing the curtains. Again we melted in a passionate embrace as my hand went up the inside of the back of the white jersey and fumbled with the bra strap. I had to use both hands in the end, but my clumsiness hardly mattered as her body was so hard up against mine that her focal points of concentration were elsewhere on her flesh. And elsewhere on mine.

All my clothes were off, as were all of hers bar her panties, by the time we got in between the sheets. From then on things proceeded to their inevitable conclusion, with cries of excitement from both of us being overtaken by uncontrollable gasps of sheer passion.

Afterwards we lay together, breathless and spent, until I glanced at my watch and saw it was nearly four. A quick calculation and I could envisage Trevor, leaving Cheltenham immediately after his third runner and putting his foot down on an open road, coming up the drive. I whispered to the now-sleeping beauty beside me that it was high time I went.

Sarah insisted on a further passionate embrace before releasing me to my clothes and departure. She gave me the impression that she thought I was panicking for nothing but I felt a definite sense of relief when I drove through the front gate.

Try as I might, I was unable to avoid a feeling of betrayal towards Sue. Hardly Judas Iscariot stuff, I told myself, but I felt I had been wrong to give in so willingly to temptation when my heart lay with another. Or at least I would like it to lie with another.

'Stop fiddling with words,' I told myself as I passed the end-of-speed limit sign coming out of Lambourn and accelerated away. 'You know you shouldn't have done that,' I muttered. 'What if someone told Sue? She would be disgusted. Probably wouldn't want to know me.'

Guilt dominated my thoughts on the journey back to my cottage on the edge of the Downs, particularly as I was putting Sue through two changes of train the following morning so that she could spend the night with me.

As it got dark, though, I found it was Jimmy Brownson who was increasingly on my mind, in particular what Sarah said he told Trevor: 'He would kill you – even if it was the last thing he ever did.'

An icy chill kept sweeping through me. So much so that I went to the central heating controls and turned up the temperature five degrees. I switched on Sky News to take my mind off the threat while I poured myself a beer and debated what to have for supper.

I was in the middle of scrambled egg on toast when the front door bell rang. It made me jump. I went cautiously to the door, flicked on the outside light and peered through the window at the side.

The man on the doorstep looked to be in his twenties, quite big and burly, with a windcheater and a cap. He had a clipboard in one hand and a large envelope in the other. Beyond him was a van. He looked harmless enough and, when I opened the door, he said politely in an accent I immediately recognised as cockney: 'Mister 'utchinson, Mister Rodney 'utchinson?'

'Yep, that's me.'

'Got a delivery for you.' He held up the envelope. Probably some press handout from a race sponsor, I presumed. I often got them.

'Just need you to sign 'ere.' I took the clipboard and the proffered biro. I was just signing my name when some movement at the side of the van made me glance up. There was a man there and, when I looked more closely, there was another on the other side.

'Just sign please,' said the man holding the envelope, but more urgently this time. I looked up again. The two by the van were now out in the open. I thought I saw a glint of something metallic in the hand of the man on the left of the van.

I ducked back hastily as the courier made a lunge at me. He grasped the edge of the door as I tried to pull it shut behind me. With the other two now also pulling it in the opposite direction, I knew I was fighting a losing battle. I turned and ran down the passage to the kitchen, flicking off the light as I went.

As I bolted through the half-open kitchen door I remembered what the letting agent had pointed out to me when she showed me round the first time. 'See this,' she said, indicating an inset switch on the wall, at shoulder height beside the door. 'It's a security alarm. Just flick the switch, the alarm will go off and it will register in the security company's office. They will then ring you to check whether they should send somebody out.'

I had thought little more about it but, with all three men shoving their collective weight against the door, I realised I probably had only seconds left to live. I felt for the switch and snapped it down. Immediately there was the sort of horrific wail you saw in old films signifying a dangerous inmate had escaped from Dartmoor.

I wondered if it was in time – my nearest neighbours were all of 150 yards away. I was knocked to the floor as the combined weight of the three men swept aside both me and my feeble attempts to block their path.

A vicious kick thudded into my ribs. A second one hammered into my stomach. I was doubled up and retching when I saw the knife. It was poised above my throat like the sword of Damocles – and it was just as deadly

'Let's get of 'ere – now,' said a voice I recognised as belonging to the man with the clipboard. But it was a lot louder, and considerably more urgent, than it had been at the front door. 'The security people will be 'ere any minute.'

'Yea,' said a second voice, also cockney. 'Could be the cops too. I'm not going back inside, not for ten grand.'

'Don't be so fuckin' chicken,' ordered the third in a slightly different accent – traces of Birmingham perhaps. 'We've still got time to kill him and drive away. At least we'll then get our money.'

'C'mon Jerry,' urged the clipboard man. 'Get a friggin' move on for Christ's sake. 'Arry's already gone to the van. 'E'll go without us if you don't get a shifty on.'

'OK,' said the Birmingham accent, reluctance evident in every syllable. 'You're a right pair of effin' cowards.'

He bent over me. 'You fuckin' shit,' he spat into my face before standing up and levelling a further kick into my battered ribs. 'You got lucky this time but, remember, the big man always gets his way – and he wants you dead.'

I lay in the pitch dark – clutching my stomach and trying not breathe into my own vomit – for what felt like an eternity. I alone knew there was no cavalry coming to the rescue. I'd thought the risk of being attacked so slight that I hadn't even bothered to register with the security company.

Eventually I managed to struggle painfully to my feet, take a bottle of brandy out of one of the kitchen cupboards and pour myself a generous measure. I then made the mistake of trying to put the pain behind me with a hefty swig, and choked most of it up. I dropped the glass in the process but, much to my relief, the sideboard broke the fall without breaking the glass.

Sitting down at the kitchen table I managed a couple of sips and felt a comforting warmth as the liquid went down my throat. Ten minutes, and three sips, later I was beginning to feel well again with the pain in my stomach reduced to manageable proportions.

It had to be Jimmy Brownson. The cockney accents of two of the murderous trio pointed to the Belmarsh area, at least one of them had been in prison and – above all else – there was the warning Sarah had relayed.

Clearly my value on the murder market wasn't that great. Ten grand to kill me. Even if it was ten grand for each of the three, it still didn't make me worth much. It had been the same thing with the John Roberts bribe. Jimmy Brownson – assuming I was right and he was behind it all – thought my integrity could be bought with a wad of notes. Clearly my reputation left a lot to be desired. Or maybe Jimmy shared the unfortunately, not uncommon, view that racing as a whole is crooked.

I thought again about the parting comments of Birmingham accent – 'You got lucky this time but the big man always gets his way – and he wants you dead.'

It reminded me of what I'd read about Margaret Thatcher and the Brighton bomb of 1984: 'Remember, we only have to be lucky once,' said the IRA. 'You will have to be lucky always.'

That didn't scare her, and nor must I let Jimmy Brownson scare me. Furthermore I would prove my innocence to the BHA beyond all doubt, and return to both the saddle and my job, despite that bastard Gavin Chesterfield having it in for me.

But, swallowing the last of the brandy, I made a mental note to get on to the security company first thing in the morning. It might be a Saturday but there had to be people on duty, if only to answer alarm calls.

I had never been to Swindon station before but I arrived there with twenty minutes to spare. I got directions to the platform where the London train would be stopping, and found it deserted apart from a mother with three children, all under twelve and all wanting to go in different directions. She gave me a harassed smile as I sat down on a seat adjacent to the exit, reckoning that was where Sue was most likely to get out.

I heard the train coming with a sense of excitement matched only by the three children whose shouts of 'Daddy' were promptly drowned by the noise. I counted eight carriages and saw no Sue on any of them. I had an awful feeling that she had decided not to come. I walked hurriedly along the platform towards the rear. No-one getting out. I glanced back and saw a figure some forty yards away busily waving at me. As I got closer I could see she was wearing the camel-hair coat she had worn for our first date. She was smiling broadly and clutching a blue oblong-shaped case in one hand and her handbag in the other.

'Sue, you look lovely,' I said as I put my arms round her, gave her a hug and a kiss on the lips before taking charge of the case. We walked hand in hand to the exit and from there to the car park while she told me about the journey: 'The train from Twickenham was dreadfully late – I thought I was going to miss my connection – but the one coming here was also behind schedule so I was alright.'

We chatted happily all the way to the cottage which she seemed to take to immediately: 'How lovely, a cottage in the country. So picturesque.' Even the inside, which I knew was pretty basic, failed to dispel her impression of quaint charm.

I carried her case upstairs and she followed. I had debated long and hard about where I was going to put it. Obviously I wanted her to share my bedroom and its double bed, but I didn't want her to think I was being presumptuous. She might feel I was taking her for granted if I put the case in my room. So I went to the spare room that was directly opposite mine and which I had hastily decorated with a vase of the various flowers I had found in the rather overgrown garden.

Would she like a cup of coffee, I asked, as we went back downstairs into the kitchen. 'Love one,' she replied, her gaze sweeping round the room. 'But let me do it. Just tell me where everything is.'

I sat at the kitchen table, last night's brandy put away in the cupboard out of sight, while she busied herself with cups, coffee, milk and sugar. She had taken off her coat to reveal a pair of tight-fitting jeans and a red jumper that also fitted her shapely figure like a second skin.

'Any further developments on the detective front?' she inquired as the percolator started to bubble.

I gave her an edited (and censored) account of my lunch with Sarah Brownson and how I was now sure I could rule out her husband; that her brother-in-law was in Belmarsh Prison and had moved to the top of the suspect list. But I was careful to make no mention of either Jimmy's threat or the three men he had sent to kill me.

As we sipped our coffees Sue told me about her brother Philip, and what he had been able to find out from Paddington Couriers. Not a lot apparently. There was nothing he was able to discover beyond what she herself had been told when she visited the firm on Thursday, namely the sender was John Roberts with a false mobile number. But Philip had other ideas he wanted to explore, he needed certain information from me and wanted Sue to set up a meeting.

'I suggested my flat tomorrow evening, say around 6.00pm. But,' she smiled, 'I'm possibly presuming a bit much.'

'In what way?'

She was still smiling. 'That you are going to be a real gentleman and drive me home rather than put me back on the train.'

It was my turn to smile. 'Of course. I'm certainly not going to subject you to that again. Tell him all three of us will meet at six.'

Conversation switched to lunch. Sue suggested she cook something but readily agreed to my counter idea and 1.00pm saw us in the Hare & Hound, where a bald-headed man I took to be Old Harry was busy pulling pints. On the wall behind him was a large painting of three horses jumping an Aintree fence, and the long-stirruped styles of their jockeys indicated that this dated a long way back.

'What year was that?' I inquired innocently.

'1930, Sean Goilin.' Harry answered in a broad West Country accent, putting a now full pint glass in front of a middle-aged man with a cloth cap that he hadn't bothered to take off.

'Don't get Harry started on Sean Goilin,' the man cautioned. 'You'll be here all day.'

'Was Sean Goilin trained round here?' I asked as the well-named Old Harry – his face was gnarled and wrinkled, as were his neck and the backs of his hands. He looked all of seventy, and quite possibly several years more.

'Nah. He was with the 'Artigans over Weyhill way but they would bring him 'ere to gallop sometimes. So the story goes, 'e did his final piece of work up on the downs above Paddy O'Reilly's place before winning the National.'

'Not Paddy O'Reilly's place anymore,' said the customer, wiping traces of froth off his mouth. 'Young fellow there now. Charlie somebody.'

'Charterman,' filled in Old Harry, disapproval written all over his face. 'Reckon Paddy 'll be back, though. He's a real racehorse trainer. An Irishman. Been all over the world. Was usually 'ere at the weekend with the wife. But young Charlie's too grand for this place.'

Old Harry sniffed in obvious disdain. Seemingly it was Charter-man's failure to support his local that accounted for the landlord's disapproval and dislike. 'Any roads, Paddy's coming out of 'ospital on Monday – so I've 'eard.'

'Sean Goilin,' I wanted to bring the subject back to the horse and local legend, not least because it looked a good story for when I was back writing. 'I heard that the regular jockey lost the ride and killed himself on the night of the horse winning the National.'

'Aye,' responded Old Harry. 'Not the regular jockey but someone who thought 'e was going to get the ride. Went up onto the downs above 'ere that very night and shot 'isself.'

'What was his name, do you know?'

Old Harry shook his head and, seemingly losing interest, pointed to my half pint and Sue's glass of white wine. 'That's £5.90.'

As I reached into my back pocket, he pushed the menu in my direction.

'You seemed to be having a long conversation?' said Sue inquiringly as I returned to the small table where she was sitting on a leather-covered bench. I put the wine glass in front of her and handed her the menu.

'Just checking on local legend and that big painting behind the bar.'

Sue looked in that direction as she inquired: 'Are your horses trained near here? I would love to see them.'

'Yes,' I said hesitantly. 'But I think it will have to be next time you come.' I explained about trainers frowning on unannounced visits from owners. 'Charlie's got runners at Cheltenham this afternoon and on Sunday mornings Christopher Mayhew often invites his partners in his horses.'

I didn't add that some of them might not welcome the appearance of somebody on the banned list. But it was much in my mind, and the last thing I wanted was to upset Christopher. I needed him to stick to his commitment to put me up whenever one of the stable's runners had a chance, and indeed to support me when I was in a position to prove my innocence to the BHA.

'What I thought we might do this afternoon,' I said, taking her hand and giving it a squeeze that was promptly reciprocated, 'is go up to the Downs and, if you feel energetic enough, we can go for a walk along where the horses work.'

She seemed happy with that, and indeed with the day's special which proved to be a rather tasty steak pie with a good choice of vegetables.

After driving up the rough track we stopped just short of Goilin's Gate and, as we got out of the car, I related the story about the Grand National winner and the jockey who was so upset at missing the ride that he shot himself at this very point.

'Ooh. How gruesome,' she exclaimed, staring at the otherwise rather pointless gate, standing on its own and keeping nothing in or out.

'I know,' I said taking her hand, 'but I am going to link it in with a piece on Charlie Charterman as soon as I'm allowed to resume. He's a rising star.'

I told her about the two top trainers Charlie had been with before taking over Christopher Mayhew's stable. 'In the racing world that's like going to the Harvard Business School and getting an honours degree. He's destined for the top, I'm convinced. But also he has gone out of his way to help and support me. I want to repay him.'

We returned to the cottage in time for tea, refreshed and rosy-cheeked, after a lengthy walk on top of the bracingly windswept Downs.

The sight of Sue, smiling happily and clearly taken with my

company, as she put the kettle on and then searched through the various biscuit tins, stirred feelings that had been developing ever since we set out on the walk. And I could restrain them no longer.

'Sue,' I began tentatively, not at all sure how she would react, as I grasped her shoulders from behind and turned her towards me. 'It's you I want. Not tea. And I want you now.'

I kissed her before she had a chance to reply. If her passionate response was anything to go by, and I was certain it was, she felt the same way. As my hands sought her breasts beneath her jersey, she whispered: 'Not in the kitchen, Rod darling. Let's go upstairs.'

Thirty passionate minutes later, and finally lying side by side in companionable silence, her right hand began to trace erotically down my stomach.

'Aah.' I cried out in agony as her fingers pressed on part of the area that Birmingham accent's shoes had hammered like a chef tenderising a steak. Trying to pretend my cry hadn't happened, I froze as Sue lifted the duvet to see what the fuss was about.

'Rod,' she exclaimed, her voice expressing the shock now written all over her face. 'Your stomach is black. It's a mass of bruises. When did this happen? And how?'

By this time she had pulled the duvet right back to reveal the dreadful state of my front. The beauty of her naked body, and her perfectly shaped breasts, somehow made my own torso seem like an exhibit in the Chamber of Horrors. I was deeply embarrassed.

'Who did this to you?' she demanded, her tone turning to anger. 'And why didn't you tell me?'

'I don't know for sure,' I began slowly. 'But a man came here yesterday evening, saying he was from a courier company, and wanted me to sign for something. Then two more men appeared. I ran to the kitchen and pressed the alarm bell.'

'And? Don't stop now, Rodney Hutchinson.' She was propped up on one elbow, her angry face only inches from mine. 'I want the full story. And don't you dare hide anything.'

I told her about the kicks delivered by one of the three but I tried to play down my coming so close to being knifed to death. 'They'd been paid to kill me. One of them said something about ten grand. But the alarm saved me. They thought the security company was on its way – and they took off.'

'And did the security company people get here?'

'No. I hadn't registered with them.' Sue's expression changed from horror back to anger. Before she had a chance to say what was obviously on her mind, I added hastily: 'But I did so this morning …. before heading to Reading to meet you.'

'Who was behind all this? John Roberts? Or rather the people who paid him?'

'I'm pretty sure it must have been Jimmy Brownson, the man who got life for the Cheltenham bomb. The one that killed Charles Alvernon.'

'And was meant for you?' She said this in a much quieter, more thoughtful tone, her anger seemingly spent.

'Yes. Brownson's sister-in-law Sarah said something about him threatening to get me when her husband went to see him in Belmarsh. Plus at least one of the three men who came yesterday evening had been in prison.'

'So what are we going to do? We can't just carry on as before and wait for them to try again.'

I was glad that she was using the word we. At least this suggested she wasn't preparing to leave me for a boyfriend who didn't have a price on his head. Not yet anyway.

'I guess I have to uncover Brownson's part in me losing my riding licence, and then prove it to the BHA. Once that's done I should be safe because everybody will know it was Brownson yet again. And that should be enough to keep him locked up for a very long time. No early remission anyway.'

'Hmm. I hope you're right.' She carefully replaced the duvet over my battered body, reached for her jersey on the chair beside the bed, pulled it over her head and down her body. Then she leapt out of bed, retrieved her panties and jeans, and quickly put them on too. 'Have you got any ointment of any sort? That bruising needs treatment.'

'Should be something in the bathroom cupboard,' I answered, sitting up but wrapping the duvet round me. By this time she was in the bathroom. 'Eureka!' I heard her cry with all the satisfaction of a modern-day Archimedes. 'Just the job.'

She returned with a tube of Active Arnaca in her right hand and a look of triumph on her face. 'Now lie down and let Nurse Susan get to work.'

She was gentle – certainly over the worst affected areas where it was all I could do to stay still, such was the pain. After ten uneasy minutes, she told me to turn over, gave me a slap on the bottom and declared: 'Now be a good boy and we will repeat the treatment this evening.'

We returned to the kitchen where Sue promptly put the kettle back on. As we belatedly drank the tea, I put on the TV to watch the replays of Cheltenham. I had taken to looking at the recordings rather than the live racing, partly because I needed to keep up to date on what was happening so that I would be fully in the picture when I returned to reporting. But also because I discovered that it didn't hurt quite so much that way. Not being part of the action

– even when I was only writing about it – was something I found painful in the extreme.

I was particularly interested in the performance of Charlie's two runners. They both ran similar races, amongst the backmarkers for much of the way but running on really strongly over the last two fences and making further ground on the uphill climb to the winning post. In other words not really out to win but to get them ready for the next time when, presumably, they would be in with a really good chance.

Over supper I brought up the delicate subject of Sue's ex-husband. This time there were no tears. She smiled and shook her head as if to flick a few stray hairs away from her face. But seemingly the gesture was more about replacing the tone of last time's conversation with a less emotional, and more realistic, reaction.

'I know I was upset that last evening,' she began. 'But I had only just heard about Richard planning to get married again, and Margaret being pregnant. But not now. Life moves on and he is no part of mine. Hasn't been for some time. Nor do I want him to be.' She shivered. 'God forbid.'

'But you were in love with him at one time?' Maybe I should have simply changed the subject. But this was something I needed to be sure about. I knew I wasn't in love with Sue – after Emma I didn't think I could ever love anybody else – but my feelings for her were increasing in intensity by the day.

'Yes, I was,' she said quietly.' Very much so. But, as I told you, we were too alike for it to last. It's true what they say about opposites attract. That way things work out between a couple. If you think the same things all the time, life is going to be boring. There isn't going to be any spark. Not a lasting one anyway.'

She sniffed, and reached for her bag to find a tissue. She blew her nose and then dabbed her eyes as the tears started to flow. 'Sorry. I'm hopeless,' she smilingly declared. 'Once I start on about my feelings I can't stop crying.'

I took hold of her hand, not quite sure what to say but kicking myself for upsetting her. 'I'm such a selfish cow,' she said through the tears. 'What I lost is nothing compared to what happened to you and Emma. That was real heartbreak,' she squeezed my hand. 'Rod, my darling. I know you lost the love of your life. Nobody could ever fill her place in your affections.'

I pulled her to her feet and the ensuing embrace was filled with emotion for both of us. 'Time for bed,' I whispered.

'Not yet,' was the whispered response. 'Nurse Susan still has work to do.'

But upstairs the massage soon gave way to passion, and the way she cried out my name when she reached her climax suggested that any feelings left for Richard really did amount to very little.

9

'Jaysus. What's he doing with those horses?' Paddy O'Reilly, voice raised in indignation, was in full flow, the Irish accent accentuated by the passion with which he spoke. I could see other Rutherford Sunday morning visitors looking our way, presumably wondering what he was getting so agitated about.

He still looked on the thin side but his appearance was markedly different from that of the obviously-ill man of a week earlier. There was a glow to his cheeks and I could see that even his hair was starting to grow back. An open-necked shirt, red jersey and grey slacks had replaced the dressing gown and slippers – seemingly regulation issue for most of the other patients – and marked him out as someone for whom all the famed Rutherford care and attention had done wonders.

'That Blue Marine could have won the three mile if he had been ridden handier. But what did the bloody jockey do? Sat at the back, strangling him, until it was too late. I'm surprised the stewards didn't have him in – and the trainer. They certainly should have done.'

'Maybe he was being got ready for next time,' I ventured. 'One of those good races at Christmas, perhaps. He would be spot on after yesterday's run.'

'He should have been spot on yesterday – he was weighted to win.' The volume was still high and the audience seemingly even larger as Paddy warmed to his task. 'I wouldn't have let him go unbacked. But I'm sure Charlie had nothing on him 'cause he knew the horse wasn't off. Doesn't do the animal any good, you know, being messed about like that.'

I nodded to show my agreement. Sue said nothing but she was smiling as she listened to the rhetoric, the traces of its Irish origin becoming more and more pronounced.

'When are you coming out of here, Paddy?' I asked in a bid to change the subject and quieten the speaker.

'Didn't I tell you'se? It's tomorrow – and I can't wait.'

'Gosh, that's fantastic,' said Sue, her first contribution to the conversation after the initial introductions.

'To be sure,' replied Paddy. 'But I told Rod before the op that I would be coming out in a week assuming it all went well. And it did. Touch wood.' He leaned forward and put his fingertips to the small round table in front of him.

'Where will you go? To the flat in Reading?'

'To begin with, yes. But I'm going to tell Christopher to go ahead with that house near the stables.' He frowned. Both the volume and tone of his voice were lowered. 'Then I'll be able to keep an eye on what that no-good nephew of his is up to. And I'll be ready to resume once he gets the boot.'

I said nothing. I didn't want to tell him that this was pie in the sky.

'Did you watch Boss Baxter's race?' Paddy looked up as he changed the subject, at least in part.

I nodded. 'Ran much the same sort of race as Blue Marine. Presumably also on a get-fit mission?'

'Balls.' Paddy's raised voice had the audience all ears once more.

'He was stopped. Wouldn't be surprised if the so-called trainer hadn't tipped off the bookies in return for a back-hander.'

'Well. That might be a bit...' I wasn't given a chance to finish what I was trying to say.

'I don't know what he tinks he's doing.' Paddy's complexion was reddening in annoyance. 'Those owners are not betting people. Sure, they might have a few quid on but what they want is to win races, not money. They've got plenty of that. They want to able to tell their friends their horse is in with a shout. Not to put them away with false information so they can have the price for themselves.'

I could see his point. The owners were all friends of Christopher and I knew that he had a share in several of their horses. It wasn't a betting stable in any way. The horses were all trying, certainly once they were racing fit. Christopher wouldn't have it any other way. He had a reputation for honesty and he had made it clear that he was intent on keeping it that way.

I spotted Rebecca in the distance, and I waved. She broke into a broad smile and came over. 'Good morning, Mr Rod,' she said. 'What do you think of our patient now?'

'I'm amazed, Rebecca. He's improved almost out of recognition. You have worked a miracle with him.'

'Not me,' she said with a broad smile across her dark features. 'It's Paddy and his determination to get back into your racing world.'

'It's amazing that he is able to go home only a week after a major operation,' intervened Sue. 'When my grandfather had something similar he was in hospital for weeks.'

'The doctors here are exceptional, and the latest 2025 thinking is that people recover better in their home surroundings,' a still-smiling Rebecca explained. 'We send somebody with them when they leave and we keep visiting them to make sure all is well.'

'I've got work to do,' said Paddy, a note of steely determination in his voice. 'The sooner I get back to it the better for all concerned.'

Rebecca laughed. 'That's the spirit, Mr O'Reilly. Nice to see you again, Mr Rod. And you too.' She thrust her right hand towards Sue who stood up and shook it.

'What about them jigger twins?' Paddy asked me as the nurse moved on to a neighbouring patient and her relatives. 'Have you made any further progress?'

'Yes and no.' I told him what Chris Thomas had said about Tom Swarter and Bob Arrows having gone quiet. I then gave him a watered-down version of Friday's attack and what had led me to believe that Jimmy Brownson was behind it.

'Jaysus, Rod.' He seemed shocked. 'You's going to have to be careful.'

'That's what I keep telling him,' interjected Sue. 'Danger seems to be always lurking round the corner with Rodney Hutchinson even though he is not writing anything at the moment.'

'Sure, your boyfriend don't know the meaning of fear,' grinned Paddy. 'Could be that's his problem.' Turning to me he added, in a much more serious tone. 'I still tink it's the jigger twins. Brownson is locked away for years but Swarter and Arrows are still around – and I reckon they want to keep you'se out of the way so they can resume their villainy.'

Paddy was now visibly tiring. His face had gone pale while his speech was slowing and becoming quieter.

I stood up and managed to catch Rebecca's eye. I raised a finger – and she came over immediately. 'We're going now Rebecca but I'm a bit worried we have overtired Paddy.'

She looked closely at his face. 'Paddy, time for a brief lie-down. Let's go.' She took his arm as he got to his feet, raised a hand in my direction and slowly walked off with Rebecca.

'What a wonderful character. I'm so glad he is on the mend,' said Sue, standing up and watching the disappearing back view.

In the car, though, she made it clear that her concerns about my safety were the priority. 'Do you think Paddy is right about the two trainers he calls the jigger twins being the ones behind the attack on Friday evening?'

'I don't think so,' I replied hesitantly – by this stage I wasn't that sure in my own mind. 'Tom Swarter and Bob Arrows certainly have good reason for wanting me well away from writing on a website or in a newspaper, and they probably know I would expose their cruelty if I got the chance. But last Friday's attack had Brownson written all over it, and some of the things the men said pointed pretty clearly to somebody who is behind bars. That could only be Brownson.'

Sue seemed unhappy about my answer, I suspect because she was hoping for reassurance and didn't get it. Wanting her boyfriend well away from the criminal fraternity was understandable, possibly even more so for a solicitor. But, despite what Paddy obviously thought, in my mind it all pointed to Trevor's brother.

I detected a certain coolness in the over-crowded pub near Windsor Castle where we had lunch. Sue never really relaxed although she did seem more her usual self by the time we drew up outside her Twickenham flat just after three. Philip was expected an hour later.

He arrived on a scooter that he parked outside the front door and, removing his helmet, he took the stairs two at a time. Tall – he can't have been less than six-foot two – and wafer thin, he wore horn-rimmed glasses and looked older than the sixteen I knew him to be.

His sister, reaching up to give him a peck on the cheek, bid him to sit on the sofa and tell me what he planned while she made us both a cup of tea.

By the time she returned with a tray, a pot and three cups, plus milk and sugar and a plate of biscuits, Philip had virtually ruled out finding John Roberts without any new leads.

'There's nothing to go on – no mobile, no clue as to his real name and his appearance when you met him is unlikely to be anywhere near what he actually looks like.' He spoke with an authority that belied his tender years and I soon put behind me the mental image I had conjured up of an overgrown schoolboy pretending to be something he was not.

'Maybe we could go into this from another angle,' he said as he helped himself to a chocolate-coated digestive before passing the plate to me. 'Sue mentioned something about two trainers up to no good and a man who owns some of the horses that have been hooked.'

Seemingly he wasn't a total ignoramus about racing either. I'd been pretty sure he would be and that I would find myself having to explain how everything worked – probably just to humour Sue – and that his involvement would prove to be a complete waste of time.

'The trainers presumably have mobiles,' he continued. 'And the people they train for would be on their contact lists?'

I nodded as Sue put a full cup and saucer on the small table beside me, and moved the fast-disappearing pile of biscuits from the arm of Philip's chair to mine.

'If you can get me the names and numbers of the two trainers there is a good chance that I can get into their contacts and find the number of the rogue owner. I could then get into his phone. Chances are there is something in his contacts that will enable us to find where he lives and what he does.'

Philip reached over to the biscuit plate, took three of the six left and renewed his munching. I glanced at his sister who silently, but expressively, raised her pencilled eyebrows.

'I can find the trainers' numbers easily enough. They'll be in the *Horses In Training* book. But can you really get into someone's mobile?'

'Takes a bit of doing,' Philip grinned, helping himself to yet another biscuit. 'But it can be done. You can't with some of this year's phones – the manufacturers have cottoned on and have built in barring– but you still can with the rest of them. Chances are though that your two men haven't changed their phones that recently. Certainly worth a try.'

I told him that I would text the names and numbers to him in the morning. Philip asked about what the men had been doing and he didn't seem all that surprised when he heard about the electric whips.

'Yes,' he said. 'Sue told me about you being set up with a bribe and a doctored tape but,' his serious expression broke into a grin, 'I guess that sort of thing is par for the course in horseracing.'

'I don't know why everybody thinks racing is crooked,' I said, acutely conscious of the note of exasperation in my voice. 'It's not. And anyway it's very effectively policed. But I guess it has got an image problem.'

'You can say that again,' answered Philip, grinning broadly before launching into an account of how a friend of his had been told to back a certain horse 'because it had had its back teeth pulled out race after race and this time it was trying.' The friend had collected a small fortune.

'Time I went,' Philip stood up, helped himself to the last two biscuits and picked up his helmet. 'Get those numbers to me tomorrow. In the morning if you can. Then give me a couple of days.' He nodded in my direction, gave Sue a wave and was gone.

'What did you think of Boss Baxter and Blue Marine on Saturday?' We were on our way back from the Downs after 15 of the string had worked half speed over six furlongs, and Charlie came up alongside me on a liver chestnut I didn't recognise. The trainer was grinning like the proverbial Cheshire cat as he posed his question.

'Well, frankly, I thought they both would have won if they hadn't spent so much of their races out of their ground.' I wasn't going to beat about the bush.

'That's what the jockeys said. Words to that effect anyway.' Charlie was still grinning. 'Billy Black seemed to think I'd put him away.'

'And had you?' It was my turn to smile.

'Uh-uh.' Charlie's expression switched from cheerful to serious. 'One of the things I learned in my two years with Major Vauxhall was not to be in too much of a hurry to win races. 'Charlie,' he would say, 'remember this and you won't go too far wrong: never win two handicaps in a row and make sure you have always got 7lb in your pocket.'

'Yes, Blue Marine could have won. But the handicapper would have put him up 10lb if he had and the horse would have done nothing else all season. Handicappers neither forget or forgive. That was another of the Major's maxims.

'I'm not sure about Boss Baxter,' Charlie continued. 'He would have had to be given a hard race to get up, and I'm far from convinced he would have beaten Brass Farthing. Probably wouldn't, and then he would have gone up several pounds for nothing. Probably wouldn't have been able to win off his new mark. Now, though, he should be pretty much right for next time.'

Charlie's reasoning made a lot of sense, and I could see why several shrewd judges regarded him as a future champion jumps trainer. His understanding of his horses, and of their mentality, would have done justice to a man with decades in the job. Paddy O'Reilly's methods, learned over years at the bottom end of the racing ladder – and from modest horses, looked basic and unsophisticated by comparison.

'Talking about next time,' Charlie continued as he slipped his feet out of the irons to make his mount feel relaxed. 'Any progress with the investigation?'

'Not progress as such but I am working on several leads. And I'm hopeful.' I was deliberately vague. I didn't want Charlie, or anybody else for that matter, to have even an inkling of what Philip was up to. And I certainly didn't want him to know about last Friday's attack. It might make him think I would never get the BHA to reverse its findings. He might also get the impression that I was somehow mixed up with crooks or, worst of all, dopers.

'Christopher still wants you to ride many of the horses when you do come back,' Charlie continued.' Blue Marine will be going again at Christmas and your 7lb claim would make him a good thing. Be a nice one on which to announce your return, wouldn't it?'

I couldn't help smiling. The thought of me riding him to victory in a good race sent a warm glow right through me. Somehow I had to come up with the evidence the BHA was going to need, and I had do so soon.

Back at the stables I steered my mount towards his box, slipped my feet out of the irons and swung to the ground. I led the horse into his stable without him having to break stride. His lad was already there.

'Morning Rod,' he said cheerfully. 'How did he go?'

Before I had time to answer, a gruff voice came from the other side of the stable door. 'Hurry up John. There's a lot to do.'

Barry glared at me before moving on to chivvy the dark-haired girl mucking out the next box. Clearly the antagonism was still very much there, despite Charlie ticking him off about his attitude towards me.

I thought again about the head lad's possible involvement in the bribe and last Friday's attack. But he wouldn't have had ten grand to splash on getting me beaten up, let alone thirty. However revenge for losing his job with Trevor could take other forms, and he probably wouldn't have much hesitation in assisting the villains. From now on I was going to have to check my reins, bridle and stirrup leathers with special care every time I rode exercise.

I was driving through the stable gates and heading towards the road when my phone rang. 'Rod. Tom Cameron. When are you racing next?'

'No specific plans Tom. Did you want to see me?'

'Well, I've got a fair bit on Gavin Chesterfield. Nothing incriminating but you might want to hear it, even if only to exclude him from the suspects.'

With Blue Marine now attracting me like a powerful magnet, even negative news was important. It could narrow the target list and so make it easier to find the source of injustice. 'Where are you today, Tom?'

'Plumpton. First race 12.30. I'll be there about an hour beforehand.'

I wasn't sure how long it would take me. I knew it was a fair way. But I had never regarded distance being any bar to a racing journalist worth the name.

'I'll be there, Tom. If not for the first, certainly by the second or third.'

'Great. See you later.'

Plumpton was one of the few racecourses in the southern half of the country that I had never been to – mainly because it only staged minor meetings – and, once back at the cottage, a look at the map put the Sussex racecourse at around 120 miles by road. According to Google, it was going to take me about two and a half hours. For the first time since yesterday I felt grateful to Sue for vetoing my suggestion of spending Sunday night at the Twickenham flat, and then making a 6.00am start to be at the stables for first lot. 'No Rod,' she had insisted, pulling away from me on the sofa. 'I need to be fresh for work, and so do you.'

As it happened I didn't get to the Sussex course until just before the third – I was late leaving and I took a wrong turning coming off the A23 – but I need not have worried. The ultra-diligent red-haired *Racing Post* man was in his customary press room position, at the table nearest the TV.

He raised a hand in greeting. 'Glad you could make it.' The other two scribes also said friendly 'hellos' with the elder of the pair making a point of shaking me by the hand. Clearly I was not guilty in his book.

When the race – a two mile chase that took the eight runners nearly twice round the tight circuit – was over all three men got up to make for the quotes in the winner's enclosure. 'I'll be back in a minute,' said Cameron. 'We can talk then.'

In fact it was ten minutes before he reappeared. 'Let's go outside,' he said, before leading the way through the small crowd towards the now-deserted rails by the last fence.

'Our friend Gavin Chesterfield,' he began. 'I made a few inquiries. Quite a lot in fact. I got most information from one of the Disciplinary Panel members. I don't want to tell you his name – you will know it, for sure – but he insisted that what he told me was totally off the record.

'Basically Chesterfield is held in the highest regard by the Panel and seemingly by the BHA board as a whole. Yes, they agree he is possibly over-keen to pounce on wrong-doers, but they regard that as a good thing with so many grey areas often making it difficult to prosecute. Seemingly Chesterfield has injected new life into the disciplinary scene and he doesn't hesitate to speak up if he believes someone is cheating. Cheating was the word my man used.

'I suggested that maybe he could take a dislike to someone and go all out to get him – or her; apparently Chesterfield is considered immune to female wiles. All cases have to be given the OK by the Panel before they are proceeded with. And never so far – my man's words – has he put forward a case that didn't stand up. And there have been a few since yours.'

'Hmm,' I rubbed my chin, deep in thought. 'So, if it wasn't Chesterfield, who was responsible for trumping up the charges against me?'

'I don't know,' said Cameron. 'But maybe you do without realising it. Somebody you've upset? Somebody you've been critical of in print? Could be even somebody who has lost money on a horse you got beaten on.'

'Good God, Tom. That could include half the racecourse, let alone the thousands in the betting shops. How the hell could I trace all those?'

Cameron grinned. 'I know. A needle in a haystack's got nothing on this. But Rod, cross Chesterfield off the list and then see who it might be. Maybe you could find that man who offered you the bribe. He would surely know who was behind it.'

'Yea,' I said slowly, wondering how much I dared tell him. 'I am looking at other possibilities. And working on other angles. It's just that it would have been so straightforward to convince the BHA if Chesterfield had been involved in some way.'

'Listen Rod. You're innocent, and most of the racecourse believe that. You were framed. I'll help in any way I can but I suspect only you really know who it could be. Possibly you don't yet know but take a tip from me for what it's worth: go back over everything. Consider anybody and everybody who it might be. It's going to take you time, and I know you want to be back racing as soon as possible, but you'll get there. And, if in the meantime I can do anything to help, I will.'

'Thanks Tom.' I looked up as the runners for the next race came galloping up the course towards us. 'There is something you could do. Speak to Ambitious Arthur. He won't talk to me but I know several people in Hedgers lost their jobs as a result of what I did – and wrote. It could be one of them, or indeed several of them.'

'Consider it done,' said Cameron as, gripping my arm, he added: 'Come on, we must get back for the next.'

Calling Sue at around 7.00pm was now a daily – and most enjoyable – routine and, after the initial pleasantries, she asked me if Philip had been in touch. 'I know he's found something but it seemed complicated. I suggested he ring you and I gave him your number.'

Once our conversation was over I rang Philip. It was indeed complicated – two Rickards on both trainers' phones, seemingly father and son, and all far from straightforward. I soon realised that I wasn't going to get it anything like clear in my mind over the phone. I asked him where he would be the following day.

'At the supermarket. My gap year job,' he replied. The supermarket turned out to be in Twickenham, his lunch hour started at noon and he suggested meeting at a café nearby.

I was there shortly after 11.45am, took an empty table, informed the waitress that I was waiting for a friend and idly studied the menu to pass the time. It wasn't exactly a smart place – maybe Philip knew I was out of a job, but maybe he had chosen it for its convenience. It was less than 50 yards from Sainsbury's.

He arrived just after twelve in red jersey, black jeans and bubbling to tell all. Breaking off only to inform the returning waitress that he would have steak and chips, he launched into his highly detailed account. As I made notes on the pad I'd brought with me, frequently telling him to slow down, he explained that he had been able to get into the contact list of both trainers and from there the contact list of both George Rickards and a Greg Rickards. Most of the calls were to the latter but Greg's contact list had George's number listed as Dad.

Dad's list included 'the home' (which appeared on Greg's phone as the Bluebell Retirement Home in Nottingham) and Philip's further research had revealed that Greg was the boss of a second hand car company based on the Mansfield Road on the outskirts of the city. Philip looked suitably pleased with himself as he gave me a piece of paper with the addresses and telephone numbers of the company, the retirement home and both Rickards.

Seconds later the waitress came up with our food – I'd chosen the same as Philip – and, fascinated by his ability to come up with all this information after being given just the mobile numbers of the two trainers, I asked him what he intended to do between now and the start of his degree course in nine months' time.

Between mouthfuls he told me that he aimed to save up enough money to go round Europe in the summer before knuckling down to a three-year accountancy degree course in Edinburgh.

'Is that really what you want to do?' I asked, looking round and being surprised at how quickly the place had filled up. All the empty tables were now occupied and there was a growing group of people just inside the door, presumably waiting for empty spaces.

My question to Philip was more than just idle curiosity. Somehow being an accountant seemed too conventional a career for someone capable of tapping into people's phones and extracting information that most of the world expected to remain confidential. I didn't want him to waste years, making the same sort of mistake as I had, just assuming that it was the natural career choice as one's father had done well out of it and seemingly enjoyed it

'Good question,' answered Philip as he took off his glasses and polished them. 'Dad qualified as a chartered accountant before going into commerce and becoming a director of a big furniture company, and he's keen for me to do the same. He's going to pay the Edinburgh fees which are over £30,000 a year so I'll row along with that unless something better turns up.

'But, and this is between you and me, mind,' he added hastily before picking up his large glass of milk shake and drinking half of it in one go. 'Don't tell Sue. She's dead keen for me to do the degree – and dead against me going more into the likes of what I did for you. But that is what really interests me. Something in that direction anyway. Maybe some sort of private investigator.'

I smiled. 'I guess she's right, looking at it the way she would with her legal training. But you obviously have a lot of natural technical ability. I'm amazed at what you've come up with for me, that's for sure.'

I was warming to Philip, and not just because I knew I was falling for his sister.

He grinned. 'Maybe I could try something to do with betting? From what I hear the racecourse can be a pretty lucrative place if you do things right.'

My phone started ringing. I fished it out of my pocket and it promptly stopped. I glanced at the number. It wasn't one I recognised. Probably somebody trying to tell me something but it served as a reminder that I needed to get on with things if I was going to go to Nottingham the next day. With Blue Marine as my own personal carrot, I couldn't afford to waste time.

I got to my feet, picking up the bill as I did so. Philip also stood up, and four people promptly claimed the table. I paid the bill at the door, shook hands with Philip as I thanked him once again and headed for the multi-storey.

I hadn't gone more than a mile out of Twickenham when my phone rang again. It looked to be the same number. 'Rod?' inquired a voice I thought I recognised but couldn't place. 'It's Chris. Chris Thomas. Our friends are back, at least Bob Arrows is. Truncator backed from 20–1 to 7–4 in the first at Lingfield. String of noughts behind its name. Absolutely pissed in. Taken a small fortune off the books.'

'Bloody hell. Was the horse in a muck sweat in the winner's enclosure?' If it was that would prove – to my mind at least – that Arrows was up to his old tricks. 'Was there any inquiry into the improved form?'

'Didn't go to the winner's enclosure – I was in the ring with the bookies. But I did speak to one of the stewards. He said they interviewed the trainer and noted his explanation. Something about a change in training routine.'

'I'll bet there was.' I was trying to concentrate on the traffic while my mind was playing a video of an electric whip being used on the Green Hill gallops.

'Just thought you ought to know. If I hear anything more I'll give you a bell.'

I was coming off the M4 nearly an hour later when he rang again. 'You're not going to believe this, Rod. But they've done it again. Tom Swarter this time at Hereford with a nag I'd hardly heard of, Busy Backson, opened 33–1 and started at 2–1. Won the handicap hurdle by six lengths.'

'Bloody hell. They must have won a fortune.'

'Maybe not. The Hereford layers had heard all about Truncator. Some of them took bets on the horse. They didn't half slash Busy Backson once they saw there was money for him.'

'Hmm,' My mind was working overtime. Fortunately there was hardly any traffic to worry about on the A345. 'Who's the owner of Busy Backson?

There was a lengthy pause, presumably while Chris Thomas looked through a newspaper. 'Mr George Rickards. Bloody hell – he owns Truncator as well.'

He, or rather his son, was going to get a visit from me.

10

It was nearly 9.30am by the time I left the stables. When Charlie asked me, as we were on the path from the Downs back to the yard, if I would like some breakfast before heading off, I shook my head explaining that I was going to Nottingham to find George Rickards and his son.

He was clearly fascinated when I told him about the jigger twins' return to action, and what Philip had found out. But I was careful not to say where, or how, I had come by this last piece of information. Fortunately Charlie didn't ask but, when I slipped off Brown River and returned him to his box, a grinning Charlie called out 'Good hunting.'

I'd calculated that the near 150-mile journey would take me the best part of three hours but it seemed to take forever to reach the M1 at Newport Pagnall and, when I did, I was so hungry that I decided to stop at the service area for something to eat and a just-as-much-needed cup of coffee.

As a result, I got to Nottingham much later than I'd planned and I decided to head straight for the Bluebell Retirement Home, even though the residents were probably having their lunch.

My GPS took me into a quiet and clearly-expensive residential area of large tree-surrounded houses with big lawns. Bluebell was at the far end of a cul-de-sac, with a prominent notice giving its name and telephone number near the front gate. This was shut.

I parked in the road outside, went through the small gate by the side of the main one, walked up a 30-yard drive to the front door and rang the bell.

The door was opened by a small grey-haired woman I guessed to be in her early fifties. She was wearing a dark tweed skirt and a thick navy sweater. 'Yes?' she said, clearly expecting me to announce the reason for my visit.

'Er, hello,' I began hesitantly, even though I had rehearsed over and over again on the journey exactly what I was going to say. 'My name is James Watson. I'm in Nottingham on business and my father asked me to call in and say hello to George Rickards.'

The mention of Rickards' name brought a smile to the woman's face, making me feel a lot more confident. 'We used to live out Arnold way, and George and my father were great friends in those days.'

'Please come in,' she said, opening the door wide and taking a step back to allow me through. 'You've timed it well. Mr Rickards has just finished lunch and he's in the sitting room before he goes for his rest.'

She led the way down a wide passage - decorated with framed landscapes on the walls and a large vase of flowers at each end - into a large room. I was confronted by a dozen or so old people sitting on chairs placed around the walls. Some of them looked up as we entered but others just stared straight ahead. None of them spoke.

My guide walked over to a bald-headed man in a tweed suit which had clearly seen better days. 'George,' she said. 'This young man is a son of a friend of yours, a Mr Watson who used to live in Arnold.'

George Rickards opened his mouth to reveal several gaps in his nicotine-stained teeth but no words came out, just an unhealthy-sounding gurgle. Drops of spittle began dribbling down his chin.

'Sorry,' said the woman, turning to me. 'It's not one of George's better days. Would you like to sit and talk to him for a bit?' She pointed to an uncomfortable-looking wooden chair nearby. 'He might take in something if you speak slowly and keep repeating what you say.'

I picked up the wooden chair, turned it to face Rickards and sat down. The place was giving me the horrors: all these people who had clearly lost much of their minds, sitting here in silence and seemingly waiting for death. But if I simply turned away I would hardly look the part of someone bringing greetings from an old friend.

'I'll leave you to talk for a few minutes,' said the woman. 'Come back down the passage when you've finished and I'll let you out. But make sure you shut the door of this room behind you.' She gestured to the door in question. 'Some of them are apt to go exploring.'

I watched her retreating back and then looked round the room. Only two of the residents, both women, were looking towards me. The rest were staring straight ahead, seemingly seeing nothing, their minds as vacant as a recently-emptied dustbin..

'My father asked me to call in and say hello,' I struggled to make the effort, just in case any of the staff were watching out of my sight. I suspected that somebody was keeping an eye on the inmates via a closed-circuit TV camera. They could hardly be left untended.

'He was telling me that you were such good mates when we lived in Arnold.' George gave no sign of having heard. He just stared straight ahead. It was then that I saw that the two women were taking nothing in either. They continued to look at me but their expressions were blank.

I got to my feet, and still George looked straight ahead. So did all except the two women. Their heads turned in my direction as I began to move away. But there was nothing on their faces to suggest anything at all.

I went to the door, this time looking neither left or right. It was like the chamber of horrors I'd been to as a boy. And, just as I was on that occasion, I couldn't wait to get out.

I breathed a mental sigh of relief when I reached the door, slipped through it and carefully shut it behind me.

'As I told you, it's not one of George's better days,' said the tweed-skirted woman. 'I don't think he's got long actually.'

She said this as matter-of-factly as if she was talking about the postman being a bit late.

'Yes,' I agreed. 'But you are doing a great job with him. And with the others. My father will be pleased.'

She smiled as she opened the front door for me. I put out my hand as I stepped through. She made no move to shake it and silently shut the door behind me.

I had to stop myself hurrying as I made for the gate. I couldn't wait to be away from the place, but I assumed my exit was being observed. And I had a part to play.

It was just gone 2.15pm by the time I found Rickard Autos. It wasn't exactly on the Mansfield Road but no more than a few yards up a turning off it and it was an impressive place with a huge showroom. The front section, clearly arranged to display the most attractive vehicles, was given over to a Merc, three Jaguars and two BMWs, each with their prices prominently displayed.

Emblazoned across the top of the building was the sales come-on: 'Rickard Autos. Every car sold with a 12-month unconditional guarantee.'

I parked in one of the customer spaces in front of the building, walked through the open front door towards the white Mercedes 220 whose apparent well-being was emphasised by its highly polished sheen.

I walked around it a couple of times and was on the point of opening the driver's side door when a salesman appeared. A big burly man in a dark blue suit with tie to match. 'Good afternoon sir,' he said. 'Nice piece of work, this one. Only 30,000 on the clock and just one owner. Changes his car every two years and the Merc dealer in the city passed it straight on to us.'

'Hmm,' I replied as I continued to show interest. 'Is Greg in?' I asked casually. 'I'd like a word.'

'Not sure, sir. He was here an hour ago,' the salesman was clearly being deliberately noncommittal. 'Who shall I say I wants him?'

'James Mason. I'm interested in this car.'

'I'll just check, sir. Won't be a minute.'

I continued my inspection of the car, opening the boot as the salesman disappeared through a door marked 'Office.'

Two minutes later he was back, smiling deferentially and saying: 'Come this way, sir.'

He opened the office door for me and sitting behind a desk was a small, balding man of about forty with horn-rimmed glasses and a smart dark grey suit. Behind him was an almost carbon copy of the salesman except that this one was even bigger and burlier. To my eyes he looked almost menacing.

'James Mason, I presume,' said Greg Rickards, his tone positively unpleasant. 'Alias James Watson. Known on the racecourse as Rodney Hutchinson - and a first class crook.'

He turned to the big man behind him and nodded. The man came round the desk and stood close to me. The salesman did the same. I felt like a mouse unsuspectingly lured into a trap and now wishing with all his heart that he hadn't been so foolish.

'What do you want?' said Rickards, still sitting in his chair - but his expression and tone were now decidedly threatening.

'Truncator and Busy Backson yesterday,' I said with all the confidence I could muster. I felt it could be fatal to show the fear that was building up inside me like an explosive about to go off. 'Were they both victims of your trainers' electric whip treatment?'

Richards seemed to be unbelievably calm. I had more than half expected the two minders to be told to take me apart.

'Mr Hutchinson,' he began, pointing a biro accusingly at me. 'You have the audacity to come here, giving a false name at my father's nursing home and now making unfounded accusations about my horses. Yet you are a disgraced journalist, a provenly bent amateur jockey who has been suspended for God knows how long. You're shit.'

He stood up, his face now flushed and his whole body starting to shake with anger. 'Gentlemen,' he turned to the two burly men I now regarded as minders. 'Take a good look at this man. If you ever see him here again, you are to take him straight to the police. And, if he requires roughing up on the way, you know what to do.'

The salesman and his opposite number grabbed me none-too-gently, taking an arm each. They frog-marched me out of the office, through the showroom and the front entrance before throwing me forward so violently that I ended up hitting the tarmac - with such force that my face smashed into the ground at the same time as the front of my body.

I could sense the blood in my mouth as I slowly and painfully picked myself up, staggering as I got to my feet. It was the best part of a minute before I was able to walk towards my car. As I fished in my pocket for the remote, I could feel bits of gravel agonisingly entrenched in the palms of my hands.

For several minutes I just sat in the car, unable to do anything more, my mind as shocked as my body. The taste of blood on my lips somehow mixed with the pain from my cheeks and, increasingly, from my hands which were hurting as badly as if they had been stung by several angry bees.

I looked down at them, my vision blurred by my watery eyes. I fished in the box of tissues lying on the passenger seat and gingerly dabbed at them. I looked in the mirror. I was horrified. There was blood all over my face, some of it drying smears but other parts were still bleeding from the cuts where I had scraped against the ground.

I hadn't had much experience of first aid - other than on the racecourse where there were ambulance men and doctors to take care of everything. But I knew enough to realise that the gravel had to be cleaned away, and the wounds treated with Dettol as soon as possible.

I forced myself to pull the seat belt across, click it in and turn the ignition. I decided to head back in the direction of the city centre. I vaguely remembered passing a couple of shopping centres, both full of people. Not surprising, Christmas was only a week away. But there had to be a chemist's shop in there somewhere.

What I was looking for appeared after not much more than a mile, and the Oregon Pharmacy did me proud. The middle-aged bespectacled blonde woman behind the counter tut-tutted at my explanation that I had been knocked flying by teenagers on powerful, noisy motor bikes who simply laughed when I'd tried to remonstrate with them.

'We've got several of those louts round here,' she began. 'Personally I blame the parents. If they'd given their kids a good hiding when they deserved it, they wouldn't have grown up the way they have.

'This might sting a bit,' she added, dabbing at the palms of my hands with disinfectant-soaked cotton wool before carefully scraping away the embedded gravel-chips. She was right - it hurt like hell.

'Sorry,' she said as I winced, involuntarily pulling my hand away from her. 'Not too much more to do. Then I'll put Elastoplast on the worst bits. That 'll keep them clean and stop them hurting when you touch anything.'

She then turned her attention to my face. 'Hmm, I don't think you are in any danger of losing your looks.' She chuckled at her own joke, more disinfectant-soaked cotton wool being carefully dabbed on my painfully-scraped nose and cheeks.

Three minutes later, as she handed me the slip to be handed over at the cash desk, she added: 'You've had a bit of a shock. What you need now is a strong cup of tea with plenty of sugar. I can recommend Maeve's Tea Rooms fifty yards up the road. She serves some lovely cakes, very sugary but that's what you need.'

I walked up in the direction indicated but, when I saw how full Maeve's was – there seemed to be a queue just to get in – I decided to stop at the first service station on the motorway. There I followed the chemist's advice with a mug of well-sweetened tea and a hefty slice of cream-filled cake.

By now it was almost 4.00pm and I had a long way to travel. And I wasn't long off the motorway before the doubts began to creep in. Maybe it was a mistake to go over what Rickards had said but, despite the increasing traffic as office-closing drew near, his words were filling my thoughts.

Perhaps I shouldn't have used false names, either at the retirement home or the showroom. They didn't fool him and, in his eyes at least, they compounded the impression of dishonesty which he – and the general public too – now clearly associated with anything connected to me.

'A disgraced journalist' was a label that was going to stick until I cleared my name completely, and identified the guilty parties beyond all doubt. The same with a 'bent amateur jockey.' For the time being nobody was going to believe me about anything I said or did. It was a patently obvious case of giving a dog a bad name - and I was the dog. No newspaper would employ me with that tag hanging round my neck. And Brett wouldn't touch me with a barge pole.

Even if I succeeded in getting my amateur licence back the public would view me as a crook. In all probability I would be booed when I reappeared on the racecourse – if I reappeared. In fact I was already scarred for life.

As I neared the Oxford bypass I made a determined effort to blank out all these negative thoughts by trying to concentrate on Rickards who, I told myself, was the real crook. But could he have been the man who framed me? He didn't seem the sort to do anything as intricate as setting me up with a bribe. His behaviour at the showroom – and his use of the two minders – indicated brute force, not subtlety.

When I eventually got home I had to force myself to ring Sue. I was in such a state of depression that I had almost convinced myself that she couldn't help. And probably didn't want to.

I had got no further than the pointlessness of my visiting the retirement home when she interrupted, seemingly sensing the despondency in my voice.

'But surely this confirmed that his son was the villain in the set-up, not him?'

I then gave her a brief account of what happened at the car showrooms, leaving out the minders and what they did to me, but including what Rickards jnr had said about my being a bent jockey and a disgraced journalist.

'But that's all rubbish,' she countered. 'Everybody knows that. Look at what that man wrote in the *Racing Post*. That's how most people will see you.'

'Hmm.' I knew I sounded doubtful. I was.

'Alright, you are going to get some knockers and doubters. That's only human nature,' she conceded. 'It's now up to you to prove otherwise, and firstly to the BHA. Their lifting the suspension, and renewing you licence, will be enough to convince most people.'

'Hmm,' I repeated slowly. Amazingly, or so it seemed, I could feel my spirits rising like a cake in the oven.

'It's only natural that you should feel down now and again. Everyone does,' Sue continued in the same ultra-positive tone. 'In your case you are bound to because you've got an arch villain out there who's got it in for you for reasons we still don't know. But you have made so much progress with this thing that you should feel uplifted and encouraged. Certainly I am because I know we are going to get there.'

It was the first time she had used the word we in this particular context. I was almost cheerful.

'Now I want to talk to you about Christmas,' she said, changing tack. 'It's only a week away. What are your plans?'

I had almost forgotten about Christmas. It was one of the busiest, and most enjoyable, times of the year for me with top class racing on Boxing Day and the following few days. Indeed I'd ridden at a couple of the minor meetings in each of the last two years. But it was a reminder I could have done without. One of the few certainties was that I wouldn't be riding anywhere this time.

'Most of our office are taking the week off,' she continued in the same upbeat tone. 'I said I would work Monday but I'm thinking of hiring a car and coming down to you on Friday evening.'

That did sound good - I had a vision of her in my bedroom, and I could feel myself smiling in delight.

She mistook my silence for doubt. 'I won't come if you don't want me to,' she said slowly, her disappointment travelling all too clearly down the line.

'Sue darling, of course I want you with me. It would be fantastic. But would you rather go away somewhere for a few days? We could go to a nice hotel in, say, Cornwall or on the South Coast. Brighton or somewhere.'

She laughed. 'A dirty weekend you mean? No Rod, I think we ought to keep up the hunt. Maybe we should go racing on Saturday. Are there not more people you need to quiz?'

There were, and Hedgers was pretty near top of the list now that Greg Rickards no longer appeared to fit the modus operandi.

Or was I making a big mistake with that assumption?

I didn't need to look out of the window to realise the weather had changed. It was freezing – at least that was how it felt – even in my bedroom. I put on a thermal vest and a second jersey, and grabbed a pair of pigskin gloves, before heading downstairs for a hasty cup of tea.

I could see many of the fields were white with frost, particularly as I neared the stables where the staff were hurrying to get the horses ready for first lot. But the cold did nothing to dampen the enthusiasm for jokes at the expense of my face.

'Did she beat you up?' inquired Jake in a tone that suggested he firmly believed the unspecified she had done just that.

'Nah, Rod's had a facelift,' chipped in Seamus in his broad Irish accent. 'Doesn't want the BHA to recognise him.'

This brought laughter all round. Even the blonde Brenda, normally on my side, joined in. 'Might be an improvement,' she said, peering closely at the marks left by the gravel.

But the subject had been dropped by the time everybody's surplus energy had been used up in a brisk work-out over four furlongs up on the Downs where the ground seemed as cushioning as always, despite the top-surface white frost.

On the way down Charlie again asked me if I would like some breakfast before heading off, and this time I had no hesitation in accepting.

I filled him in on the mental and physical state of Rickards snr while he cooked the bacon, and I had given him a resume of my unpleasant encounter with Greg Rickards by the time we had taken our seats on the stools by the counter.

'I somehow don't think he's behind the attempted bribery and setting me up with the BHA,' I said. 'He strikes me as much more of a physical violence type. The sort who will go in with threats, not hesitating to carry them out, rather than something requiring a lot of careful planning.'

Charlie, chewing on his bacon, said nothing for the best part of half a minute as if considering my comment. 'I don't know,' he said eventually. 'I wonder if that's so.'

'Just think about it, Rod.' He was holding his fork upright and looking straight at me. 'Who stands to gain most from you being discredited? And barred from expressing your views in print?'

He turned his attention back to the little that was left on his plate. 'No-one, at least so far as I can see, wants you out of the way more than Tom Swarter and Bob Arrows. You are a walking, talking, living threat to both of them. They stand to lose their licences if you get back into business.'

I realised he was right. And Charlie hadn't finished: 'Rod. I think you encountered the real Greg Rickards yesterday. He knew exactly who you are, and his reaction shows that he knows just what you can do. True, he tried to frighten you off. But that doesn't mean he is not capable of resorting to subtlety. And I still think he is the brains behind the betting coups. You must be very careful.'

Charlie's warning dominated my thoughts throughout the drive home and, by the time I got there, I had more than half convinced myself that he was right. But there were other possibilities, and I had other enemies. I shuddered at the thought. I had to ring Tom Cameron.

Yes, he would be at Newbury and no later than three-quarters of an hour before the first. In fact he was just getting out of his car when I arrived almost 75 minutes ahead of the opener. We were among the first to arrive, bar the officials and the racecourse staff.

'Morning Rod,' said the red-haired Racing Post man as he got out of his car, shrugging his way into a browny-green waxed Barbour and taking a bulky laptop case out of the boot. 'I've found out a fair bit on the Hedgers' front. Come on, we can talk inside. It's bloody cold out here.'

Indeed it was and the sky was ominously dark, hinting at the possibility of snow. The press room, though, was warm. Some thoughtful member of the racecourse staff had turned on the heating. We both took off our coats as Cameron began elaborating on his researches.

'I started with Ambitious Arthur,' he said, taking his laptop out of its case and plugging the cable into a power point. 'I told him this was all off the record but I was curious as to who could have had it in for Rod Hutchinson. I said I was convinced you'd been set up.

'He was hesitant at first, saying it had to be off the record. Could I give him my word that none of this would appear in print, or at least could not be attributed to him in any way? I promised him that Rod, so be careful how you use it. OK?'

'Of course.' I said, taking my coat off the back of my chair and hanging it on the row of hooks on the far wall, before resuming my seat across the table from Cameron.

'I said that I'd heard some staff members had lost their jobs because they'd been involved in the blackmailing of the Major, as had a couple more who had set up the receipt of his tips, even though they themselves had done nothing wrong. I said I didn't need names – I wasn't going to write anything – I just wanted the facts because you are a friend as well as a colleague.

'Arthur said that Hedgers had suffered badly in the publicity over the bomb and the directors were adamant that the bad eggs should be cleaned out – and paid off handsomely to lessen the possibility of further bad publicity from unfair dismissal cases. I gather they got pretty big sums.

'Arthur also told me that there had been an investigation by the auditors into the share registrations, how Jimmy Brownson had been able to build up such a big shareholding under false names without anybody smelling a rat. But they were unable to find evidence of fraud among the staff in that department. Seemingly they concluded that it was negligence rather than collusion with Brownson, and they have now appointed somebody with specific responsibility for examining share transfers.' Cameron grinned at me: 'What you might call shutting the stable door after the horse has bolted.'

I laughed but Cameron's expression was serious once more. 'I also spoke to a friend of my wife. She is a section manager in Hedger's. She said it was meant to be hush-hush, even internally, but she knew that two people in one of the other sections had been retired early and the word was that three others had been too. According to the grapevine, it was all in connection with the Cheltenham bomb but she didn't know any more.

'Going back to Ambitious Arthur,' Cameron continued but paused when the press room door opened.

'Morning gents,' said the racecourse manager, putting his head round. 'Glad to see some people are here early. Doubt we'll get much of a crowd with the weather so threatening. But the Met Office says we should get through the card alright.'

Cameron waited, seemingly to be sure the manager wasn't coming back. 'Yea. Arthur said none of the on-course people were involved in the hoo-hah over the bomb, blackmailing the Major or the share registrations. But there was – and apparently there still is – a widespread feeling of resentment towards you for blowing the gaffe. Even bitterness, and not just among the people who lost their jobs.

'I asked him whether that bitterness could extend to setting you up with an attempt at bribery. He didn't answer, just shrugged his shoulders and muttered something about not knowing anything more. He again made me promise not to say anything that could be attributed to him.'

'Hmm.' I considered the implications. 'What do you think?'

'I don't think there's much doubt.' Cameron scribbled something on the shorthand pad in front of him, as if writing a must-do note to himself, before looking me straight in the eye. 'Rod, Hedgers is obviously littered with resentment and those who lost their jobs have good reason to want revenge. There are surely some amongst them who would have been capable of setting up the bribery and engaging that man. What was his name - Richards? Roberts? But how you go about finding him, or just possibly her, that I don't know.'

Further conversation was halted by the noisy arrival of two other pressmen who both dumped their laptop cases on the table and, after saying 'Hi Tom, Hi Rod,' continued with their discussion about who was going to win the first.

I stood up, thanked Tom, and decided to go outside and digest his findings in surroundings where I could concentrate on the implications of what I'd been told.

I walked towards the winner's enclosure, acutely conscious that this was a return to the scene of the crime – or at least where the self-styled John Roberts attempted the bribery that had had such devastating consequences. And from there I went out onto the course and up the straight as I considered Tom Cameron's comments and conclusions.

Maybe it wasn't the most sensible move – my shoes were little protection against the wet grass, and my socks were soaked within a matter of strides – but at least there was no-one about to disturb my thought processes. If Tom was right, and logic suggested he was, finding the culprit would be like searching for the proverbial needle in a haystack. I didn't know anybody in Hedgers, bar Arthur Jackson, and nor was I likely to find anyone in a position to help me pinpoint who it might be. Even a list of the people who had left the company in the past year would be just about unobtainable for somebody with no connection to the betting firm. Furthermore any suggestion that I might be shortlisting possible ex-employees could bring, even if not further retribution, a closing of the ranks.

By this stage I was nearing the second last fence and the bottom few inches of my trousers were as soaked as my feet. I cursed myself for my stupidity, walked across to the road used by the ambulance that followed the runners, and headed back towards the stands.

I paused by the bookmakers, all of them well-wrapped up against the cold, and reflected what a tough life they had during the winter months, exposed to the elements for hours at a time. One of them greeted me by name and called me over to his stand. Seemingly he wanted to talk about the Truncator and Billy Backson stings of two days earlier.

'Them Arrows and Swarter, Rod?' he asked. 'They the ones you wrote about before?'

'Well, I did write something about their previous coups,' I admitted. 'But I didn't actually say they had broken any rules. I couldn't. Their lawyers would have had a field day.'

'Yea, suppose so,' he agreed, tucking his scarf inside his coat and stepping down from his stand. 'You just about the only one that writes about anything like that. We need you back.'

I laughed. 'I'm trying to get back but I have to prove that I was set up - and that's turning out to be difficult.'

'That man that tried to bribe you? What was his name?' said George Godden – at least that was the title on his board.

'John Roberts, although I doubt that he would have used his real name. Seems to have been an actor of some sort, probably little known and disguised.'

'Listen Rod, I'm going to ask around,' said Godden quietly, his tone turning serious. 'Somebody must know him, or know who he might be. As I said, we want you back writing that column on *sports-all*. It's just tips and reports since you left. No meat on it whatsoever.'

I thanked him and walked on, feeling considerably cheered. I'd only gone four bookies further down the line when I was hailed by one whose name I did know. 'Fearless Fred. No bet too small or too big,' proclaimed his board.

Fred Masters, moustached but bald as a coot, jumped down and shook my hand, his broad grin and cheerful manner as infectious as 'flu in February.

'Now Rod, I'm opening a book on you,' he enthused. '6-4 to be back by Cheltenham. That a fair price? Do you want a bit on?'

I laughed, and clapped him on the shoulder. 'Me backing myself might be the kiss of death, Fred. In any case 6-4 sounds a bit short. I know I'm innocent but I've got to find out who set me up in order to convince the BHA.'

'Can you do that?' Masters' tone was serious. So was his expression. But his enthusiasm was heartening.

'I bloody well hope so,' I replied. 'In fact I know I can. But, by Cheltenham? That's a tall order.' I chuckled. 'Maybe 5-1. But by this time next year? I'd say I was odds-on.'

I stayed for the first two races, passing the time of day with three or four trainers and a couple of the jockeys. None of them appeared surprised to see me, or asked how I was progressing with my investigation. Indeed they seemed to view me as much a part of the regular racing furniture as I viewed them.

Only on the drive home did the difference hit me. They were at Newbury in their professional capacities whereas I had no function there at all. Indeed I had no racing function, full stop. And nor would I until I came up with incontrovertible evidence to place before the BHA.

All I had was a number of people with motives. The only person I knew for certain to be involved was John Roberts. I was nowhere near finding him and, apart from a loose undertaking from one bookmaker, I was not likely to either.

By the time I reached home, I was as depressed as I'd ever been. I forced myself to sit down at my computer and, after checking my emails (nothing of any relevance), I typed out a further list of the possibles and then put them in order of probability.

An hour later, fortified by a mug of strong tea and several chocolate biscuits, I read it through:

1. Greg Rickards. Strong motive: me resuming journalistic career could mean exposure, disgrace and prison for him.

2. Tom Swarter and Bob Arrows. Both would lose their licences if I put in print what they had been doing to their horses. Would also face public disgrace and possible imprisonment.

3. Someone sacked from Hedgers. But who? And could I find him or (less likely) her?

4. Jimmy Brownson. Already convicted, disgraced and imprisoned. Seemingly had sworn to kill me.

5. Likewise the man who Brownson paid to plant the bomb.

I also listed those I had suspected previously but now looked unlikely:

1. Barry. His surly manner seemingly not just directed at me.

2. Trevor Brownson. Sarah apparently adamant he wouldn't go that far - and I believed her.

3. Somebody I had upset/criticised in print. Possible, but nobody obvious coming to mind.

What I needed was a plan of action. I decided I would sound out Charlie, Sue and maybe Paddy O'Reilly as well.

11

But it was Emma I thought about as I tossed and turned, unable to sleep. As so often when she reappeared in my thoughts, she was dressed in the clothes she had on when I first met her. She was working as a temporary receptionist in my brother-in-law's surgery. It was a Saturday morning and I had gone to see him for treatment for a cracked forearm injured in a fall at Sandown the previous day. The striking-looking blonde was wearing a white roll-neck jersey and black trousers that fitted her shapely bottom and legs like a second skin. I'd had trouble taking my eyes off her.

While I had much more recently fallen for Sue, I couldn't help wondering if you could be in love with two women at the same time. Indeed was it permissible, or even possible, to fall in love with another so soon after the first one had died?

I turned over to my right and, after ten restless minutes, back again but still sleep wouldn't come. I decided not to fight with my subconscious anymore and let it go back over my all-too-brief association with Emma. My thoughts progressed to her death – something I'd usually been reluctant to do because it invariably made me sad. But this time I let my mind wander. Somehow it drifted, in a background of angel-inspired music, to her floating up to heaven, wearing wings to help her progress.

But, as she floated upwards and became smaller and smaller the further she went, I felt the air becoming hotter. And hotter. It suddenly dawned on me that, while she had gone to heaven, I was descending into hell. Indeed there were several ugly red devils with horn-like helmets, each holding a hot fork. They looked a bit like Martians in a comic strip, only a whole lot more frightening. They were barring my progress and the sweat was pouring off me as the heat intensified. I pleaded with them to let me pass.

'No,' they declared in unison, rushing forward and driving the prongs of their forks into my stomach. The pain was intense, so much so that I woke up. My pyjamas were soaked in sweat and I was as hot as the hell I'd been dreaming about.

I could hear a crackling noise from downstairs and there seemed to be some sort of flickering light outside the bedroom window. I got out of bed, went to the window and realised the house was on fire. I hurried to the door and down the stairs. The fire was in the left-hand side of the house and appeared to be coming from the kitchen. Maybe I'd left the cooker on. I knew there was a fire extinguisher on the wall by the side of the fridge. I made for the door, tried to open it and – to my horror – was confronted by a veritable Dante's Inferno.

I hastily shut the door and rushed for the stairs. Back in the bedroom I grabbed my clothes, put on my trousers, a vest, two jerseys and a windcheater plus my shoes in record time. I snatched my phone, wallet and car keys off the bedside table, plus my passport from the drawer, went back down the stairs two at a time and unlocked the front door. But it wouldn't open. I pulled at it with all my might but it seemed to be stuck tight. I went for the sitting room window. The handle turned but that too wouldn't open.

I panicked and started yelling for help. The futility then struck me. Nobody was going to hear me: the cottage was too isolated for anyone to be even aware of the fire, let alone hear anybody shouting. The flames were now spreading from the kitchen into the sitting room. There was a frightening whoosh as the sofa burst into flames.

I choked as the toxic fumes from the burning sofa spread rapidly through the room. I knew I had to get out before they poisoned my system.

I ran for the stairs and back into the bedroom. I prayed, silently and hurriedly, that these windows would open. The one at the back of the house did but it was above the kitchen and the flames were lapping at the window sill.

I rushed to the other side of the room. There were flames there too but nothing like as bad. I opened the window, pulled myself up onto the sill, squeezed through the narrow gap and threw myself forward. I hit the gravel even harder than I did when the Rickards' bouncers threw me out of the showroom. This time it was the flames that made me pick myself up. I ran forward only to trip over a large stone and fall headlong onto more gravel. My hands, still sore from Wednesday, suffered again. The pain was acute. Only the roaring behind me persuaded me to get to my feet. I trod carefully this time but the heat at my back was the motivating force. I knew I had to keep moving or I would go up in flames, suffering a truly agonising death.

When I reached the lawn I tripped again. This time I was so badly winded that I couldn't get up. I glanced fearfully behind me and saw, to my intense relief, that I was a good twenty yards away from what had become a raging inferno.

But something out of the corner of my eye caught my attention. I stared hard. It was the wooden garage on the far side of the house, and I thought I could see flames at its base. The implications were horrific – and they were more than enough to have me staggering to my feet. I walked towards it and tried to break into a run. But I couldn't do it, not to begin with anyway. I just didn't have the strength.

But the closer I got, the faster I walked. The flames were lapping at the side nearest me but the rest of the garage looked OK. Now I could run. I had to. I knew that, if the fire took hold, my beloved BMW would turn into a bomb of incredible violence and devastation, destroying God knows what.

I wrenched open the right hand wooden door, and then the left where the nearest flames were only feet away. I tried to tell myself that I was being stupid, if not suicidal. But I had to do it. I rushed inside, my left hand trying to shield my face from the intense heat and my right giving the remote a click. I opened the car door, threw myself inside, inserted the key and turned on the engine. By now the flames were sweeping right across the open garage front.

There was no turning back. At least no trying to get out on foot. I would be burned alive. As I stamped hard on the accelerator I could see nothing but a solid wall of flame. 'Please God, let me live,' I yelled out loud as the car shot into it and, miraculously, reached the other side.

I slammed on the brakes as the burning house loomed up, opened the car door and rolled onto tarmac. I kept rolling for a couple of yards, picked myself up and ran across a small stretch of grass before crashing into a thick thorn hedge.

I looked round, first to the left and then to the right. Everywhere was lit up like a vast Santa Claus grotto. The house was on fire from floor to roof and from back to front. So was the garage from which I had just escaped. But my car was a good twenty yards from either, and there was not even a spark to suggest it was in any danger.

It was then that I heard the clanging bells. I saw the headlights almost immediately and I found myself lit up like a spotlight in the circus as the headlights of the fire engine picked me out. Half a dozen helmeted men emerged from it, some jumping down even before it had come to a halt. One ran towards me while the others unrolled the grey tubes, changing from flattened rubber into violently kicking pipes as they filled with fluid.

'You alright mate?' shouted the man who came towards me and began helping me to my feet.   Once I was standing, he was off to join his five colleagues. I watched in something approaching awe as they went about their business with unbelievable speed and efficiency. Within ten minutes of their arrival they had the flames under control, and within twenty almost everything was doused down. Only the brick skeleton outline of the house was visible in the headlights of the fire engine as a police car drew up. Two uniformed officers got out and spoke briefly to some of the fire crew who pointed in my direction.

'You alright, sir?' said the first policeman as I walked towards where the fire had been.

When I assured him that I was OK – 'Just a bit shocked at the way the house went up in flames' – he wanted to know if I knew what had started it.

I shook my head. 'No, not really except that it began in the kitchen.' I hesitated. 'I suppose I might have left the cooker on when I went to bed. But I don't think I did.'

The second policeman, who hadn't uttered a word, wrote my answer down in his small notebook before snapping it shut and putting it back in his breast pocket.

'Could I have your full name and mobile number?' asked his colleague, presumably the senior of the two. The second man took out his notebook once again, this time to write down my details, while the first told me I could expect a call later this morning and advised going to a friend or neighbour for what was left of the night. 'Sometimes the shock only sets in afterwards. I recommend a mug of strong tea.'

'With a tot of whisky in it,' added the other man with a wink.

After a quick word with the fire crew they were gone. Ten minutes later there was only me – and the ruin – left. I looked at my watch. 2.30am. What the hell was I going to do?

I thought of driving to Sue's flat in Twickenham, ringing her on the way to alert her. But it was quite a long way and there was a disturbing feeling of jelly about my limbs. Charlie's house would be a lot easier.

After twenty seconds of ringing, during which I wondered if he kept his phone downstairs rather than by his bed, there was a sleepy, questioning 'Hello?'

I quickly explained what had happened and asked if he could give me a bed for what was left of the night. 'Sure.' He didn't hesitate. 'Come straight away.'

During the 15-minute drive I pondered over who or what might have been responsible. The more I thought about it, the more convinced I became that I had not left anything on in the kitchen. That could only mean it had been another attempt at killing me.

And it had to be Greg Rickards. Even if somebody with a Hedgers' connection wanted me dead, it was too much of a coincidence for the attack to have come only hours after Tom Cameron was telling me of possible enemies connected with the betting firm. Rickards, on the other hand, had been threatening me with maximum violence only two days ago. More than ever, he looked the sort to carry out his threats.

When I got to the trainer's house Charlie was in his dressing gown with a half-drunk mug of tea in his hand. He ushered me into the kitchen, poured another mug out of the pot and bid me tell him what had happened. Fifteen minutes later I was in the spare bedroom and, while it took me some time to get to sleep, it was daylight when I woke up.

I was in the wrong side of the house to be able to see the yard but I could hear the unmistakeable sounds of the string getting ready to leave and, five minutes later, I saw them heading in single file up the track leading to the Downs.

I looked at my watch. Just after 8.00am. Time to ring Sue. She was on the tube and it was noisy but she left me in no doubt about her reaction. She was horrified. 'Rod, this is appalling,' she began. 'I'm so frightened for you. It keeps happening. First those thugs pretending to be from the courier company, then that horrible man in Nottingham and now they have burned down your house. What are we going to do?'

Clearly, whatever course of action was decided upon, she intended to be part of it – despite the obvious dangers. 'The police came to the house, or what was left of it, before the fire people left and I gather they will be coming back,' I told her. 'In the meantime I'd better contact the letting agent and give her the bad news. Plus find somewhere else to live'.

'Do you want to come to me? At least we don't have arsonists in Twickenham.' I could picture her smiling at her own joke. But she was immediately serious again. 'Rod, you must go somewhere less isolated. Somewhere in a town. Didn't you say you were in Reading before? That would be much safer.

'And Rod. When the police are talking to you again, tell them everything. Please. For my sake. I'll be a nervous wreck worrying about you until I know you are going to be safe.'

'OK,' I knew I sounded hesitant but I was mulling over the possible options. Maybe going back to Reading would be a good idea. Quite a drive from Charlie's though. 'I'll talk to a Reading agent and see what they can come up with.'

She made me promise to ring her again by mid-morning. 'Please Rod. I love you.'

She hadn't used the L word before, and it had me thinking as I put my phone back into my pocket and gazed through the window at the now deserted path to the Downs. Maybe it was time I told her just how much I loved her.

The phone springing into action brought me back to reality. It was a number I didn't recognise. 'Mr Hutchinson?' inquired an authoritative-sounding voice. 'This is Detective-Inspector Hodgkinson. Can you be at your cottage in half-an-hour?'

I hesitated and looked at my watch. 'Could we make that three-quarters?'

'Yes. 9.00am. I will see you then.' His tone was firm, as if he was accustomed to people doing what he said. I wasn't even given a chance to say anything further. He had already disconnected.

The sight of the house – little more than the blackened four walls, charred woodwork and a caved-in roof – shook me to the chore. And a heap of burnt wood – all that was left of the garage – made me realise just how stupid I'd been to attempt to save my car.

Detective-Inspector Hodgkinson, a craggy-faced, tough-looking six foot-plus individual in his mid-forties, did little to assuage my feelings. His manner was antagonistic from the start. He ignored my outstretched hand and went for the jugular.

'Mr Hutchinson,' he began coldly. 'I understand you have a criminal record with the horseracing authorities. They gave you a five-year ban for accepting a bribe to stop a favourite. Perhaps you would care to explain your part in all this.'

He indicated the burnt-out house with a broad sweep of his right arm, and his gimlet-like brown eyes bore into my own as he waited for an answer.

I was taken aback, and I hesitated. Clearly it was going to be one of those 'anything you say may be taken down and used in evidence against you' interviews. If not actually 'guilty unless proved otherwise.'

'Detective-Inspector.' I began, doing my best to match his coldness with my own. 'I will have you know that I am as innocent of the British Horseracing Authority charges as I am of anything to do with this fire, and I have spent most of the last fortnight gathering evidence to prove my point to the BHA.

'My part in all this' I added, 'was waking up in the middle of the night to find that I was in danger of being burned alive. I escaped only in the nick of time and, frankly, I'd hoped you would be able to tell me who did it. Not accuse me of trying to turn myself into a modern-day equivalent of Guy Fawkes.'

'OK.' The Detective-Inspector seemed to accept I had a point, although the expression on his face was hardly suggestive of being suitably chastened.

'I understand from the fire officer's report that the fire started in the kitchen and that you had to jump from your bedroom window,' he continued. 'Did you get a chance to try either the front door or the downstairs windows first?'

'No. Or rather I did but I couldn't open either the door or the windows. I only had time to try the sitting-room window because the sofa had caught fire by that stage and the fumes were beginning to choke me.'

His tone changed slightly and his voice dropped as if imparting something that was being kept secret: 'Our preliminary forensic examination found traces of Super Glue on both the front door and the two windows that weren't completely destroyed.' He paused, took a step closer and seemed to deliberately bore into my eyes with his own. 'Who do you think would have done that, Mr Hutchinson?'

Super Glue. I was shocked. But, if I was a bookmaker, Greg Rickards would now be 1–2 favourite. I tried to blank out the image of that flushed face and his body shaking with anger. I didn't want Hodgkinson to read my mind. Not yet anyway. I could be wrong. Maybe it was somebody from Hedgers after all.

'Burning down someone's house, preferably with him in it, is a common way of enforcing threats, Mr Hutchinson. As I suspect you are beginning to realise.'

I said nothing. But I digested carefully what he was saying. Seemingly, though, he was far from finished.

'I said earlier that you have a criminal record with the racing authorities. It may surprise you, or it may not,' his bushy eyebrows were raised in tandem with his questioning expression, 'that you also have a record with the police. A record for being attacked.'

I tried to look puzzled, although I feared I knew what was coming. 'You were beaten up in the racecourse car park at Ludlow last year and in December you were almost killed by a bomb in the Cheltenham car park.'

I fleetingly wondered if he also knew about the recent Friday the 13th courier company attack. Again I tried to make my mind think of something else. Doubtless telepathy was taught in wherever they trained detectives.

'Yea,' I conceded. 'But that was last year. Those responsible are now in prison. They can hardly have done this.'

'I wouldn't be so sure,' said Hodgkinson. 'In my experience it isn't just the law that has long arms.'

I said nothing. I was only too well aware of what he was implying.

But could I really be certain that it was Rickards and not someone in Hedgers? Or one of the jigger twins, or both of them; after all they trained practically in each other's pockets, and for the same man. And there was Jimmy Brownson, with both the money and the motive for murdering me. Not to mention the avowed intent!

'Mr Hutchinson.' The detective's accusing tone brought my mind sharply back from conjecture to confrontation. I immediately resolved not to argue. He was not going to let go unless he was convinced I was on the side of the law. And, despite my answers, he still seemed to think I was a crook.

'I will need to speak to you again. I trust you are not planning to go anywhere over Christmas?'

'I've got to find somewhere else to live,' I answered. 'This place is going to take six months to put right.'

'Where are you thinking of?' His tone suggested he was not going to drop this particular bone.

'At this stage Reading looks odds-on,' I answered. 'That's where I was before I came here, and I'm going there now to see what I can find.'

'I need you to keep me informed. Ring me once you know anymore.' He gave me his number and I put it into my phone.

'Right,' he said and walked off to his car without another word. I watched him get into the black Rover and drive off. I went to my car and rang the letting agent. She was predictably horrified.

I was about to drive off when Sue rang. 'I'm on my way,' she said. 'Where should I meet you?' I thought I could detect a note of excitement in her voice. 'I've taken the rest of the day off. Jeremy is standing in for me and I'm going in on Monday in return.'

'Great. Are you on the train? To Reading?'

She laughed. 'No, I'm under my own steam. I've hired a car for the next few days.'

'Great.' I repeated, thinking quickly. Obviously it was vital that we found a flat, today if at all possible, and it needed to be furnished.

'Go to the station car park. The one where I parked the last time. Ring me when you get there. If I'm there first I'll ring you.'

'You probably will be. I'm going home now to pick up some clothes.'

As she rang off, realisation began to dawn. I had no clothes other than those I was wearing. Furthermore I'd lost both my laptop and my desktop computer, and – just as bad – my file of racing statistics together with my form books and all my old articles. Just about the only good thing was that I'd had the presence of my mind to pick up my wallet with its bank and credit cards before I ran for the window. But I hardly knew where to start.

I did by the time I reached the car park in Reading. First stop was the insurance brokers in Broad Street. The younger of the two grey-haired ladies behind the front desk proved as helpful as she was efficient and, after expressing horror at what had happened, she filled out the claim form, got me to sign it, said she would get an official report from both the fire department and the police and submit the lot to General Accident.

I'd just about finished buying a new laptop and printer when Sue rang. She was in the station car park. Where was I? I told her to stay put and I would meet her outside the front entrance in fifteen minutes.

It was a further fifteen before we reached the letting agents in Minster Street. I thought they might be reluctant to offer me anything at all after losing a property to an obvious case of arson. But Mary Bradshaw, after having two hours to get over her initial shock, was back to her normal ultra-helpful self. She had, she explained, emailed the Florida-based owner and followed up with the initial police and fire station reports. Did I want somewhere in the same area or was I considering moving back to town.

'Back to town,' said Sue firmly, before I had a chance to say anything. Dressed in her smart dark grey suit and camel hair overcoat, her appearance brooked no argument.

'In that case I might have just the place,' Mary replied, and from that point on she addressed most of her comments to Sue. 'It's a two-bedroomed flat very near where Rod was before. Backing onto it in fact, in a similar designed complex and this one is fully furnished.'

That last comment was played like the trump card she knew it to be, and played with a smile.

'Sounds as if it might be OK,' said Sue with a slight amount of doubt in her voice. As she explained afterwards, it was inadvisable to sound too keen no matter how good it might appear. Rental agents, in her experience, were no better than estate agents.

Five minutes later we were all squeezed into Mary's VW … and a further five saw us driving slowly past the old Kennet Walk flat, turning right then left, and drawing up outside its twin sister in a similar block of four, each with its own garage.

It was much the same layout inside too. Sue went slowly from to room, closely followed by Mary pointing out various selling points, and me bringing up the rear saying nothing.

'No TV?' queried Sue.

'No, that's for the tenant,' said Mary. 'Normally they have their own. But it does have full sets of crockey, cutlery and kitchen equipment including toaster, microwave, washing machine and dishwasher.'

Sue nodded, her expression suggesting she wouldn't have expected anything less. 'How much?'

Mary quoted a figure £500 a month more than I had paid for the Kennet Walk flat. I said as much.

'True,' said Mary. 'But that was a good 18 months ago and this part of Reading has become very popular. Also it's fitted out to a much higher standard than your old one.'

'Just give us a private word,' said Sue.

'Sure,' came the answer. 'You two chat away while I go and get my appointment book out of the car. I've got another couple coming here this afternoon and I need to check what time.'

'That's sales talk,' said Sue as Mary shut the door behind her. 'But it is very nice. What do you think?'

I hesitated. It was expensive, particularly for someone who had no salary and whose capital was largely tied up in two racehorses almost guaranteed to be running at a loss. I did a quick mental calculation. I had enough in the bank to cover the next six months but, if I wasn't back working by then, I would have to turn to some other work or try my luck elsewhere in the world. Either way I wouldn't need to stay here.

'OK, we'll take it,' I told her hesitantly, the uncertainty in my voice all too evident.

'You're going to be back writing in a few months, I just know it.' Sue's confident tone was in marked contrast. I had to hope she was right. That saying about a faint heart never winning a fair lady came to mind. Even though this one had light brown hair!

I was about to kiss her when the door opened. Mary, desk diary in hand, said: 'They're coming at three. I know they're keen. It's a first class property and I wanted to give you first refusal, Rod, because you are already a client of ours and I feel it would suit you. Don't you agree, Sue?'

She was now playing the sisterhood card. So was Sue. 'I think it's ideal,' she agreed. 'Maybe the price is a bit high but rents are going up, particularly in the Home Counties.'

'OK,' I said, trying not to think about the money. 'I'll take it.'

By the time we had completed the paperwork back in Minster Street it was nearly 2.00pm. 'Lunch,' I said to Sue as we turned right out of the office and headed towards the town centre. We found a café that looked promising, and was fast emptying of office workers. I walked in but, glancing behind, I realised Sue was no longer with me.

I back-tracked and found her staring at the window of the next door-travel agent. 'What's so appealing?' I asked. Her answer was to point at a large poster in the top right of the window. 'Christmas in Kenya,' was emblazoned across a beach scene of scarcely believable brightness.

'Come on,' I said, taking her hand and steering her back towards the restaurant.

But she was reluctant to move. 'You go and grab a table. Order us something. I'll be with you in five minutes.' She disentangled her fingers from mine and disappeared through the travel agency door.

I chose a table near the front of the restaurant where I could keep a lookout for her, told the waitress who brought the menu that I was waiting for my girlfriend, and began to feel annoyed. There was no way I could afford a holiday, not after paying so much for the flat. Surely she knew that? Or was she one of those women who milked their men of every last pound?

When she did arrive she was clutching a large brochure and

smiling happily. My heart felt as if it was going to melt.

'Listen,' she said. 'It's Christmas, and I want to give you a present. How do you feel about flying to Mombasa on Monday and spending a week in the sun?'

'Sue, I can't let you do that. It's probably ridiculously expensive, particularly at this time of year. It would be different if I was working – then I could take you.'

Before she had a chance to argue, the waitress thrust a menu between her and the brochure. 'Can I take your orders, please?' Her tone seemed to demand an immediate answer and even Sue, whose appetite was clearly for the holiday, put off further discussion while she scanned the menu. After a minute's deliberation, she opted for plaice, boiled potatoes and broccoli. I told the waitress I would have the same.

'Listen,' said Sue, brochure in hand and clearly not giving up. 'I'll make a deal with you. I'm meant to be working Monday and then I'm off until the following Monday. If I ring my boss and he agrees to give me both those Mondays as holiday, we go. If he doesn't, we won't. How about that?'

I couldn't quite see the logic but her melting smile would have had me signing up for the North Pole. 'Alright,' I agreed.

She got out her phone, pressed a few buttons and I could hear it ringing. 'Hi Gordon,' she said. 'I'm working all Monday but something's cropped up and I need to take the afternoon off. As you know the office is then closed until the following Monday, the 29th. I want to take that off and the Tuesday as well. I've got a few days due to me for that last court case so I'm going to take part of that. I just wanted to check you have nothing lined up for me on either of those days. I will be back in the office sometime during the morning on the Wednesday, New Year's Eve.'

I could hear the male voice at the other end – I presumed it was Gordon Watson – but not what he was saying. Sue had a broad smile on her face as she listened to his answer. 'Yes, it's him,' she said, looking in my direction and her smile turning into a grin. She rang off, folded her phone and reached for her handbag. 'No problem,' she said, placing the phone in a pocket in the leather bag. 'I think my boss approves of you.'

I was curious. 'He knows we go out together, then?'

'I told him after you had asked me out that time in the office. Conflict of interest and all that. It wouldn't do if I hadn't done so, and somebody found out when we continued seeing each other. I've kept him informed ever since.' She smiled. 'Not the intimate details, though.'

'Glad to hear it.'

'Just one thing, Rod.' She was serious once more. 'Christmas is big for racing, isn't it? Will you be OK missing those few days?'

A week ago I would have said that I wouldn't. But privately I was rather relieved that I would be abroad and unaware of what was going on. With no reason to be at the races – either as a rider or a reporter – I would be feeling as out of place as a teetotaller at a beer festival.

I explained the situation, Sue gave my hand a squeeze and said she would be back in two minutes. It turned out to be nearer ten. 'All fixed,' she said on resuming her seat. 'We just have to take in your passport. You did say it was in your car?'

When I grabbed it from the drawer of the bedside table my intention had been to avoid the long-drawn out process of applying for a replacement. Not to use it within days. But perhaps the Gods were shining on me. If they were, it certainly wasn't before time.

The rest of the afternoon was spent shopping in Broad Street for clothes (mainly at Marks & Spencer) and for food (Sainsburys) to put in the flat, with Sue spurring me on whenever I showed signs of tiring. When we reached my new home we parked my car in the lock-up garage and Sue's rented one right up against the garage door. She cooked supper and the lengthy love-making session that followed felt the most natural – and satisfying – thing in the world.

But stark reality hit home in the early hours. It was Detective-Inspector Hodgkinson who woke me, or rather his words: 'I trust you are not planning to go anywhere over Christmas,' and the forbidding tone in which he had spoken them. What was he going to say when I told him about the Kenya trip? Would he try to stop me?

From there it was but a short step to wondering whether I should be going at all. At the moment the trail to Greg Rickards was as hot as the temperature in Mombasa. If I let it go cold I would have only myself to blame. And, despite that promise to Sue about telling the police everything, I'd done no such thing. Frankly I didn't deserve to save myself.

But how was I going to explain all this to Sue? She would be so upset. If she then felt that she should ditch me, well, I couldn't blame her. She deserved better than a complex, mixed-up loser. Yet if I took the easy way out and went ahead with the Kenya trip, Rickards would have more than enough time to cover his tracks.

No, I had to tell Hodgkinson everything before we left. But, if I did, I could hardly expect him to put the squeeze on Rickards with me saying: 'You deal with it. I'm off on holiday.' And would Sue be able to get a refund at this late stage?

I tossed and turned, unable to find a solution. About the fourth time I did so, a loud grunt came from the other side of the bed. 'Come here,' she muttered, pulling me towards her. 'Turn over,' she ordered sleepily, pushing me onto my side before pressing her front against my back and putting her left arm around my chest. With that the solution came to me: in the morning I would tell Sue my worries and let her decide. I promptly fell back to sleep.

12

'You can come with me in the Discovery,' said a beaming Charlie when I introduced him to Sue shortly before 8.00am the following morning.

Several of the lads were already mounted and circling. I could see them all glancing at Sue as she stood next to Charlie, looking pretty special in her white trousers and red windcheater.

'Your girlfriend is lovely,' said Brenda as she legged me onto Ezekiel. I was thankful that there were no crude comments from any of the lads as I joined the circle but, with Charlie in earshot, they seemed to be on their best behaviour.

Having agreed a plan of action with Sue on the drive to the stables, I was in a particularly good frame of mind. She had listened carefully to my worries and concerns during the forty-mile journey and then, as I knew she would, she came up with a relatively straightforward course of action.

We would go to the police station in Reading on our return, ask for the Detective-Inspector, tell him about Greg Rickards, his two trainers, the electric whips and his threats when I went to his Nottingham showroom. We would also tell Hodgkinson how I believed Rickards had set me up with the attempted bribery – and that we were telling him now because we were leaving for a week's Christmas holiday on Monday evening. We would give Hodgkinson the name of the hotel and both our mobile numbers.

With my worries no longer much of a concern, I found the four-furlong spin across the Downs particularly exhilarating despite the biting wind, and I was more than ready to accept Charlie's offer of breakfast when we returned to the yard.

Before I had a chance to say anything Sue informed him, with what struck me as exaggerated coolness: 'We must go. We've got a busy schedule.'

'Rod, I'm going to the car,' she added unsmilingly and set off across the yard. After thanking both Charlie and Brenda, I followed suit.

Sue said nothing when I joined her, or when we drove out of the gate and onto the road. 'Is something wrong, honey,' I asked, putting a hand affectionately on her thigh. She brushed it aside. 'Please don't. I've had enough for one morning.'

When I turned to look at her, she seemed close to tears. I slowed the car and pulled in to the side of the road.

'Sue darling. What's the matter. Is something wrong? Is it the holiday?' I had a vision of Gordon ringing her about some crisis or other that meant we couldn't go.

She pulled a tissue out of the box below the dashboard and blew her nose noisily. She was smiling through her tears when she turned to me. 'Sorry darling. I'm being silly. But that horrible Charlie put his hand on my thigh and started feeling me. Quite high up too.'

Further questioning revealed that he had apologised after she told him to 'take that hand away.' But, Sue explained, she was upset and annoyed in equal measure.

I said I was surprised at his behaviour, and that I shared and understood her feelings. But, in truth, I wasn't surprised at all. Sue was an extremely attractive woman and Charlie was, in all probability, as red-blooded as any man in his early twenties.

The police station was easy enough to find – a big, red-brick building in Castle Street – and easy enough to find parking within reasonable distance. We went up half a dozen steps and into Reception only to be told that Detective-Inspector Hodgkinson was off duty. Could anybody else help?

I gave my name and addresses – both previous and present, told the officer behind the counter about the arson attack, that I had some additional information and would like to speak to someone dealing with the case. The man, I guessed to be in his late twenties, picked up the phone on his side of the counter and relayed the information. 'Detective-Sergeant Johnstone will be with you shortly sir.'

The Detective-Sergeant proved to be tall, thin, almost bald, about forty and blunt. 'Yes?' was all he said by way of introduction. I explained that I now thought I knew who was responsible.

We were ushered down a corridor and into a room at the far end. It consisted of not much more than a long table and half a dozen pretty basic chairs. The Detective-Sergeant took the seat at the head of the table and gestured myself and Sue to the nearest chairs on each side. He took a pen from his breast pocket and a notepad from a pile on the centre of the table. Looking straight at me, he said again: 'Yes?'

I explained that I had been to see Greg Rickards at his Nottingham car dealership on Tuesday, that his minders had thrown me out bodily, and he had reason to fear what I might write when I returned to my job as a racing journalist.

'This man? Rickards, you say? What's his address?'

Johnstone wrote it down. 'What might you write?' he asked.

I explained about the gambles on his horses and that some of the training methods used were against the Rules of Racing.

Johnstone wrote this down too. 'OK, Detective-Inspector Hodgkinson will contact you on Monday. You gave him your telephone number, I take it?'

Sue, who had been showing signs of impatience with the policeman's somewhat pedantic progress, intervened. 'You see, the thing is Detective-Sergeant, we are going abroad for a week's Christmas holiday on Monday evening so we want to give you my number as well as Rod's, and the number of the hotel where we are staying.'

'Good,' said Johnstone. 'Fire away.' He carefully wrote down both numbers and read them back to Sue before standing up. 'Thank you,' he said. 'You know the way out? Left out of the door and keep going.'

Ascot's pre-Christmas jump meeting bore about as much resemblance to the high fashion allure of the mid-summer Royal meeting as an ordinary foot soldier to the beplumed, breast-plated glamour of the Household Cavalry. But Sue was relieved: 'When you said Ascot I couldn't see how it could be anything except fashion, even in the middle of winter, and I would look like a tramp.'

She had exchanged her red waterproof for a camel hair coat and, with her white trousers showing beneath the hem, she looked stunning. I told her so only to be met with a smile and a whispered 'you are only saying that to make me feel better.'

Certainly the male-dominated press corps looked up with undisguised interest when she made her entrance alongside me. 'Hello Rod,' said a few of the dozen or so already seated, laptops open, but the majority of the eyes were for Sue.

'Any news for me?' inquired Tom Cameron after I had introduced him to Sue.

'Yes, indeed. Another attack. This time they tried to burn me alive.'

'Seriously?' said the *Racing Post* reporter, looking round to see if anyone else had heard what sounded like a sensational piece of news. 'Say no more now,' he said quietly. 'Let's talk outside after the first. See you by the winner's enclosure?'

I nodded, and did the same to a number of others who looked my way as I led Sue out of the room. I took her on a conducted tour of the grandstand, pointing out various places of relevance. But the whole place had an empty look about it with most racegoers seemingly waiting for Kempton's King George VI Chase meeting on Boxing Day.

The favourite won the first, with Charlie's runner a well-beaten fifth. No question of being given an easy race this time. The four-year-old hurdler was a 20–1 chance, inexperienced and clearly not good enough.

We joined up with Tom as he finished talking to the winning trainer. 'Come on, let's go over there where there is nobody about,' he said, pointing in the direction of the last fence and final hurdle. As we walked, I told him how I had been woken by the heat as the fire was about to spread from the kitchen, how I had jumped from the bedroom window, driven my car out of the garage through the flames, and how the house had been totally destroyed.

'And you think it was deliberate, rather than a short circuit or something in the kitchen?' asked Tom as we reached the rails.

'I've no doubt. Not after the police told me that the ground floor windows and door had been stuck tight with super glue.'

'Bloody hell, Rod.' Tom was clearly shocked. 'This is getting really nasty. What are the police doing about all this? Are they going to give you some sort of protection?'

'They are investigating, pretty seriously too.' I gave him Detective-Inspector Hodgkinson's name and that of the Detective-Sergeant we saw during the morning.

'We are going abroad for a week on Monday evening,' added Sue. 'But we don't want to say where, just in case.'

'Sure,' said Tom. 'I hope the police won't tell anybody either. I presume you have told them?'

I nodded.

'Good story,' he said by way of reply, and grinned. 'Sorry, I know I shouldn't look at it that way. But, by God, it will certainly help to prove your innocence. It shows that somebody has had it in for you right from the attempted bribery at the start. Who do you think is behind the whole thing? Off the record.'

'I really don't know, Tom.' I wasn't going to mention anything about Rickards. Saying things to journalists 'off the record' was asking for trouble. At the very least, they were likely to drop heavy hints in future articles.

'Listen, I'll put it in tomorrow's paper and, if my bosses let me, I'll add something to the effect that it's about time the BHA lifted your suspension. I presume your editor at *sports-all* reads the *Post*? I'll email him a copy anyway. With a bit of luck, he will reprint it on his website.'

As Tom headed back towards the press room, Sue and I went towards the bookmakers with me explaining that I wanted to see the prices on the next race.

We were greeted with a shout. It was George Godden, gesticulating as feverishly as an old-fashioned tic tac man. 'Rod,' he shouted. 'I've been trying to contact you. That man John Roberts: have you got a copy of the film showing him? One of the press boys said it was used at the inquiry.'

'I did have George but it was destroyed in a fire at my house the other night.'

'I've still got my copy,' intervened Sue. 'It's in my office.'

'Can you get it to me, love? My friend thinks he can help. He's in the business.'

'I have to keep my copy,' she replied, glancing at me as if for approval. 'But I could make a duplicate on Monday morning and email it to you.'

'Perfect,' replied George, giving her his email address. 'Probably be after Christmas by the time my man looks at it. But he's some sort of actors' agent. He thinks there's just a chance he might recognize that geyser.'

We watched the race from the stands but I could sense Sue becoming bored and, feeling she wouldn't relish the prospect of another four races, I said I wanted to see how Charlie's runner went in the next and then we would head off.

Grand Gatsby had the form to win the two and a half mile chase, leading jockey Billy Black was riding him for the first time and the eight-year-old was second favourite. Handily placed throughout, the bay gelding jumped well, went to the front between the last two fences and won comfortably.

I went down to the winner's enclosure while Sue said she would wait for me in the stands. Charlie was in understandably confident mood, both when talking to the owner and when addressing the press. 'This horse has a big future,' he said, his voice full of conviction. 'He's definitely Cheltenham material. I'll give him a bit of break now and he'll have just the one run before the Festival.'

I congratulated Charlie and shook his hand. 'Thanks Rod. Let's hope you're back by March.'

Did he mean that, if I was, I would get the mount? It seemed an impossible dream. But there had been that undertaking from Christopher Mayhew early in the season when he said he wanted me to be champion amateur, and ride most of the stable's runners that were in with a chance.

I headed back to the stands telling myself to get a grip and face reality. But I was in buoyant mood when I greeted Sue with a kiss, took her arm and told her it was time we went to the flat for tea.

'Do you think George's friend will be able to trace that John Roberts man?' she asked as we drove out of the car park.

'Possibly. But there are thousands of actors, aren't there? And I'm sure he would have been heavily disguised the day he tried to bribe me.'

Coming down from the cloud nine inspired by Charlie's remark, I was hit by an equally decisive dose of reality. George Godden was trying to be helpful but, if I was a bookmaker, I would assess his contact's chances of success at no better than 20–1.

The nearest newsagents, only three streets away from my new accommodation, was very different from Joshi Shah's shop. For a start there was no chatty turbaned proprietor behind the counter – just two rather harassed-looking women, busily dealing with a string of customers, many of them seemingly in a great hurry even on a Sunday morning.

I glanced at the papers spread out over the big counter searching for the one I wanted. I found half a dozen copies of the *Racing Post* half-hidden under a much bigger pile of *The Sunday Times*.

No mention of me on the front page, nor anything hinted at in the list of principal contents. I bought it anyway, and I managed to resist the temptation to start looking for Tom Cameron's article until I was back inside the flat.

I didn't have to look far. I was the lead on page five with a large head and shoulders shot of me in race-riding gear. *Amateur jockey and journalist Rod Hutchinson lucky to survive arson attack* screamed the headline.

Tom related how I had been woken in the early hours of Friday by a fire – seemingly starting in the kitchen – and how, unable to get out of a ground-floor door or window, I had jumped from the bedroom window and had then been forced to drive through flames in order to rescue my car from the burning garage.

I was quoted as saying that the police told me the downstairs door and windows had been stuck with super glue. Detective-Sergeant Johnstone was quoted as saying: 'Our inquiries are continuing but, as of now, we are treating this as arson.'

The article referred to the Cheltenham bomb as well as the previous incident in the Ludlow car park. It also recapped the details of the bribery case that saw me banned from riding for five years and being suspended by *sports-all.com*.

The article concluded: 'Hutchinson has maintained all along that he was set up, and for much of the last three weeks he has been trying to establish who was responsible. He believes he is close to finding out and says that this latest incident points to one particular individual. For legal reasons we cannot name that person but the fire, life-endangering though it undoubtedly was, must surely cast some doubt on the validity of the BHA's conviction.'

Some doubt? I thought Tom could have made that bit stronger. After all I'd given him an exclusive on a pretty sensational story. It was attempted murder.

Paddy O'Reilly's new home was just off the Caversham Road and it was long-suffering wife Mary who opened the door of the first floor flat. She seemed delighted to see me and said she would put the kettle on as she showed me into the sitting room.

'Look who's here, Paddy,' she said as she directed me towards an empty armchair.

Her husband thrust out a hand in greeting as he began to get to his feet. 'Rod. Jaysus, you'se living dangerously,' he said, grinning broadly and pointing to the *Post* on the small table in front of him, open at Cameron's story.

'Was it the jigger twins, do you think?' he asked. 'They'd be quite capable of doing that – or rather paying somebody to do it.'

I told him about Greg Rickards and my visit to Nottingham. 'Didn't know about the son but it all adds up,' he concluded thoughtfully. 'I presume you've told the police?'

I hedged. 'I went to see Detective-Inspector Hodgkinson at the police station in Castle Street yesterday but he wasn't there. He's to ring me tomorrow.'

'Tell him everything Rod,' Paddy leaned forward in his armchair, his index finger raised in my direction as if to emphasise his point. 'Rickards is dangerous, and Arrows and Swarter are not much better. I guess they know how close they are to being exposed. They'll try again unless they realise the police are onto them.'

Mary's arrival with the tea brought a temporary halt to the warning and switched my attention to the pieces of paper he had been holding and were now being carefully placed on the small table beside him.

'Just doing my entries,' he said.

'Entries for what?' I was puzzled.

'For when I resume at the yard. I want to keep up to date, and make sure I put the horses in their proper races once more.'

I was none the wiser. 'Are you going back there? Is Charlie leaving?'

'He needs to. He's destroying whole careers at the moment. Look at the way he pitched that poor four-year-old in at the deep end yesterday. Fancy running him at Ascot first time out. That horse should have been at the likes of Taunton or Exeter to give him confidence and belief in himself. But no. What does the young fool do? He runs him against some of the best novices in the country.'

Seemingly the old hobby horse was being given another airing. I didn't want to argue but, in fairness to Charlie, I pointed out that he had had a winner at Ascot, something not every trainer managed in a whole career.

'With those horses how could he fail?' Paddy was clearly unimpressed. But he looked well in himself. Seemingly he had put the worst of the cancer behind him, at least in the short term. But resuming training? I decided I shouldn't try to disillusion him. It was probably hope that was keeping him going, as well as turning the corner for him medically.

For the next half an hour I listened to Paddy's plans for each of the horses in the yard. Mary then brought the flow to a halt with a reminder that it was time for his medication, giving me an opening to leave. I told them about the Mombasa holiday and that I had shopping to do.

Back at the new flat I made a list. Mainly clothes. The food items I kept to a minimum. Sue had left early for Twickenham, saying she had a lot to do. We were to meet up at Heathrow at 2.00pm the next day with the Kenya Airways flight leaving at 5.25pm.

What I didn't have was my Covid certificate but I was able to print a copy off the central register, and I folded it carefully into my passport. According to Sue, who had discussed the requirements with the travel agent before paying for the tickets, that was all we needed.

Parking my car at Heathrow I still felt that I shouldn't be going but that all changed when I met up with Sue in Terminal 4. She was beaming from ear to ear, hugged me tight and declared: 'I'm so glad you agreed to come. This is going to do us both the world of good.'

She was right. Once we recovered from a somewhat gruelling flight – we had to change in Nairobi where we had a three-hour wait – we found ourselves in a different world. The Mombasa Beach Hotel proved to be the sort of thing holidays were sold on: wall-to-wall sunshine from dawn to dusk, broad sweeps of sand to the right and to the left as far as the eye could see, and the Indian Ocean the temperature of a warm bath.

And that wasn't all. The romantic evenings, with a band playing gentle music by the pool, had an aphrodisiac effect on Sue who threw aside all inhibitions. We made love enthusiastically and passionately every night. Usually in the morning too. Indeed her apparent eagerness for this aspect of life made me realise just how much her demanding career sapped her energy at home. Even the prospect of her ex-husband fathering the children she wanted so much seemed to be bothering her not one iota.

As went up to our room on the fourth evening, the day after Boxing Day, I decided to ask her to marry me. When we entered the room I led her to the huge window looking out over the ocean and got down on one knee.

'No Rod, not here. Not now,' she said, forestalling the proposal.

'This place is too much like paradise. Wait until we are back in reality. Then, if you still feel the same way....' Her lips went to mine and she gave a whispered murmur of delight as I began to peel off her clothes.

Three-quarters of an hour later, when she was sound asleep beside me, I mentally ran through my situation, the reality facing me when we returned home, and what I had so far failed to do.

Greg Rickards had tried to get me burned alive and he had very nearly succeeded, but I had still to give his name to the police. Nor had I told Detective-Inspector Hodgkinson of the possible Hedgers' suspects. Jimmy Brownson he had probably worked out for himself. Similarly the man who planted the Cheltenham bomb. But the fact that I had gone off on holiday, after doing no more than leaving a message with an underling, would hardly stand me in good stead.

Tuesday, December 30. I switched on my phone for the first time in a week. Sue had made me turn it off when we were waiting in Nairobi airport for the connecting flight. 'I want us to get maximum benefit from this holiday – and it won't be a holiday at all if we are constantly in touch with things at home,' she had insisted.

There were about a dozen messages, including one from my sister – 'Happy Xmas. But where are you? Have tried to ring several times. Am worried. Hope you are OK.' But nothing from the police. I couldn't decide whether that was good or bad – but at least Hodgkinson wasn't screaming for my blood.

However there was one from Tom Cameron. Sent on Saturday afternoon, it said: 'Hi Rod. George Godden (bookmaker) came into Newbury press room this afternoon, asking me for your mobile number. I said I couldn't give it to him but I could ask you to ring him.'

Tom had given me Godden's mobile number. I was about to ring when I realised it was only 5.00am in the UK. Four hours later I decided there was nothing to be gained by not waiting until we were back at Heathrow. But I couldn't help wondering. Had he, or rather his friend, found John Roberts? My hopes soared. At least they did until we were taking off from Nairobi. Then reality hit me.

For a start, as I had already told the bookmaker, John Roberts can't have been the man's real name. Also there were literally thousands of actors, and this one would have deliberately disguised himself to look very different from the real Roberts. If I found him, and he denied any involvement, how could I prove otherwise? By the time the lights were dimmed I was as depressed as I had been before the holiday.

Sue, taking my hand and giving it a squeeze, provided comforting reassurance – particularly when she said: 'I've decided to buy a car as soon as we get back. That way I can get backwards and forwards from my place to yours whenever I want. I used to have a car when I was married but in those days it was more of a nuisance than anything else, with me worrying it was going to get damaged when I left it outside the flat all day. Now they've opened a special all-day car park near the station.'

Arriving at a grey, drizzling Heathrow at 6.30am, I went first to Twickenham to drop Sue off at her place. The weather was no better by the time I got to the Reading flat shortly after nine. But by this stage the suspense was killing me.

I crossed my fingers, said a silent prayer and rang Godden. I apologised to the bookmaker for not ringing before but explained that I had been abroad and had only just seen the message asking me to ring him.

'No problem,' George replied cheerily. 'It's just that I got a bit of information about who that John Roberts character might be. Will you be at Cheltenham today?'

I explained that I had been in a plane all night and I was too exhausted to go anywhere, adding 'Could you give me the details over the phone?'

'Sure. At least I'll try. My contact is a theatrical agent. He's not 100% sure by any means but he thinks he recognises the man. He says, if he's right, it's a character named Danny De Dresden.'

'Danny De who?'

'Dresden. You know, that German town that got bombed to bits in the War. I think they make china there now. Dresden China.'

'Yes, sorry. I'm with you now. Do you have an address for him?'

'No, but if my man is right, he's in Liverpool at the moment. He's in a pantomime, Aladdin at the Empire. Danny De Dresden isn't his real name, of course. God knows what that is but they all use their stage names all the time. Might be worth your while going up there. I guess you'd probably know whether it's the same man when you see him.'

I said I would go up there within the next few days and thanked him for taking so much trouble.

'Good hunting,' said the cheerful voice at the other end. 'I'll be interested to hear how you get on.'

I googled the Liverpool Empire Theatre, found the cast list for Aladdin and there he was. Head Palace Guard: Danny De Dresden. No picture although there were head shots of the principal characters. Performances at 2.00pm and 7.00pm. The theatre was in Lime Street, very near Lime Street Station. I remembered that from my first visit to the Grand National. Most of the press contingent stayed at a motel nearer Southport than Liverpool but, wanting to savour the atmosphere of Nationals past, I had booked myself into the Adelphi. The hotel was part of Grand National folklore.

I looked at my watch. It was getting on for 10.00am. If I left in an hour I could be in Liverpool by 3.00pm, plenty of time to find accommodation before the evening performance. I rang Sue to tell her what I was planning. I thought she might want to come with me. She did but said she couldn't afford to take another day off.

13

The more I saw of the Head Palace Guard the more uncertain I became. Danny De Dresden, like the rest of the cast, was heavily made up and his was a relatively minor role so there were few chances to study him. From three rows back – the closest to the stage that I could get – it was well-nigh impossible to equate him with the John Roberts who had begun the whole vicious cycle. He looked about the same height and there were no obviously different facial characteristics. But nor were there any clear similarities.

Back in the hotel, just about the cheapest I could find within reasonable distance of the theatre, I resolved to go for broke. I would go to the theatre the following morning and play my cards like a blackjack player with a marked deck.

I waited until 10.30am before walking up to the Empire. I explained to the lady on the ticket desk that I was a big fan of Danny De Dresden, I had been at the previous evening's performance and wanted to get a selfie with the actor.

'That's lovely,' said the middle-aged lady as she picked up the phone at her elbow. 'George, is Danny in yet?'

I could hear the voice at the other end but not what he was saying. Only the lady in front of me: 'There's one of his fans at the desk. Wants to get a selfie with him.'

Again I could hear somebody saying something. 'OK, I'll tell him,' she replied before putting the phone down and smiling at me. 'No rehearsals this morning so he won't be in until around twelve. If you can come back at 12.30, I'm sure he'll be glad to see you.'

Back at the hotel, I began typing into my laptop. When I had finished, and was satisfied that I'd included everything I needed, I went to the reception desk, said I wanted to print off a letter that I would email to the hotel. If the cheerful red-haired receptionist thought this an unusual request, she showed no sign. She gave me the hotel's email address, picked out my letter two minutes after I'd sent it and printed off a copy without looking to see what it said. 'No problem. Any time,' she said as I thanked her.

I was back at the theatre just after 12.30pm and was directed to a side door. This was opened by an overalled man who looked well past retirement age. 'Danny you want?' he inquired. When I nodded, he ushered me inside and down a dark passage. He knocked at the fourth door on the right. 'Danny. Fan for you,' he announced in a loud voice.

'Thanks Jim,' said the grease-painted actor as he opened the door. 'Come in,' he said to me, smiling broadly and showing no sign of recognition. Nor did he when I explained that I'd been a fan for years, had loved his show yesterday evening and would like to take a selfie.

He seemed delighted and posed happily while I clicked away on my phone, getting several shots. I still didn't know if it was the same man but I knew I would never get a better chance. I asked him for his autograph, giving him a piece of paper I'd taken from my hotel room.

'What name did you say?' he asked, taking the biro I'd handed to him.

'I didn't but it's Rodney Hutchinson.' No reaction or sign of recognition from Danny De Dresden. Smilingly, he signed his name.

I picked up the piece of hotel notepaper, studied it and said: 'You've put Danny De Dresden. I know you as John Roberts.'

He looked puzzled. 'Sorry?'

'John Roberts,' I repeated.

Again no reaction, and certainly no recognition. 'Newbury racecourse. Friday, November 28. You tried to give me money. Remember? A wad of fivers in a brown envelope. You said you'd won a lot of money from my tips. Said your name was John Roberts.'

Now he knew who I was – and that I knew who he was. I could see it in his expression which turned from delight to fury as if I had flipped a switch.

He reached for the door, wrenched it open and shouted down the passageway: 'Jim. Come here, quick.'

I grabbed hold of him by the collar and yanked him back inside. 'Listen, Danny,' I said as he stared at me, almost blind fury in his eyes. 'If I'm thrown out of this place, the police will be here inside an hour and I can guarantee you will never act again.

'But I'm not interested in getting you arrested. All I want to do is clear my name with the racing authorities and, if you help me by signing a piece of paper, I can guarantee that you will never hear from me again. And I will say nothing to the police.'

I knew the last bit was a complete lie. But needs must and it certainly had the desired effect on Danny. As the door opened, with Jim putting his head enquiringly round it, Danny lifted his right hand in acknowledgement of the man's arrival. 'It's OK, Jim. We've sorted it. But don't go too far away. I might yet need you.'

As his footsteps could be heard retreating up the passage, I took the piece of paper out of my jacket pocket, smoothed it out and handed it to Danny. He took hold of it as gingerly as if it was coated in poisonous powder. I watched his face as he slowly read it through.

'To whom it may concern,' it began. 'At Newbury racecourse on Friday November 28 2025 I tried to hand racing journalist and amateur jockey Rodney Hutchinson a considerable sum in bank notes but he refused to accept them. I was paid to do this by persons unknown. I had never met Rodney Hutchinson before.

.... Danny De Dresden

January 1 2026

'That all?' he asked.

'That's it. Sign that and I'll call it quits. You can carry on acting as long as you want. But Danny,' I grabbed him by the throat, 'if you don't sign, I am going straight to the police and they'll arrest you within the hour. Whoever got you involved is facing charges of arson and attempted murder. If you don't believe me, you can ring Detective-Inspector Hodgkinson at Reading CID.'

'How can I know what you are telling me is the truth?' Danny seemed reluctant.

'Ring Detective-Inspector Hodgkinson and ask him.'

'Alright, I'll sign.' I watched him as he scribbled an undecipherable signature on the paper and handed it back. 'Now will you please leave,' he said firmly. 'I've got to get ready for the performance.'

I smiled and moved for the door. As I opened it, I turned and said: 'One last thing Danny. The man who paid you to try and give me that money. What did he look like? And tell me the truth. If I find you have lied to me, it 'll be me who rings the Detective-Inspector – and I'll tell him where he can find his murder suspect.'

I received a glare, bordering on hatred. 'I can't be sure,' Danny began slowly as he appeared to cast his mind back. 'He was definitely disguised, and I thought afterwards that it might have been another actor. He was about average height, maybe a couple of inches more, early twenties. No real distinguishing features, dark hair and spoke with a slight accent. I'm sure it was a false one. But there was a definite trace of Midlands to it. My guess is that he had been paid by someone to give me the instructions. I don't think he was the principal, if you know what I mean. Now would you please go. I need to get back into character and that's going to take me some time after what you've done to me, barging in under false pretences and threatening me.'

He looked weak and tired. I could see that the Head Palace Guard's matinee performance might not win too many plaudits. I smiled as I shut the door behind me, and making for the exit, I took my phone out of my trouser pocket and switched off the recording device.

It took me a good two hours to play it all back at the hotel. I typed the whole transcript and emailed it to Sue, together with a copy of the signed statement, before setting off for Reading.

I had got as far as the outskirts of Birmingham when she rang. 'That's absolutely fantastic,' she said. 'I've spoken to Gordon and he says it should be enough for the BHA to regard the conviction as unsafe.'

'Meaning?' I thought I knew but I wanted to hear it for myself.

'Meaning that they will no longer consider your five-year ban safe to uphold, given what the actor has said. Gordon suggests that I prepare a submission to go the BHA and give him a copy. He will then tell the BHA that, in his capacity as legal assessor, he considers that your conviction does not legally stand up. Words to that effect anyway.'

I slowed from 70pmh to not much more than 50mph as I

considered the implications – and was almost blown off the road by a huge spray-blinding lorry whose driver sat on his horn in protest at having to pull out and overtake.

'Where are you?' Sue sounded almost as anxious as I was. 'M1. Somewhere near Spaghetti Junction. Can't see too well. Spray everywhere. And it's chucking it down.'

'OK. Don't talk now. But Rod, drive straight to Twickenham. Then we can put this thing together this evening and I'll get the finished version into the BHA tomorrow morning.'

As the call ended visions of Cheltenham swept through my mind. Me going down to the start on a fancied runner, soaring over those fences up the back straight, over the open ditch at the top of the course and then thundering down towards that so often-fatal third last. I put my foot down in excitement, pulled out into the fast lane and, glancing at the speedometer, saw I was doing over 100mph. I put my foot down further and, only when it topped 120mph, did I realise what a dangerous game I was playing. Particularly in these wet conditions.

'Get a grip, Rod,' I told myself out loud as I eased down to just over seventy. No good suffering all the hell of the past few weeks if you don't live to tell the tale. And tell the tale I would: how I had been stitched up, beaten up and nearly burnt alive. It would make riveting reading. Probably get offers to join one of the national dailies, maybe even write a book.

I was still on a high as I parked outside Sue's flat, rushed up the steps and embraced her passionately even before she had had a chance to shut the door behind me. 'Rod,' she smiled breathlessly as she unwrapped my arms from around her. 'Take it easy. We've got a lot of work in front of us.'

As we sat down at the dining room table, she quickly made it clear that the whole BHA approach was to be done on the low-key lines already agreed between her and her boss. No 'justice at last' trumpeting, or accusations of BHA incompetence. Quite the reverse. In fact not a word was to be said in any form of media before racing's ruling body issued a statement.

'If you do say anything in the Press, or to your *Racing Post* friend, there is a very real danger that the BHA will feel they are being backed into a corner and insist on a review of the whole case, or even on an appeal hearing,' Sue explained. 'Either would mean a delay which could run into weeks. Not to mention hefty legal fees. What we want is to get the ban lifted and you back with *sports-all. com* as soon as possible.'

I wasn't sure I agreed. Not after all I'd been through in the last month. 'But what about people like Charlie and Christopher Mayhew? They're the ones who will be giving me rides, and they won't if they remain unaware that I'm going to be cleared and back in business. It's important that they know the position, that I was innocent all along.'

'OK. I take your point.' Sue seemed uncertain, her agreement being given hesitantly and apparently unwillingly. 'But it's vital that they don't say anything to anybody. Otherwise we are going to face BHA proceedings and delays. Once you get your licence back – and your job – then you can tell the world, and write exclusives about the whole saga to your heart's content. It'll be even better for your career if it all comes from you. Won't it?'

I had to agree she was right. Compromise also came in the form of me cooking supper while she got down to work on the submission to the BHA. It was nearly ten by the time she declared that the initial draft was finished. Next I had to read it through to make sure the facts were correct. It was well after midnight before we had a version that satisfied both Sue's legal arguments and my desire for proof of innocence.

Even so I was on such a high that I was unable to get much in the way of sleep and Sue, beside me, kept tossing and turning. Several times she appeared to be talking in her sleep but I couldn't make much sense of the words.

I must have got some sleep, though, because when all the lights came on at 6.30am I was conscious of being woken up. 'Sorry,' she said. 'But I have to get ready for the office and I need to leave here in little more than half an hour.'

I waited until she had gone before ringing Charlie. 'Good morning,' I began. It was a good morning – the clear sky suggested that the sun was going to shine and, despite my lack of sleep, I felt on top of the world. 'Charlie, I'm in London so I won't make it for first lot but I'll be there for the second.'

'OK.' He sounded decidedly unenthusiastic.

'Charlie, I've got some good news.'

'Good, I could do with some. Jackson Jim's tendon has flared up. Going to be out for the rest of the season.'

'Shit.' The gelding was one of those I might have been looking forward to. 'I am sorry. But Charlie, it looks like I'm going to be back racing soon. Don't say anything to anyone yet. It's to be kept hush-hush for a week or two. I'll tell you more when I see you.'

'Rod, that's fantastic,' he enthused. 'Listen, got to go. See you later.'

I looked at my watch. It would take me the best part of ninety minutes, and that was allowing for most of the traffic going the other way. I scraped a two-minute shave, golloped down a plate of cereal and headed for the door. I reached the yard just as first lot were returning.

Charlie was going round the stables talking to each rider about how their horses went. When he saw me, he gave a wave and came along the path to meet me. He shook me by the hand, smiling broadly, and said: 'Come and have some coffee and you can tell me what's happened.'

In the kitchen he told me to make some toast while he busied himself with the coffee percolator. 'Now, what's the news?' he asked, smiling broadly.

I told him about my visit to Liverpool, what Danny De Dresden had confessed to and how the details were being presented to the BHA. 'But Charlie,' I said, my voice deliberately hushed. 'Whatever you do, for God's sake say nothing to nobody about this. It's essential that the initiative comes from the BHA. If they feel they are being pressurised in any way they will get difficult and, in all probability, drag their feet. The whole approach is aimed at them being the ones who will tell the world.'

'Yes, I can understand that,' he replied, speaking slowly as he considered the implications. 'But Rod, you must now get fit. And I mean fit. None of this part-time amateur approach. I'll need you here for both lots from now on.'

Clearly he was still thinking in terms of me taking many of the rides, and I noticed the difference when we went out into the yard with Charlie making straight for the head lad. He raised a finger as he approached, signifying he had something to say. 'Barry, Rod is riding Boss Baxter. He'll canter four furlongs and come back at a good half speed.'

'OK boss,' was the reply with Barry touching his cap in acknow-ledgement. 'Let's get you out,' he said to me.

I followed him to the row of stables on the left side of the yard where he flipped open the catches that were keeping the inmate of the second box inside his home. The bay, ears pricked, was already saddled and bridled and was chomping on his bit, clearly keen to get moving.

Barry gave me a leg up, saying in a quiet voice, the tone almost threatening: 'This is a Cheltenham horse. Keep hold of his head. If you fuck him up I'll kill you.'

As I thrust my feet into the irons, and shortened the reins to stop the by-now highly excited horse taking off, I couldn't help but wonder if I'd been wrong to rule out Barry. It was only too apparent that he still bitterly resented my presence.

But Boss Baxter felt something special, certainly when we were up on the Downs and doing the first part of the planned work. He moved with effortless grace, exuding power and class from every muscle, and he seemed to cover an almost impossible amount of ground with each stride. I could see why Paddy O'Reilly was so aggrieved at the way the horse had been ridden last time out.

Boss Baxter was even more impressive doing the half-speed. He positively floated over the ground and his galloping companion was having to work quite a bit harder just to stay level. 'That bugger is a bloody good horse,' shouted across a breathless Jake beside me as we pulled up.

Charlie, watching by the Discovery, seemed well pleased when we came to a halt in front of him. 'Told you last time's run would pay dividends,' he said, winking at me.

Boss Baxter's work had impressed several of the other lads too and there was much comment on the sort of price he would be at the Festival meeting. I wondered if they would be quite so keen on the horse's chance when they found out I would be riding him.

Back in the yard I handed the horse back to his regular girl, Janice, a small pleasant-faced brunette who clearly doted on him, and I confirmed with Charlie that I would be there for both lots the next day.

Back at the car I checked my phone. There was one message:

'Please ring Detective-Sergeant Hastings at Reading Police Station.' I rang the number and gave my name when it answered.

'Ah good morning sir,' said a female voice. 'I've taken over your arson case from Detective-Inspector Hodgkinson. Any chance you could come into the station later this morning?'

'Sure. I'm on my way to Reading now.'

'Good. Can we make it around twelve?'

I confirmed I would be there at that time. Half an hour later the phone rang. It was Charlie.

'Rod, are you on the way to Reading?'

'Yea. Should be at the new flat shortly.'

'Could I use your computer if I call in? Mine's on the blink and I've got to get entries in this morning.'

'Sure.' I gave him the address and directions. 'I have to leave in time to be at the police station at noon. New person in charge, a she – and she wants to see me.'

'Sounds interesting.' Charlie laughed. 'Have you got a printer?'

I told him I had.

'Great. I always like to print off a copy when I've entered anything. Just to be on the safe side.'

Detective-Sergeant Hastings proved to be a dark-haired woman in her mid-thirties with a deceptively friendly manner. I soon discovered that it only barely disguised an exceptionally shrewd brain and an attacking approach. As we sat down in an interview room she asked me who I thought was responsible for the fire.

When I said I wasn't really sure, she made it very clear that she didn't believe me.

'Come off it Mr Hutchinson,' she said. 'Somebody, or probably some people, try to burn you alive and you can't even hazard a guess. Pull the other one. Nobody gets that sort of treatment without good reason. Who have you made into an enemy? And why are you so reluctant to tell me?'

I searched for an answer. And I couldn't find one. 'You're hiding something,' she continued, this time with more than a note of steel in her voice. 'You'd better tell me because, sure as hell, I'm going to find out. I have already discussed you with Detective-Inspector Hodgkinson. He's convinced you are involved in various criminal activities and that it's you we should be concentrating on. Not your attackers.'

'Well,' I hesitated. This was going badly in the wrong direction. Seemingly the time for procrastination was over, and to hell with the consequences for the jigger twins – everyone else too, for that matter.

She switched on the recorder as I began to tell her about John Roberts and Danny De Dresden, and how his attempt at bribery had cost me my riding licence and my job. I said that there were a number of people who, for varying reasons, wanted me to have a voice in print no longer. I mentioned Hedgers, Greg Rickards and his two trainers, and Jimmy Brownson.

My interviewer made a few notes as I spoke but asked no questions until I'd finished. 'And who would you make favourite - to use the terminology of your world?' She smiled for the first time in our twenty minute interview.

'Greg Rickards, I suppose.' I glanced across at the recorder. It was still on.

'Why?'

I told her about my visit to his Nottingham showroom, what he had said and how his two thugs had forcibly ejected me.

'Interesting. We'll pay him a visit.'

I winced as I pictured what he might do. Not for some time - he couldn't afford to have the police coming down on him. But he would be sure to want revenge. And be sure to find a way of exacting it.

Back at the flat I made myself a sandwich before switching on the computer. I idly flicked through the recent Sent Items in Outlook, and then the latest Word items. I was keen to see what Charlie had entered and at which racecourses. But there was nothing. Obviously he had permanently deleted his work, at least so far as an ordinary user like myself could detect.

I turned my attention to my phone. Two missed calls from Sue. I rang. No answer. Two minutes later the phone pinged: 'With a client. Will ring when free.'

I was debating whether to ring my sister and how much I should tell her about Sue – Belinda took an overly keen interest in my love life - when Sue's call came through.

'Hi. Good news,' she began. 'I took our submission into the BHA this morning. Gordon had already telephoned them so they knew what to expect. The man I spoke to, Graham somebody, said they had already set up a meeting of the various people who need to be involved for Monday. Gordon says they have no option but to reconsider, given the statement the actor man signed. It's just a question of what they feel they need to say to the press, and how and when they do that. His guess is within the next fortnight but in the meantime we mustn't try to pre-empt them by saying anything to anyone.'

'What about me mentioning what is going on to Brett, my boss at *sports-all.com*? Is it Ok for me to tip him off, do you think?'

'Definitely not, Rod. We must assume that any type of media is going to go public if they get wind of it. It's a good story for them.'

'Hmm. I guess you're right,' I grudgingly acknowledged. 'I know that if I got wind of something like this I wouldn't hesitate.'

She laughed, before continuing: 'Listen, I told you I was buying a car. I've got one in mind but I need your advice. If I stay put tonight, will you come to Twickenham in the morning after you've done your riding? Then we can look at it together. I don't really want to do it all on my own in case I make a mistake.'

'Sure. I should be with you around half eleven. That OK?'

'Perfect. Must go now, Rod. Got another client coming. Love you.'

Supper with my sister and her husband at their house in one of the smarter Reading suburbs made for an enjoyable and relaxing evening. I had always got on well with Belinda and the death of our parents in the first few months of Covid seemed to somehow give us a special bond.

As she did most of the talking – her doctor husband Stuart was a quiet type outside surgery hours and the twins had been dispatched to bed soon after my arrival – I was happy to listen and answer the questions as she put them. Even those concerning Sue.

I filled her in on my recent progress in Liverpool but both she and Stuart were horrified to hear about the fire. 'My God,' she exclaimed. 'You were so close to being killed,' while Stuart wanted to know what the police were doing about it.

I told them about Detective-Inspector Hodgkinson and Detective-Sergeant Hastings, the submission to the BHA and the part Sue was playing. 'I suppose after Emma it's difficult to get close to anyone,' fished Belinda.

'I guess so,' I answered hesitantly. I had been pondering a similar question until Mombasa provided the answer. 'But I like her a lot.'

Fortunately that seemed to satisfy my sister, at least for the time being. There was no further probing, and shortly after ten I made my excuses – having to get up early to ride out – and headed home to the flat.

The garage for my car was the second of the four in a line underneath the flats. I expected a light to come on as I turned off the road to my garage but nothing did. Not even when I pressed the remote to open the garage door. I made a mental note to ring Mary Bradshaw on Monday.

I locked the car and pressed the remote to shut the garage door behind me. As it swung down I sensed movement. I looked round but I could see nothing in the blackness. Not to begin with anyway. When I did it was almost too late. I just had time to raise my right elbow and it was my upper arm that took the full force of the blow. I heard a curse and then a rattle as something metallic hit the concrete. It was only then that I realised there were two of them. 'My fucking knife's gone,' said the man who had hit me.

'Shut up,' muttered the other mugger. At least that is what I presumed him to be. The second man, bigger and burlier that the first, closed in fast and knocked me to the ground, shouting: 'Grab 'im and don't let the bastard go.'

I was rolled onto my back and given a vicious kick in the ribs. It had me gasping for breath. My hands were gripped by the first man and pulled painfully over my head. The other man stood over me and, as he raised his right arm, I made out the shape of a knife. It was more of a large dagger than a knife - and he seemed about to bring it down into my neck.

I knew this was the end. People say your life flashes before you when you are about to die. I was too terrified for anything like that. As the blade was lifted to give the deadly blow extra force I screamed.

The noise was almost enough to put the man off his aim. It certainly took away some of the force. My attacker hesitated as if unsure whether to proceed or raise his arm and re-aim. I twisted sideways and screamed again as I saw the blade come down. I managed to twist my body a second time. But it was not enough. I felt a searing pain in my thigh. Somehow, despite the agony, I managed to shout: 'Help. Murder.'

The whole area was suddenly flooded with light.

'What the hell's going on?' came an elderly male voice from the window of the number one flat. 'I'm going to ring the police. They'll be here in two minutes.'

'Come on Johnny,' shouted the smaller of the two men. 'It's not worth getting ten years for twenty grand.'

'Are you alright, young man?' called out my saviour.

'I think so. My thigh's been stabbed,' I called back. 'I'm going to drive straight to the hospital.'

'I could ring 999,' the man shouted.

'Thanks,' I said, pressing the remote to open the garage door. 'But it'll be quicker if I drive.'

I managed to limp painfully to the car door and get in behind the wheel. I felt my thigh. It didn't hurt that much but, judging by the amount of blood that was turning my trousers into a sticky mess, that was probably my body's defensive mechanism kicking in. I knew I had to somehow staunch the flow. And quickly.

I rang Stuart as I drove back to his house as fast as I dared. The front door opened even before I had a chance to get out. Belinda was in her dressing gown and Stuart was pulling on a jersey. Both came down the steps.

'Should really go to hospital for this,' said Stuart. 'But let's see how bad the damage is.'

I limped into the kitchen and was instructed to take my trousers off. The flow of blood had resumed on the journey, and I had to painfully peel the sodden section away from my right thigh.

Stuart dabbed at the cut with a Dettol-soaked cloth and cleaned it with another while I tried, none too successfully, to blank out the pain. He then covered the cut with a thick piece of ointment-smeared gauze and put a large piece of Elastoplast over the lot.

'I'm going to give you a tetanus jab just to be on the safe side,' he added, reaching for the syringe Belinda was taking from the top shelf of a nearby cupboard. 'The cut's not too bad, actually. When you rang I feared far worse.'

'Me too.' said Belinda. 'Rod, are you sure it was just muggers? Not the same people who set fire to the cottage?'

I shook my head. 'No. It was muggers alright. They ran for it when one of the other tenants stuck his head out of the window and said he was going to call the police.'

'Even so, I think you should inform the police here in Reading.'

Stuart's tone was decisive but Belinda interrupted. 'It's gone eleven, Stuart,' she said. 'We've all got to get some sleep. I don't see what harm it will do to wait until the morning. The muggers will be well away by now anyway.'

'Yes, I suppose you're right.' Stuart seemed reluctant to concede but my sister was already a stage ahead of him.

'Come on Rod. There's a bed made up for you in the spare room.'

Personally I would have preferred to drive home but I knew from long experience that once Belinda's mind was made up there was little point in arguing.

I also knew that I would find it difficult to sleep after such a traumatic experience. As I lay in the strange bed I ran through the attack that had taken me so close to death, and the more I thought about it the more I felt that I could have met at least one of the would-be killers before.

The bit about not worth getting ten years for twenty grand bore an uncanny resemblance to what that cockney had said (about not going back inside just for the sake of ten grand), when the so-called courier and his gang attacked me at the cottage three weeks ago. Confusingly, though, this one's accent was not cockney. More English Midlands. But, I smiled to myself, the price on my head appeared to have doubled!

Could this really have been Greg Rickards' work, though? Presumably the police had been to see him. If so, he would hardly have risked going in again so soon. Surely he was too smart to antagonise the police, or even to make them suspicious. I knew he was a ruthless, unprincipled bastard - and probably not averse to trampling on anyone who got in his way. But he was also shrewd and clever. He would be very careful to avoid giving the police the impression he was a violent and dangerous crook.

Could it be that the attackers' language, approach and method – again they used knives rather than guns – wasn't so much Rickards as Jimmy Brownson? Certainly it was the sort of thing you might expect from murderous thugs locked up in Belmarsh. Maybe I had been wrong to rule out everyone bar Rickards. Perhaps I shouldn't have ignored the ex-Hedgers' people either, someone who had lost a well paid job and was pulling the killing strings. If it was, I was back to square one because I hadn't even an idea who could be involved from the big bookmaking firm.

I tossed and turned like a boat in a storm. When the alarm on my phone went off at 6.30am I was convinced I'd hardly slept at all. I dressed in the dark, slipped almost silently through the front door, carefully pulled it shut behind me and drove off as quietly as I could.

I reached the yard in good time, got my own horse saddled and bridled. But I couldn't get on Brown River unaided, not with all that bandaging on my thigh. Fortunately Jake saw my plight and gave me a leg-up. 'Boss is in a bad mood today,' he said, grinning broadly. 'He's already gone for Brenda and he gave John a right rollocking for nothing.'

Maybe that was why I'd been put down for my own horse rather than one of the stable stars. I could see Charlie at the far end of the yard, shouting at somebody. When I joined those already circling, though, he was as pleasant as could be - and he even thanked me for coming. Maybe he'd just got out of bed the wrong side. After all, anyone could do that from time to time.

A sharp twinge from my thigh as I rose to the trot concentrated my mind on the present, and it was a whole lot worse when we did the speed work up on the Downs. I could feel blood oozing as we walked back down the path to the yard. Only a small patch showed through my jodhpurs, fortunately.

I had already decided to skip second lot and I was careful to cover the growing dark blotch when I informed Charlie. He wasn't best pleased. 'You're going to need to be fit if your licence comes through,' he said, making no attempt to control his annoyance. 'That means riding out both lots six days a week.'

I agreed with him, and said so, but explained how I needed to be in Twickenham to assist Sue with her pending car purchase. He grunted and walked off in the direction of his house.

I still had to call in at the police station. Neither Detective-

Inspector Hodgkinson nor Detective-Sergeant Hastings were in. I got the impression that they were off-duty although nobody actually said so. The constable on the desk took down the details of what I said I thought was an attempted mugging. Bringing up the Rickards' suspicions would have made things too complicated and I needed to keep it straightforward if I was to get to Twickenham before Sue's patience ran out.

'Lot of mugging going on these days,' commented the constable who took down the details. He only looked about nineteen but spoke with a world-weary authority and in a tired tone, as if nothing would surprise him.

14

Sue had boiled it down to a straight choice between a VW Polo and a Peugeot 208. She wanted a small car for ease of parking and, after much mental debate, she had decided it had to be white. We went from a dealer in Twickenham to another in Richmond, and then back again. I felt there wasn't much to choose between their products and, after I'd said that I gave the Peugeot marginal preference, Sue plumped for the Polo!

She signed the papers, made a bank transfer for the price, gave me a hug and a kiss, and arranged to pick up the car first thing Monday morning.

Back at her flat, though, her mood changed from elation to concern as she prepared lunch and quizzed me about the latest attack. 'Rod, that's the third attempt on your life in what, three weeks? Plus that horrible Rickards man getting his bouncers to throw you out of his car showroom. We've got to get the police to give you some protection. You can't rely on luck for ever more.' She threw her arms round my neck and sobbed into my shoulder.

I held her tight, fished a tissue out of my trouser pocket and wiped her face. She took it and noisily blew her nose. 'Sorry my darling,' she sniffed. 'But I'm so afraid you will be killed.'

I pulled her to me with one hand while the other went to her right breast. Still holding her close, I told her what I thought the police were doing and of my intention to see either Hodgkinson or Hastings on Monday morning.

After lunch she insisted on cleaning the wound – it looked pretty nasty by this stage with dark brown bruising more to the fore than the actual cut – and somehow that led to sex. As we lay together in contented, companionable silence, I wondered if this was the right time to ask her to marry me. I was still mentally tossing a coin – I didn't want her to put me off a second time – when my phone rang.

It was Tom Cameron asking if there was any further news about my getting my licence back. 'Lot of talk here at Sandown about new evidence. George Godden says the BHA are going to scrap the suspension. It's the talk of the betting ring.'

Shit. That was all I needed – and probably all the BHA needed to resort to a long, drawn-out appeal hearing. 'I don't know Tom,' I said cautiously. 'I don't think things have moved all that far actually. When I do hear anything, though, I promise you will be the first to know.'

I knew I sounded ungenuine and unhelpful. 'You'll be the first to know' was what people always said to the media when they knew something but weren't saying. It invariably proved an empty promise with 'you' becoming just one of many to be told. At best.

'What was that?' Sue inquired, dreamily as she gently stroked my thigh. When I told her she shot upright as if she had been stung by a wasp. 'For God's sake he mustn't do that. It will put us back weeks. Doesn't he know that? We've got to stop him.'

I explained that Tom's priority was to get the news into his paper before any other journalist beat him to it. She seemed disgusted. 'Surely he must know that we can't afford to upset the BHA. That must come before any stupid media rivalry.'

She was only partly mollified when I told her that all he had got from me was an undertaking to give him the news when we were in a position to know, and before I gave it to anybody else.

But the mood was gone. No question now about this being the right moment to propose. Only several hours later, after she had dressed the wound a second time and we were making love once more, did it return. 'Roll over,' she commanded as she lay on top of me. 'I need you underneath me this time.'

Two minutes, and several passionate thrusts later, she came, crying out 'Oh darling. I want your baby.'

Back in Reading by mid-afternoon on Sunday I decided duty calls and drove to Paddy's O'Reilly's flat off the Caversham Road. He opened the door himself and, ushering me into the sitting room, he indicated the chair nearest the radiator.

'Going to get really cold tomorrow. Could be snow,' he said cheerily. 'That's when the test will come. Yer man could struggle when the Downs gallops are unusable.'

There was no getting away from the relish with which he started on the familiar hobby horse. Charlie's faults and failures were trotted out like the stable's string, one after another. Horses would go lame, others would break down or get sick. Far from the best going to Cheltenham, they would be out of action for the rest of the season.

Mary, bringing in tea and biscuits on a tray, gave a knowing wink in my direction. Obviously she had heard it all before and, in all probability, more times than she cared to remember. 'Now Paddy, don't get yourself too worked up. You know what the doctor said.'

Her husband's attention switched to me as his wife poured out the tea. 'Any progress with the BHA, Rod?' he enquired, helping himself to a chocolate digestive.

I told him about Danny De Dresden's signed confession, the submission to the BHA and Gordon Watson's view that my suspension would be dropped, quite possibly in this coming week.

'About time too,' said Paddy. 'Looks like you'll be back before me. I spoke to Christopher about me coming back and he said he wants to give myself time to make a full recovery. Also said something about giving Charlie a bit longer. Hmph.'

Paddy, spluttering over his tea, continued: 'He's still there only because I was sick. And because blood's thicker than water.'

'What about those nasty men who were trying to silence you, Rod?' asked Mary with more than a hint of concern in her voice.

'Aye,' agreed Paddy. 'Do them jigger twins know you are on the point of being cleared? Watch out, Rod. They will be running scared when they do know. They will be out to silence you before you can go to town on them in print.'

I didn't get a chance to answer. There was no stopping Paddy: 'Did you tell the police about them? As I told you before, it's essential that you keep the detectives fully informed. Don't hold anything back. They think racing is dodgy enough as it is. If they feel you are not telling them everything, they won't exactly come rushing if you get attacked again.'

When I got back to the flat it wasn't the police I rang but Christopher Mayhew. I told him about the Danny De Dresden confession, its delivery to the BHA and Gordon Watson's opinion. Maybe I shouldn't have done so – I knew Sue would be horrified – but I felt I had to convince the man who was not only a former BHA board member but also the key to my making a success of my riding career. Without his horses I would struggle to increase my winner tally from a humble four. With them, I could be champion amateur.

He wasn't the slightest surprised. 'Yes, they rang me tell me a fair bit of this,' he said. 'I've been pressing them for some time. As I told you before, it's my reputation that's on the line, not just yours. I gather the lifting of your suspension, and the granting of your riding licence, will be in this week's *Racing Calendar*. They want to keep it all low key so no press announcement or anything like that.'

'Are you happy with that?' I queried. 'Shouldn't there be some sort of press release explaining things?'

Christopher laughed. 'That's not how the BHA does things – as I am sure you know. But Rod,' his tone turned serious. 'Charlie tells me that you are nowhere near racing fit and that you frequently skip riding out.'

'Well, yes and no.' I told him about so much of my time being taken up with finding the evidence to prove my innocence.

'I understand that but Charlie is against you being given the ride on so many of the best horses. Like any trainer, he wants the best jockey he can get. I'm sticking my neck out for you and I can't go on doing that if you're not fit.'

I assured him that I would be riding out both lots every day from now on and, with nothing further to do on the innocence-proving front, I would soon be race fit once more.

This seemed to satisfy Christopher who said: 'Good. I have to keep my trainer happy you know. Particularly this one with him being my nephew.'

I rode Boss Baxter first lot and Blue Marine in the second, Sue's bandaging holding up well and the knife injury itself hardly troubling me.

Clearly I was back in Charlie's good books. Both horses worked like the future stars last months' Cheltenham running suggested they might be, and the significance of me being given the leg-up was not lost on the stable staff.

'I hear you're getting your licence back,' said Jake as we pulled up at the end of a four furlong three-quarter speed that had both of us struggling for breath, and forgetting all about the bitterly cold wind that had the forecast snow written right through it.

'Where did you hear that?' I asked incredulously as we headed towards Charlie in his Discovery.

'Somebody told Brenda at Sandown on Saturday,' Jake continued. 'Or rather one of the press boys asked her if it was true.' Jake continued. 'No smoke without fire and all that. And now the guv'nor puts you up on the two big Cheltenham hopes. It's obvious, isn't? Boss Baxter will go for the Kim Muir and that one' – he pointed his gloved index finger at Blue Marine's handsome head – is ready-made for the National Hunt Chase.'

The two races Jake mentioned were both restricted to amateur jockeys. Maybe Charlie was paying lip service to Christopher Mayhew so that he would have a free hand in the choice of jockey for his other runners at the Festival, and go for one of the top professionals.

He said nothing after either horse worked. And there was not even an invitation to have a cup of coffee let alone breakfast. But, as I was walking away towards my car, he called out to me, raising his finger as if he had just remembered something. 'Rod. We must go through riding plans and runners. Can you call round this evening? Say around half five?'

'Sure.'

'Great. See you then.' The words weren't spoken with any great enthusiasm. But they had me fired with excitement.

A message on my phone went some way towards bringing me

back down to earth. It was Detective-Sergeant Hastings: she wanted me to go to Reading police station to see her as soon as possible. I drove straight there.

I was shown into the same interview room as on the previous Friday. Five minutes later she came bustling in, a file under her arm, and an I-mean-business expression on her face. There was no apology for keeping me waiting or, for that matter, any explanation for immediately switching on the recorder.

'Now Mr Hutchinson,' she began. 'Tell me about those so-called muggers on Friday night.'

I explained what had happened: how I had been saved by the occupant of number one flat, the stab wound, its treatment by my brother-in-law, my sister's decision to put sleep before an immediate report, and my visit to the police station the following morning.

'Had you seen either of these men before, Mr Hutchinson?'

I hesitated. 'No. At least I am pretty sure I hadn't. But there was something about what they said that reminded me of the attempted attack by the courier people.'

She leafed through the file. 'When was that?' she asked as she searched – and as I realised my mistake.

'Friday, December 12.' It felt more like Friday the 13th,' I added, trying to turn my blunder into a light-hearted joke.

'Was this reported?'

'Probably not. I didn't think much of it at the time. No damage being done and all that.' I knew I was in for a rocket, at the very least. Hence my trying to make it sound hardly worth reporting.

Detective-Sergeant Hastings sat up and looked me straight in the eye. 'Mr Hutchinson,' she began gravely. 'Withholding evidence from a police officer is a serious matter and one which could see you in a lot of trouble.

'I told you last Friday that we believe you are involved in criminal activity and that my superiors take the view that it is you we should be investigating. We can now add wasting police time to your charge sheet. Why didn't you report this courier attack?'

I explained that I had thought it to be a one-off and that, as no real damage had been done, I considered it a waste of police time if I called them in.

Ms Hastings – I had noticed that there was no ring on the third finger of her left hand – looked unimpressed but said nothing.

I decided to try and regain the initiative. 'What happened when your people visited Greg Rickards in Nottingham? What did he say? I hope he didn't simply deny the whole thing.'

The file was reopened. I could see what looked like a type-written report quite near the top.

'Nottingham police interviewed Mr Rickards on Saturday, arriving at the showrooms at 9.27am,' she read out. There was a lengthy pause while she studied the rest of it.

'Hmm,' she said. 'It appears that he recalled your visit, said you had been to see his father giving a false name. Said you were a disgraced journalist trying to cause trouble for him and his two horse trainers. Said he had told you not to come near him again. Also said you were a liar and needed to be locked up.'

She closed the file and, looking at me straight in the face, said: 'It appears that you are not to be trusted, Mr Hutchinson. And this' – she tapped the front of the file – 'bears that out.' She stood up, indicating that the interview was over. 'Be very careful. We are watching you.'

It was dark by the time I reached the stables. I could see a light on in the house and, wasting no time as it was bitterly cold, I hurried along the path leading to the door at the side.

Charlie opened it before I had a chance to ring the bell. I was a bit wary after his cool manner in the morning but I need not have worried. He was all smiles and positively welcoming. He ushered me into the sitting room, poured me a beer and bade me sit down on the sofa as he sank into the armchair nearest the fireplace and raised his glass.

'Cheers,' said, smiling broadly. 'Here's to us and to a partnership packed with winners.' He swallowed a hefty draught and, keen to be seen in the same optimistic spirit, I did the same.

Charlie, clearly relaxed in his roll-neck jersey and smart cavalry twill trousers, wasted little time in getting to the point. 'Christopher was on to the BHA this morning and was given an assurance that your licence renewal will be in this week's Calendar so we can start making plans.

'He still reckons you could be champion amateur by the end of the season and I agree with him. I reckon you'll be fit enough to start taking rides the week after next and by mid-February you should be on half the string including the main Cheltenham hopes. Boss Baxter in the Kim Muir and Blue Marine in the National Hunt Chase.

'There'll be other horses for other races. But we'll have to how things go with them and whether they prove good enough.' Still smiling, he downed the rest of his drink, stood up and reached out a hand in the direction of my glass.

'Come on, drink up. You've hardly touched yours. This is a celebration.'

I didn't want to drink much more. Apart from anything else I had to drive home. Being stopped over the limit was the last thing I needed. I was in bad enough odour with the police without adding a further offence. An image of Detective-Sergeant Hastings swam in front of my eyes. But I didn't want to disappoint Charlie. I drank the rest of my glass in one almighty swallow and held it out for a refill.

Charlie, clearly on a high, started going through the rest of the string and his hopes for them. Personally I thought some of the geese had about as much chance of turning into the swans he was depicting as I did of winning the Booker Prize. But I wasn't going to put a dampener on anything, not after being given the nod for the mounts at the greatest jump meeting of the year.

I relaxed, let the words pour over my head and just nodded in agreement. In any case I could feel the beer taking its effect, so much so that at one point I closed my eyes. I had to shake my head to avoid nodding off. But I was tired and the room was beginning to go round. I wondered if I should suggest that I stay the night.

However I needed to get home, particularly with snow threatened. I stood up and promptly fell back down onto the sofa.

'Rod, you OK? ' Charlie asked. But the note of concern on his face promptly turned into a grin. 'Now I've got you, you bugger,' he added quietly, so quietly that I thought I must have misheard. In any case it was all I could do to keep my eyes open.

'Rod, I think you're a bit drunk,' he said as he stood up. 'Come on. I'll drive you home.'

He pulled me to my feet, told me to put my arm round his shoulder and we moved unsteadily to the door, down the passage and out into the cold. Even the near zero temperature failed to sober me up and Charlie had to really struggle to get me to my car. He opened a back door and pushed me inside.

He searched in my Puffa jacket pocket for the key, got into the driver's seat and headed, not in the direction of the road, but towards the track leading to the Downs.

'Ith the wrong way,' I murmured, conscious that I could hardly get the words out, and cursing myself for not refusing that second beer.

Steadily it dawned on me that other things weren't right either. I had to get in touch with Sue to say I would be late ringing her. I fumbled in my pocket for my phone. I somehow managed to open it up and I clicked on a button. Then another but I couldn't get my fingers to do anything more.

I could hear Charlie droning on. I listened as hard as I could. Although he was looking straight ahead as we climbed that familiar path, he appeared to be either talking to me or talking to himself about me.

'I don't know how anyone could have thought I was going to let you ride all the stable's runners. An amateur who had ridden only four winners.' He said the words with undisguised contempt, almost spitting them out. 'I'd be a laughing stock: a first season trainer putting up a novice, an amateur in every sense of the word.

'Everybody would think I'd no idea what I was doing. I would hardly last the season – despite training for my own uncle.'

By this stage we were halfway up the hill and the snow was coming down in earnest, although the powerful windscreen wipers of my BMW were having little difficulty in providing Charlie with a clear view.

But the hatred in his voice was intensifying: 'The only solution was to get rid of you. But you were costing me a fortune. The more you survived, the more the price went up. These rent-a-killers seem to have some sort of connection between themselves. And after last Friday's bungling I couldn't afford any more.'

I was thrown across the back seat as the car swung sharply left. I caught a glimpse of Gideon's Gate through the driving snow as I pushed myself upright. Some of the drug that had been used to spike my drink – I now had no doubt what had made me so sleepy – was beginning to wear off. I calculated my chances of escape at around even money if I pretended to be completely drugged.

The car came to a halt. Charlie turned round to face me as he continued: 'You know what they say? If you want a job doing properly, do it yourself. This drive up here tonight has cost me nothing. And, Mister Rodney Hutchinson, disgraced racing journalist and one-time amateur jockey, tonight you are going to die. I doubt, though, if anyone is going to name a gate after you. The police will see the suicide note that I ran off on the printer at your flat, and which will be left in this car, and the verdict will be 'Taken own life while the balance of mind was disturbed.'

'And I will be left to book the best jockeys in the business, go onto the Cheltenham honours' list as one of the select few to train winners at the Festival in their first season, and proceed to become rich and famous.'

With a sickly smile of triumph on his face, he frog-marched me to the gate, hurled me to the ground, fished in his anorak pocket for what appeared to be some sort of metal chain and proceeded to attach my ankles to the bottom part of the gate.

As he fastened the contraption I recognized what it was – a hobble, normally used for tethering a troublesome horse's back feet together to stop it lashing out. My estimate of survival went from evens to 10-1. But even that price looked too short when he took from another pocket a bottle of some indeterminate liquid, thrust it between my lips and ordered me to drink.

Desperately, I turned my head away at the last moment and was rewarded with a stinging slap across the face. I got another when I did it a second time. But I had succeeded in getting rid of some of the sleeping draught which I knew would be my death warrant.

There was little left in the bottle for the third and final swig but this time he got it all down me, largely because my reserves of strength were virtually nil. I was so weak that I could make not the slightest effort to stop him when he took my phone out of my trouser pocket, wiped it on my jacket and hurled it down the path.

'You'll be dead long before I come up and untie you,' he said, making not the slightest attempt to disguise the note of triumph in his voice. 'The police blood tests will confirm that you took your own life.'

I waited until I was sure that he was heading back through the driving snow before sticking two fingers down my throat as far as I could get them. I'd seen jockeys do this after eating a hunger-satisfying sandwich before going to the scales – and it worked for me too. Never had I felt so pleased with myself after being sick.

As Charlie disappeared into the snow and down the track on foot, it dawned on me that he had not tied my hands – I wouldn't have been able to do the finger trick had he done so. Presumably he thought that the hobble would be enough. Particularly coupled with the blizzard conditions.

But how could I survive? The snow was steadily piling up on my Puffa and my trousers, and brushing it from my head and face made my hands, particularly the fingers, lose all feeling - except that of pain which was increasing to unbearable proportions by the minute.

I tried to kick my feet clear of the hobble. That also brought only more pain. Soon I was shivering uncontrollably. I wondered how long it would be before I passed out. I tried squeezing and unsqueezing my fingers. Difficult turning to impossible. Soon I couldn't even feel the fingers. In desperation I turned my attention to my toes. They wouldn't move and they hurt like hell.

I knew I was freezing to death. Literally. I tried to let my life pass before me, more as a way of keeping me going. But it was the worst bits that played before my frozen face: the death of my first pony, my Jack Russell terrier being run over, the death of both my parents within days of each other, Emma's funeral. Then my own – I could see it clearly. I could also read the heading of my obituary: 'Disgraced amateur jock commits suicide at historic spot.'

After that I was shaking so badly that I could sense nothing beyond snow and pain as I turned into a human snowball. I knew I was gone and, giving up, I felt I was drifting into a coma.

I had no idea of the time – I'm sure I passed out - and it seemed ages later when I heard a car slowly climbing up the path, its tyres slipping in the snow and its engine revving. I was convinced I was imagining things. Then the headlights briefly dazzled me.

I thought I could make out a figure coming towards me. But I knew it was a mirage - I was already dead. This was obviously the mental equivalent of the kick that a horse gives after it has been shot with a humane killer.

I heard a cry. It was a woman's voice. 'Rod, Rod,' she called out. Was this someone calling me to heaven? Or to hell? And was this hell freezing over?

'Philip, come here and help me,' I heard her shouting. 'It's Rod and he's alive.' She was wrong - I could have told her had I not been covered in snow. I presumed it was all some sort of frozen hell that I had descended into as death took over.

The next thing I knew two figures were helping me to my feet and the male one seemed somehow to break the hobble with what looked like a crowbar. I was in so much pain, as they carried me towards a small white car, that I knew I was alive after all. But I was shaking and hurting so much that I wished I was dead.

Once in the passenger seat I felt the hot air blasting me. Soon the atmosphere was like a Turkish bath and the more I was warmed up, the more the agony seeping through every vestige of my body increased.

I vaguely heard Philip – I now knew that it was him – saying 'Wait a minute, Sue. I must pick up that phone.'

He slammed the car door shut behind him while Sue leaned across, cradled me in her arms and whispered: 'Rod, my darling, darling. I knew something was very wrong when you didn't ring me at seven. I got onto Philip to track your phone and, when he said where it was, I knew that horrible man was trying to kill you.'

I tried to say something but no words would come out. Instead I was shaking uncontrollably and I was vaguely aware that tears were somehow pouring down my cheeks.

'My darling,' Sue hugged me tight. 'Don't worry. You are going to be alright. We got here as quickly as we could but then I thought you were dead. I was so upset that I wished I was dead too. just to be with you. And finding you just now feels like a miracle.'

She kissed me repeatedly.

'Found it.' I heard Philip say as a back door opened and he slipped inside, shutting the door behind him. 'The phone was right by the BMW. The leather cover seems to have saved it because the signal was still strong and the phone itself is still working. Listen.'

The voice I heard brought the horror of it all to life: 'The only solution was to get rid of you. But you were costing me a fortune. The more you survived…..'

As I listened to the rest of Charlie's words, with Sue still holding me tight against her chest, I broke into a smile.

Not only was I going to get my job back, so too was Paddy O'Reilly.

And I was going to write that book.

Printed in Great Britain
by Amazon

24924691R00134